THE ALCHEMY PRESS BOOK OF
HORRORS 2
STRANGE STORIES & WEIRD TALES

Also available

The Alchemy Press Book of Horrors

Edited by Peter Coleborn & Jan Edwards

The first volume in the series contains twenty-five tales of horror and the weird, stories that encapsulate the dark, the desolate and the downright creepy. Stories that will send that quiver of anticipation and dread down your spine and stay with you long after the lights have gone out. Who is Len Binn, a comedian or…? What secrets are locked away in Le Trénébreuse? The deadline for what? Who are the little people, the garbage men, the peelers? What lies behind the masks? And what horrors are found down along the backroads?

"The thing about anthologies is that you get a plethora of diversity, which in my humble opinion is no bad thing. The Alchemy Press Book of Horrors doesn't disappoint, with contributions from well-known names such as Ramsey Campbell, Samantha Lee, Mike Chinn and Peter Sutton, there are also a few authors there that I have never read before. Anthologies are a good way to dip your toes in the shallows of someone's writing, giving the reader, us, an idea of what to expect, should we want to read more of their work One thing is for sure, Peter Coleborn and Jan Edwards have brought together some very talented people and every story in the book 100% deserves to be included. Unthemed, this collection takes the reader to some very dark places." – *The British Fantasy Society*

THE ALCHEMY PRESS BOOK OF
HORRORS 2
STRANGE STORIES & WEIRD TALES

Edited by
Peter Coleborn & Jan Edwards

The Alchemy Press

The Alchemy Press Book of Horrors 2
© Peter Coleborn and Jan Edwards 2020

Cover art © Peter Coleborn

Interior art © Jim Pitts

This publication © The Alchemy Press 2020

Published by arrangement with the authors

First edition
ISBN 978-1-911034-07-0

Published by
The Alchemy Press, Staffordshire, UK
www.alchemypress.co.uk

CONTENTS

ACKNOWLEDGEMENTS

Beneath Namibian Sands © Pauline E Dungate 2020

Black Nore © Tim Jeffreys 2020

Digging in the Dirt © Mike Chinn 2020

Every Bad Thing © Sharon Gosling 2020

Footprints in the Snow © Eygló Karlsdóttir 2020

Henrietta Street © Gail-Nina Anderson 2020

Hydrophobia © John Llewellyn Probert 2020

I Left My Fair Homeland © Sarah Ash 2020

I Remember Everything © Debbie Bennett 2020

Lirpaloof Island © Garry Kilworth 2020

Promises © Nancy Kilpatrick 2020

The Hate Whisperer © Thana Niveau 2020

The Loneliest Place © John Grant 2020

The Primordial Light © John Howard 2020

The Secret Place © Samantha Lee 2020

We Do Like to Be Beside © Peter Sutton 2020

What Did You See? © Paul Finch 2020

PREFACE

The Merriam-Webster online dictionary defines "horror" as "the quality of inspiring horror; repulsive, horrible, or dismal quality of character". And as for "horrors": "calculated to inspire feelings of dread or horror". (Don't you love definitions that include the word you are defining!) One knows what is or what isn't horror when one stumbles over it, and that it will differ from person to person. Which is why you will find a range of stories herein, a range that captures some element of horror. Or dark fantasy. Or the macabre. Or the weird and the strange and the fantastic… This is why we've added that subtitle: Strange Stories and Weird Tales for this second volume. One thing that remains constant is quality writing. We have seventeen fabulous writers, some of whom you are undoubtedly familiar with, others perhaps less so, but we're confident you'll enjoy them all.

As we know, most readers avoid prefaces – so we'll keep it short. And all being well, we'll see you again in volume three.

—The editors

In Memory Paul Barnett (John Grant)
1949—2020

Horror is there to desolate, yes, but to demonstrate humanity, not inhumanity. To howl such dilemmas and emotions as sadness, loneliness, grief, anger – in a way that non-genre cannot
– Stephen Volk

This was a likely place to harbour supernatural horrors!
– Robert W Chambers

BENEATH NAMIBIAN SANDS

Pauline E Dungate

Elaine Harrison stared down into the huge, conical depression in the sand. Back in Koichas, she had seen the images that the drone had taken two days before but the reality was so different. The pictures didn't evoke the feeling of awe that the actuality did.

She crouched at the lip and picked up a handful dry sand, allowing it to trickle through her fingers. With no cohesion the individual grains caught the light as they tumbled down the slope. The depression, maybe thirty feet deep, had sides with a perfect slope that allowed the grains to flow unopposed to the bottom. Wind had rounded the lip but for some reason hadn't filled up the space. Except for the wreckage of the Land Rover on its side near the centre, wheels towards her, she could almost imagine a giant hand smoothing the sides daily.

"What could have made a depression like this?" she asked.

"Kettle holes." Bayron Ndume stood beside her, also looking down into the hollow. Despite his name, he was as English as she was, his grandfather having emigrated to Birmingham long ago.

"What are they?"

Bayron was a landscape geologist whereas she was only an administrator for a charity providing clean water for villages in the south of the country. She still wasn't sure why she had volunteered for this search party in the middle of the Namibian desert.

"You know how glaciers move?"

"Vaguely."

"Imagine a boulder caught in a depression in the rock. As the ice moves over it, instead of going with it, it is trapped and turns on the spot, digging its way deeper. It makes a hole."

"I'm guessing it's a bit more complicated than that, and this isn't ice."

"Think of a stick being spun round in the wind. It could dig out a hole like this."

"Could it really?"

Bayron shrugged. "I haven't thought of a better explanation yet."

"But that is Laury's Land Rover down there?" Laury Bishop was Elaine's boss. She didn't particularly like him but when he'd disappeared she felt obliged to volunteer, not expecting to be allowed to go. Her experience of desert conditions was limited.

"It is very likely," Bayron said.

The vehicle had sand piled around it and, except for its inverted position, didn't look too damaged. It was the kind of accident that people walk away from.

"We need to go down and look," she said. There had been three in the Land Rover: Laury, the driver, and a local guide. Well, local in that he lived on the outskirts of the desert. Not much could survive in areas this arid.

She rose to her feet and made to step forward but Bayron put a hand on her shoulder. "Not without ropes," he said.

"Why? I could get down there easily."

"But not back up. Have you tried walking up the face of a sand dune?"

"No, but—"

"Trust me. It is very difficult. Naheela will want to radio back that we have located the Land Rover. Then we go look."

"Okay." She didn't like waiting. It was frustrating. Elaine wanted to get this over and head back to base as soon as possible. The endless sand dunes stretching in all directions were oppressive. And she hadn't appreciated how the strength of the sun would be magnified by reflection from the loose sand.

She and Bayron walked back to the two vehicles and trailer that made up the search party. There were four others. Naheela, the other woman on the team, handed her a bottle of water. "Is it them?" she asked.

"Bayron thinks so. He says we should use ropes to go down to investigate."

"Right. I'll report in to Koichas." She waved to the three men who were standing nearby – two were armed rangers, the third doubling as cook and mechanic. "Jamie, Matias, harnesses and ropes for three, Isra line up the jeep as an anchor."

Elaine felt useless as the rest of the team hurried to follow Naheela's instructions. She felt she had only been included in the party because Laury was her boss. "I'm going down," she announced.

Naheela merely nodded; no trying to persuade her not to. "Follow Bayron's instructions," she said.

Bayron checked her harness was secure before allowing Elaine over the lip into the depression. Isra had the engine of the jeep idling and was watching them in the wing-mirrors while Naheela stood on the shady side, keeping well back. Matias tested the security of her rope. She had watched Jamie begin the descent. He had gone over the lip backwards, his rifle slung over his back, as if he were abseiling a rock face. Elaine had seen the way that the sand had shifted beneath his feet, the dry grains sliding over one another. There was no cohesion.

Elaine copied his movements. The moment her feet touched the slope she felt the sand move. The least pressure of her boots set up mini-avalanches. Unstable, she fell to her knees. If the rope hadn't been there she would have tumbled, unable to stop herself. This descent wasn't going to be as easy as she had thought. Her hand touched the surface. It was already burning hot, and the day had barely started.

She concentrated on moving her feet slowly until she backed up against the fallen Land Rover. With relief she unclipped the rope but reached to hold onto the superstructure of the vehicle.

She yelped, her skin blistering on the hot metal. Bayron, who arrived moments after her, passed her a pair of cotton gloves.

Jamie had already worked his way round to the other side where there was a little shade and was scooping sand away.

"There's no one here," he said. "Either they were thrown clear or they climbed out."

Not any other alternative, Elaine thought. The Afrikaner did sometimes state the obvious. "Is it Laury's Land Rover?" she asked.

Jamie reached in and yanked a backpack from under one seat. He opened the zip-pocket at the front. "Yep," he said. "Laurence Bishop's passport."

She looked up the slope, which from this angle was daunting. She couldn't see their vehicles, and Matias, standing on the lip, appeared small and far away shimmering in the heat. The sky overhead was an untarnished silver-blue. The surrounding dunes were invisible.

"Could they have climbed out?" she asked.

"Try it," Bayron said.

She did. Every step she took was like climbing on ice. Her weight made the grains move frictionlessly over each other and she slipped back. There was nothing to hold on to, except the rope. If they had climbed out they would be wandering aimlessly in the desert with no shelter and little water. They'd be lucky to be found. She understood why the advice was to stay with the vehicle if you break down. It was a larger target to spot.

"Does the radio work?" she asked. She knew that Laury always carried a phone and that out here there would be no signal.

"No. It was smashed in the fall."

"Then, where are they?" Laury might not be desert savvy but he'd travelled with two men who were.

"Hey!" Jamie called. He'd found a slender pole from somewhere – the radio aerial she realised – and was stabbing it into the sand, presumably looking for bodies. He had moved downslope a little to where it levelled out. From the top of the crater, the Land Rover had obscured the shape of the ground at the centre of the depression. Here the sand formed a circular hump. Bayron's kettle stone, perhaps, or like the peak you get at the moment a raindrop hits water. A meteorite strike? Would that make this kind of pattern in sand? She'd've asked Bayron but he was standing next to Jamie, looking down. She trudged over to them, the soft surface dragging at her boots.

"There's a hollow under here," Jamie said, pushing the pole into the centre of the mound. He waggled it and the sand began to cave in, leaving a hole surrounded by a foot-high barrier of sand like a much larger version of the ants' nests she'd seen around the village.

"They could have taken shelter down there," Elaine said.

"If it's big enough," Bayron said.

Jamie poked around a bit more. "It goes deep."

It started slowly, but the rush of sand rapidly increased to a torrent exposing a huge cavity beneath.

"We need to go and look," Elaine said.

"Not without torches. Stay here." Bayron trudged back round the other side of the Land Rover and clipped on one of the ropes. After a few hand signals. Elaine saw him being hauled up the slope. Presumably he'd tell Naheela what they'd found as well as gathering the equipment they'd need to explore below. Elaine sat in the meagre shade to wait. Jamie passed her a bottle of warm water. She hadn't thought to bring any with her. At least she had her hat, even though she thought it made her look ridiculous.

"Why are you here?" Jamie asked.

Before she could answer, he pointed at the ground. "Not in Namibia. Here. You could have stayed back in Koichas."

She signed and took another sip of water. "I'd never have heard the last of it if I hadn't gone looking for him – personally."

"I thought he was your boss."

"He is. My best friend, his wife, persuaded him to give me the job."

"So you could keep an eye on him?"

"I guess. She's heard about charity workers getting involved with local women."

Jamie laughed. "And she thinks Laury Bishop would do that? The only woman he'd be interested in would be one bringing him an exotic insect."

"That's what I told her." Elaine shrugged. "She's a bit of a worrier."

A scuffle of sand heralded Bayron's return. He was carrying more ropes and a rucksack. He pulled out three torches. "Naheela's told Matias to set up a tent and sort lunch while we explore. We are to be back by noon, whatever. Then we'll try to pull the Land Rover out of the hole."

"Can't afford to leave good equipment lying around," Jamie muttered.

"No, we can't," Bayron said sharply, "But we can use it as an anchor for our ropes."

"Do we really need them?" Elaine asked.

She felt a little stupid when he said, "How will we get out again?"

She wasn't an explorer and her skills didn't extend to caving so she watched as the two men set up the rope, dangling the ends into the cavity and checking they were secure. She worried that their weight would cause the vehicle to roll or slide but said nothing. She'd made enough stupid comments as it was. When they were satisfied Jamie went in first. She knew he had reached the bottom when the rope went slack.

"What can you see?" Bayron asked.

"It's a cavity, about eight feet deep and six across. The walls are disintegrating. Piles of sand all over the place."

"No sign of Bishop's team?"

"Nothing obvious."

"I want to go in," Elaine said.

"There's not much room."

"Doesn't matter." She was already clipping the rope to the harness.

"I'll lower you," Bayron said.

Jamie was right. With the two of them in the space it was claustrophobic. It wasn't just the size of the cavern but the smell. She'd once been in a loft housing a colony of bats. It reminded her of that, only drier, like the space was filled with the essence of moth wings. It was choking, tickling at her throat. She put a hand over her mouth and nose to keep out the most of it. Jamie hadn't mentioned the bones. The floor was littered with them. Most were small and crunched underfoot. She picked up the tiny skull of something that might have belonged to a lizard. There were bigger ones, too. She spotted something that resembled the tooth of an elephant. She knew that some small herds survived on the fringes of the desert. One falling into the pit wouldn't have been able to climb out. Some of the bones had what appeared to be skin clinging to them.

Elaine noted the falls of sand that obscured a lot of the bones but in one place there was a lump that didn't fit. She hadn't seen it when she first entered as Jamie had been standing in front of it.

"What's this?" she said, touching it. She'd expected it to be hard, a boulder perhaps. She still had the kettle-hole image that Bayron had described for her. The surface gave. It was more like touching the skin of a balloon that was beginning to lose air. She rubbed her fingers together. It was slightly sticky, enough for sand grains to adhere to it. She tried pinching the surface between her fingers. It was resilient. She pulled and sticky strands came away. They had the texture of spider's web or a fungal mat.

Jamie, seeing what she was doing said, "Hey, I want to collect some of that."

"Why? It's gross."

"Aren't you curious about it?"

"Not really. I want to find out what happened to Laury."

"Well, he's not here."

Something glinted in the torch light. She pulled the object out from under a pile of sand. She held it up in triumph. "He was. He never goes anywhere without this."

Jamie glanced at the iPhone she was holding. His voice had a tightness when he said, "You go up top and report that to Naheela. Bayron and I will search this pit more thoroughly."

She was about to protest when Bayron called down having obviously been listening to the conversation. "We've had more experience with this kind of thing."

"What kind of thing? You think he's dead, don't you?"

"That's not what I'm saying."

"You're thinking it, though."

"We know the desert, Elaine."

She laughed. "You don't. You spent most of your life in Birmingham."

"That's true but I have been working in Namibia for three years longer than you."

"And I'm just a useless passenger in this search!" She was angry but she also knew that he was right. Until yesterday she hadn't gone further than the outskirts of Koichas. She knew nothing about the desert or its dangers. "Pull me up then. I might be more help helping Matias cook."

By the time she got up to the level plateau, she was exhausted. Not just from the climb, which was assisted by Isra hauling on the rope, but from the heat and the frustration of feeling useless. He picked up his rifle when she was safely at the top. Naheela was in the jeep acting as the anchor. She gestured for Elaine to join her in the cab. As she opened the door a blast of cool air greeted her. She hadn't realised that the vehicle had air conditioning.

Naheela handed her water and said, "I'm going to keep nagging you to drink more. You are not acclimatised to these conditions."

Elaine climbed in and accepted the water. Naheela was right but it niggled. It was another indication that she was the passenger and not a functional part of the team.

"Tell me what you found." Naheela said.

"Laury's iPhone. He was in that cavern."

"Describe everything."

Elaine wondered if she was being humoured or distracted but did the best she could. "Where could they have gone?" she asked.

"Jamie and Bayron will be checking to see if there are any tunnels leading off the cavity. Many desert animals burrow to keep out of the heat."

"Mighty big rabbit," Elaine muttered.

Naheela laughed. "Rivers run underground as well. I wasn't aware of any in this area but there is so much unexplored out here."

"Even with modern technology?"

"That only scratches the surface, literally. When the others come up I'll update Koichas and decide the next move. Okay?"

Elaine sighed. "All I really want to know is what happened to Laury."

"We all do. We can learn from mishaps. Then they might not happen to anyone else."

"You call the Land Rover falling into that pit, a mishap."

"Until we find out otherwise, that's what it will be classed as."

~~~

Over lunch it was decided that Bayron and Isra would attempt to drag Laury's Land Rover out of the pit while Jamie collected the bones from the cavity. They would give him an idea of what animals ventured this far out into the desert. Naheela planned to fly the drone over the area and see if there were any more similar pits. Knowing how they formed would be useful information.

"And what do I do?" Elaine asked, hoping Naheela would let her help with the survey. Computers was something she could do.

"You can help me," Jamie said. "We won't be able to carry all the finds back so photographing the bones will be the best bet."

"All of them. They are horribly mixed up and we crushed a lot."

"Just the skulls. They'll give a good indication of species and give us a count."

She wasn't too happy going back underground with the pervasive musty smell but she was tired of feeling like a spare part. "Just show me how you want it done," she said.

Elaine found the situation frustrating. The space was really too small for Jamie to root around sifting the bones to find skulls and for her to set them out on the squared cloth he'd laid out on the floor. The fungus ball thing didn't help. It took up space and she was sure the funny smell was coming from it. She had to keep looking behind her at it. Her imagination told her it was flexing, almost as if it were breathing.

"We've got an ape skull here," Jamie said plonking the object in front of her. It made a change from all the tiny lizards. As she set it in position the jaw fell away. Elaine stared at it for a moment then said, "Er, Jamie. This is human."

"It can't be,"

"It's got fillings."

Jamie snatched up the skull, then whirled round.

"Where did you fund it?" Elaine asked.

"In the sand, beside the cocoon thing."

"Are there other bones?"

"It won't be Laury. It's too clean. A skull can't get this clean in a week."

"It's someone. He'll need a proper burial."

"This could have been here for years."

Elaine snatched the skull from his hands. "You look for more bones. I'll take this up to Naheela."

"Now look here…"

Elaine didn't listen. She clipped her harness onto the climbing rope and tugged twice, sharply, the signal to be hauled up.

Bayron helped her over the lip, "Given up already?" he asked.

"We've found something," she said, refusing to be baited. She crossed to where Naheela was sitting under the canvas shelter with her laptop open before her, and placed the skull beside her. "We found this."

Naheela glanced away from her screen for a moment. Then closed the lid. "This was in that cavity?"

"That's what I said."

Naheela looked up at Bayron. "Forget the Land Rover. Go and join Jamie. If there are human remains down there they must be collected."

~~~

By dusk there was an argument in the camp. Naheela made it clear that they were going to be spending a second night in the desert. It was too late to set out for Koichas and travelling in the dark was not a good idea. It made sense to camp where they were and reassess in the morning, especially as Naheela's drone had located another pit. It was old, half-filled with blown sand. Bayron was keen to examine this one more closely to work out how it had formed while Jamie wanted to examine the other one, hoping to find more animal bones. Elaine wanted to go back.

The excavations had revealed three human bodies in the cavern, all of them covered with a layer of desiccated skin. The other items found with them confirmed that it was Laury's party. Elaine felt it more important to take the bodies back for a decent burial and to inform families properly. At this moment she wasn't quite equating the skeletons with someone she'd known. That would come later. Currently, she felt the reason for them being out here was over. The others seemed to have lost the focus for their purpose. If they couldn't travel at night, her vote was to return at first light.

Naheela wanted an explanation. Yes, there had been an accident; yes, the men had probably sheltered in the cavern and without much in the way of food and water, they might have died – temperatures here dropped well below zero at night. That didn't explain the state of the bodies. Jamie said they had not been there long enough to be mummified and it was too cool underground for that. There were beetles who would clean bones that precisely and perhaps leave the skin but there wasn't any sign of them and it would take weeks to do.

"Why did Laury say he was coming out this way?" Naheela asked.

"He'd heard that big insects had been seen in this direction."

"Laury would go chasing any insect," Jamie muttered.

Elaine glared at him and continued, "He was worried that there might be a swarm of locusts forming. He'd want to stop them before they reached the crops. The growing season's been too short for several years."

"It's much too dry for devourers to emerge. There's been no rain here," Jamie said.

Elaine didn't know the exact life cycle of locusts but she could understand why Laury was concerned. "How do you know?" she said.

Naheela raised her hands. "Isra, you haven't said anything. What is your advice?"

Unlike the rest of them, he was the only one who had actually lived all his life in Namibia. He largely kept his opinions to himself. Now he said, "We should leave. There are no small devourers, only big ones."

"What about you, Matias?" she asked.

The cook/mechanic shrugged. "I go where I am told."

"In that case," Naheela said, "I will decide in the morning. But I do want a watch kept. Jamie, sort that out."

~~~

The two women shared the tent while the men bedded down in the jeeps. Elaine had been surprised by the thickness of the sleeping bags on the first night out but as the temperature plummeted after sunset she appreciated the warmth.

She lay awake listening to Naheela's gentle snore. In her mind she could see that leather-clad skeleton skull. She didn't consider herself particularly squeamish but the image of swarms of small, flesh devouring beetles was unsettling. In the end, pressure in her bladder forced her up. She remembered to put boots on before she left the tent – Jamie had pointed out scorpion tracks the previous night – grabbed a torch and stepped out into darkness. Above, the sky was a deep black punctuated by pinpricks of stars. The moon was nearing full, casting weak shadows across the sand.

She saw a gleam of torchlight beside the silhouette of one of the jeeps. Ducking behind the other one she quickly relieved herself – the wet patch would quickly dry and she didn't want to venture any closer to the pit. She walked over to where she had seen the light, making sufficient noise to alert whoever was on watch. Matias was leaning against the hood of the jeep. He looked around as she approached.

"Couldn't sleep," she said.

"And I would like to," he said.

"I don't see why there has to be a watch. There can't be anything dangerous bigger than a scorpion."

"There are Isra's big devourers."

She laughed. "Do you believe that?"

Matias shrugged. "Who knows what is out here? Do you hear that?"

"What?"

He held up a hand. "Listen."

She stood quietly. All she could hear was the shifting of sand grains and a popping sound as the metal in the vehicles cooled.

"Nothing."

"That is what is creepy."

Elaine shivered. Even if she couldn't sleep, it would be warmer in the tent. "Goodnight," she said.

As she bent down to unzip the tent flap Elaine though she heard a rustling. It reminded her of moth wings against a light, only more expansive, a host of moths. She could see nothing and assumed it must be one of the men moving around. Before she ducked inside, she glanced up at the moon. A shadow flitted across its surface. Her imagination, or one of those birds she'd heard about that made daily trips to the sea to soak their feathers before carrying the water back to their chicks hidden from predators in the desert. She tried not to picture flocks of insects pouring from the ground and she crawled back into her sleeping bag. Myriads of beetles was bad enough.

When she awoke at dawn Naheela was already about. As Elaine emerged she saw her in earnest conversation with Bayron and Isra.

"Did you see Jamie when you went out last night?" Naheela asked as she approached.

"No. Only Matias. Why?"

"He's disappeared."

"Where would he go?"

"Devoured," Isra said.

"Don't be ridiculous," Naheela told him. "And he's got too much desert craft to go wandering off."

"Maybe he fell in the pit," Elaine said.

Naheela scowled. "Get some breakfast from Matias. I'll do a drone sweep of the area. Bayron, Isra – see about getting that Land Rover up. I'm not wasting time waiting for him to show up."

"Bossy," Bayron mouthed as he moved away.

Matias had boiled water for tea and handed Elaine a mug and a meat-filled flatbread. She didn't ask what the meat was. Some things were better not to know.

"Has Jamie gone off scouting the other pit?" she asked.

Matias shrugged. "He relieved me after midnight. Not seen him since."

"Will this change our plans? Will we go straight back to Koichas?"

"Naheela won't want to abandon him out here."

"Isra's a tracker. Perhaps he can find where he went."

"He thinks a devourer got him. I heard him tell Bayron."

"Isn't that superstition?" Elaine said. "There's nothing out here that big."

"Something got Laury Bishop."

A shiver went up her spine and she had the image of millions of tiny beetles ganging up on them. "I don't want to think about that," she said, taking her breakfast and heading over to the edge of the pit.

Bayron had already attached ropes to the fallen Land Rover and Isra was steadily hauling the vehicle up the slope. Naheela came to watch.

Elaine asked, "Any sign of Jamie?"

"There are faint trails around the older pit but nothing specific. Koichas says we have to go check it out."

"We're not going back?"

"We have until mid-afternoon. Get your hat and sunscreen. We are heading out as soon as this vehicle is up."

It wasn't far to the next pit. Bayron reckoned Jamie could have easily walked it and since he wanted to look there, Naheela agreed to start the search there. Once Laury's Land Rover was raised she sent Bayron and Isra to take a look. Elaine asked to go too. She didn't see any point just hanging around while Matias tried to fix the wreck – it was either that or tow it back. Naheela wanted to stay near the radio in case further instructions came through.

~~~

Elaine stared down into the bowl. The sides were shallower, the hollow partly filled with blown sand which looked darker as if it had been exposed to the air for longer. If she wanted a word to describe it, she would have said *tarnished*. She thought that if she fell into this one she would be able to climb out.

"Why should this depression be different from the other one?" she asked.

Bayron pointed to the dune behind them. "Wind direction. To get the effect the wind has to be in the right direction."

"You still think it's like a kettle hole?"

"Why not?"

"Then what about the hole at the bottom?"

"Underground water course."

"That just happened to dump all those bones there?"

"Devourers," Isra said.

"Huh." Bayron didn't argue but he clearly didn't believe in them.

"We need to go down and look," Elaine said.

"Jamie's not here and no there's no sign that he was."

"I'm going down." Elaine stepped over the lip and allowed the sand to carry her to the bottom. Behind her she heard Bayron mutter "Stupid". It didn't worry her. She was sure she could get out, which meant Jamie could if he'd fallen in.

Reaching the bottom she stood and turned. Bayron had fixed the rope to the jeep's bumper and was about to come after her. She took a step backwards and squealed as the ground gave way beneath her.

She landed with a thump on her back, all the air knocked out of her. As she stared at the circle of sky above the light was suddenly occluded. Her heart rate increased rapidly until she realised it was Bayron.

"You okay," he asked.

"Yeah." Her voice came out croakily. "Winded."

He swung down into the cavity, sweeping a torch beam around. She glimpsed bones and smelt the same mustiness. "Just like the other one," she said.

"Not quite," Bayron stepped across to a dark sand-encrusted shape. "This is hollow," he said.

It was like that soft, fungal mass they'd found in the other one but ripped open. There was nothing inside. Elaine touched the substance. Like the other, the outside was sticky to the touch, inside it felt like smooth plastic.

"It's like a cocoon," Bayron said.

"You think something was inside it?"

"If there was, it's gone now."

Elaine shivered, thinking about the shadow she'd seen over the moon. She turned slowly, hoping nothing was lurking in the darkness at the edges of the cavity. "Let's go," she said. "Jamie isn't here."

Bayron had to help her out of the cavity and it wasn't as easy scaling the sides of the pit as she had imagined. She wouldn't admit it but she was glad of the rope. Reaching the top, she heard the radio crackle to life. She followed Bayron over to the jeep in time to hear Naheela say, "We've found Jamie." She sounded grim.

"We return," Isra said.

~~~

When Matias had brushed the sand out of the working parts of the Land Rover's engine, he'd put some of their spare fuel in the tank and taken it on a short drive to check that it was working properly. He'd found Jamie's body on the other side of a dune.

"How do you know it's Jamie?" Elaine asked. She suppressed the squeamishness she felt at the sight of the leathery skeleton. The skin was stretched over the bones as if all the soft tissues had been sucked out. Nothing, she thought, could work that fast.

"The remnants of his clothes, and his rifle," Naheela said.

It wasn't just the mummified condition of the remains that was disturbing. Several of his bones were broken as if he had fallen from a height, and his skull was crushed, the inside of which was empty.

"We go back to Koichas now," Naheela said. "Matias, can you drive the Land Rover?"

~~~

Bayron led with Isra taking shotgun. Naheela drove the second jeep with the trailer while Matias coaxed the Land Rover in their wake. Elaine rode with Naheela as they threaded their way back through the dunes. In the dips there were still traces of the tyre tracks they had made on the way out. Mostly they relied on Isra's local knowledge and a compass. Naheela's GPS signal was fleeting and unreliable.

Elaine tried to relax, not easy when the vehicle was being jolted about by the uneven surface. Naheela hung back from the lead vehicle, keeping out of the dust kicked up by the wheels. Isra dropped out of sight over the crest of a dune. Naheela gunned the engine to give them the momentum to take them over the top. The nose tipped steeply downwards and Naheela slammed on the brakes. The Jeep skidded sideways, the trailer jack-knifing and throwing Elaine heavily against the dashboard, and slid to a halt. Before them was a dep pit.

Shakily, Naheela said, "That wasn't there before."

"Where's Isra?" Elaine said.

Naheela scrambled out of the vehicle and stood on the lip. "Down there."

The other jeep lay on its side near the bottom of the

depression in a very similar position to how they had found Laury's Land Rover. Elaine couldn't see any movement. She cupped her hands to her mouth and shouted, "Are you okay?"

No response.

"Get the rope from the trailer," Naheela said. "I'm going down there."

"Is that a good idea? We should wait for Matias."

"Just do it."

Naheela attached the rope to the front bumper and started walking backwards down the slope. Elaine watched, switching her attention between Naheela and the fallen vehicle. Naheela was almost at the jeep when Elaine noticed a movement in the sand. First, she thought, hoped, it was Bayron or Isra. It was more at the centre, sand trickling down like water into a plughole. Before she could call out, something erupted from below. Elaine screamed. Naheela looked up, sensed the movement and half-turned. Huge serrated pincers fastened around her waist and pulled her under.

Elaine covered her face with her hands, her breathing fast and erratic, seeing the image of the massive head and jaws imprinted on the insides of her eyelids.

"What is it? Where are the others?" Matias grasped her wrist roughly, pulling her hand away from her eyes. She hadn't heard his vehicle arrive. She pointed.

"What happened?"

"It ... it ate her."

"What did?"

"A thing, a monster. Isra's devourer." She could hear the hysteria in her voice but couldn't do anything about it. She began to cry.

When she finally calmed down, Matias handed her a mug of hot sweet tea. He'd unloaded the stove from the trailer and heated the water. She took it and stared at the surface of the liquid. She was tempted to laugh but bit back the sound. If she started she'd never stop. It seemed such an English thing to do, to make tea, and incongruous in the situation.

"What do we do now?" she asked, her voice a whisper in case she disturbed the creature.

"I don't know. Go back to Koichas."

"We won't get back there before dark. Not now."

"We can try. Unhitch the trailer and just drive. Fast as we dare."

Elaine nodded and sipped at the tea, hearing Matias working in the background.

"Ready to go?" he asked.

She stood up then and brushed the sand off her clothes, trying to make the motions ordinary. She looked up as a shadow skimmed over her. Rising over the dune was a huge winged creature. She screamed as it fastened its jaws around Matias's head. She took an involuntary step backwards, overbalanced and began to slide. She scrabbled at the surface in a futile effort to slow her descent.

Below, she heard the susurration of dry sand grains running over each other.

THE LONELIEST PLACE

John Grant

"The loneliest place to be," Wendy said, "is forgotten."

She toyed with a strand of yellow hair so fine it looked like it had been printed on paper and then the paper thrown away.

Moto glanced at Pincus and Pincus glanced at Moto. They were sitting in one of the interview rooms at the 14th precinct house. They weren't interviewing Wendy because the cops thought she was a criminal, which was the usual reason people were brought to this room, but because they thought she could help them catch one. At least, the Loo – Lieutenant Patrick M'Troyd – thought so, and what the Loo thought was generally the law around here, or supposedly so.

"We won't forget you," Moto assured her.

He wasn't lying. She looked about twelve although she'd told them she was nineteen going on twenty.

"I know my way around," she'd said earlier. When most teenagers say this it's a sign that they probably don't, whatever they might think. But in Wendy's case it sounded like nothing more than the unadorned truth.

And yet she seemed so sweet. The daughter you never had.

"Let's go over it again," said Pincus.

"I remember it perfectly clearly," Wendy said.

"It's to make sure *we* remember it."

"Oh. Okay."

~~~

Earlier in the day the Loo had gathered all the boys and gals of the 14th together in the squad room and told them about his latest plan to stop the Kreep Killer. The cops were used to such meets as the city grew progressively more panicky about the killer's exploits, but this time a certain puzzlement hung in the air. Who was the cute child sitting in the chair next to the podium where the Loo was doing his best to inspire and uplift?

It was the press who'd invented the name "Kreep Killer". These past eight weeks he'd terrorised downtown New Amsterdam by viciously murdering seven little girls, all of them around the same age as the one sitting beside the Loo. The cops thought the Kreep's tally was probably higher than that, because three other children in the "same demographic" – to use the official term – had gone missing over that eight-week period. The public was outraged at the cops' failure to make an early arrest, the mayor was outraged because the public was outraged, the Commissioner was outraged because … and so it went on down the line until all the outrage landed on the desk of the Loo who, like the good cop he was, spared his officers the worst of it.

"Is it his daughter?" said Pincus under his breath to Moto.

The big man shrugged. "Don't think he has a daughter. Niece?"

They didn't have long to wait for an explanation.

"We've tried just about everything," Patrick M'Troyd was saying, "and some of them twice. And so —" he turned to look at the seated child, who was calmly checking her fingernails " —I've decided to try something I wish I didn't have to."

"She's bait," said Pincus.

"*Jail* bait," Moto replied.

Other cops were making the same guess. A rustle of dissatisfaction moved around the room. It was one thing putting undercover female officers out on the streets in hopes of luring a rapist, but this was a *child*, f'godsakes.

That misapprehension vanished like dew after dawn as soon as the Loo had finished introducing the "child" and she started speaking for herself.

"Don't let appearances fool you," she began. "I've been designed to be virtually indestructible."

~~~

Pincus had been dreaming most nights recently, and hot and fevered dreams many of them had been. Some of the more presentable ones he told to Laretta and Alex over the morning oatmeal, and they laughed politely as a wife and son should. But what he was keeping from them both was that most often, in these dreams, he had been younger than he was today. The dream protagonist was a youthful and swaggery Pincus, a single man, a man for whom Laretta lay some years in the future, and Alex – centre of the universe for the waking Pincus – had quite literally not yet been conceived. This was why some of the dreams weren't suitable for presentation at the family breakfast table. Even when Pincus had done no more than canoodle with the beauties of his night-time imagination – and, to be fair to him, that was as far it went, most of the time – he still felt obscurely guilty when he woke to find Laretta breathing sweetly in the bed beside him.

The guilt soon passed. What took longer to dissipate was the sense of time having been dislocated, as if by waking he'd skipped from past into future without having directly experienced the intervening decade or more.

He was feeling that same dislocation now as he and Moto sat in the unmarked in downtown New Amsterdam, with Wendy in the back. Downtown New Amsterdam at night – particularly here on Sprigg Street – is if anything about fifty per cent brighter than it is during the day, what with all the clubs, liquor stores, porno shops, and even the occasional grocer, not to mention the bushels of bling on some of the hookers, available in plenitude in every sex or combination thereof. There were a few uniformed cops around, not interfering with business but just keeping an eye out for trouble. A guy was trying to save the hookers' souls by telling them the return of the Lord was imminent, and presumably much the same message was being imparted by the two nuns who were cruising the two ends of the block with pious expressions and collection boxes; they were getting more propositions than quarters. It wasn't somewhere any decent father would take his kid, that was for sure. Since Pincus couldn't shake off the sense that he and Moto were somehow supposed to be acting in *loco parentis*, the whole scenario made him feel deeply uneasy.

He glanced sideways to see if maybe Moto felt the same, but Moto's face was as impassive as it always was. You could have taken Moto's face and stuck it on the side of Mount Rushmore, and the only people who'd notice anything amiss would be the ones bright enough to know there'd never been a Japanese-American president.

In his mirror Pincus could see Wendy's face. She was looking if anything a tad bored. Did machines get bored? Even though he knew what she was, he was finding it almost impossible not to think of her as a child, one of Alex's little friends, perhaps.

The glaring signs of Sprigg Street shone their lights across her, giving the illusion that she was wearing a constantly changing series of coloured masks.

"One last check," she said. It didn't seem unnatural, somehow, that she should be the one issuing the orders.

Moto reached out and tapped the switch on the enigmatic metal box taped to the dashboard. In the movies, thought Pincus, they wouldn't have had to use scotch tape to fasten it there, but this was New Amsterdam, where the bosses rode around in stretch limos and helicopters and everyone else had budgets to meet.

The box had a little red light on it, baleful as a serpent's eye.

"Do it," said Moto.

"I'm Wendy, please fly me," she said.

Only she didn't say anything at all. The words didn't come from behind the two cops but just from the box. They sounded a bit tinny, truth be told, but Pincus wasn't about to complain. If

Wendy were to start subvocalizing *La Traviata* or something, and he and Moto had to sit the whole way through it clapping in all the right places, then, yes, he might have had a thing or two to say about the sound quality. As it was, though, he only marvelled at the wonders of modern technology.

"Seems to be doing just hunky-dory," the tinny voice added.

Pincus watched her reflection as she pinched her own cheek.

There was a corresponding squawk from the box.

She chuckled – and the box did likewise. "You should hear it if someone lands a punch."

"It's not punches we're worried about," said Pincus.

Wendy leaned forward and ruffled his hair. "Not gonna happen," she said in her own voice, the box providing a sort of ghastly backing vocal.

The whole of downtown was crawling with cops, of course, drawn in from all over the city, not just the 14th. Pincus was pretty certain he'd recognised a couple of the johns trolling the arcade of sidewalk whores, and hoped they were cops working undercover and not just off duty.

The radio crackled.

"Everyone's in position." So did M'Troyd's voice.

"No time like the present," said Wendy, reaching to open the unmarked's rear door. "Never say die. Let's grasp the bull by the horns, shall we?"

In a moment she was out of the car and the two cops watched the back of her as she scampered along the sidewalk in her sandals, dressed in red like Little Red Riding Hood, her straight golden hair hanging to halfway down her back, the picture of innocence alongside all the jostling mercenary flesh.

"Do you think they teach her to talk like that?" said Pincus.

"Like what?" Moto replied, never shifting his eyes from the retreating red figure. Wendy was flouncing exactly the same way Karen flounced when it was her turn to fill the dishwasher or cook the supper. He admired the artifice.

"In clichés," Pincus explained.

"Oh." Moto was silent for a moment. "I was thinking she had

a rather fine way with words."

That was the trouble with the big man. You never knew if he was joking. He probably didn't himself.

~~~

Wendy wasn't really conscious of the hookers and other sidewalk fodder around her as she pushed her way along Sprigg Street. She knew exactly the kind of terrain that she wanted to find, and it wasn't here among the bustle and the dazzle. M'Troyd had suggested a couple of the downtown parks as possible hunting grounds for the Kreep, but this was exactly why Wendy wasn't going to choose either of them. Having devoured the reports in both the newspapers and the 14th's files, she knew the Kreep was exactly the opposite of dumb. He was two steps ahead of the cops and was likely to stay that way unless Wendy could out-think him. If M'Troyd believed Braceworthy Park was a likely place to trap the killer, the Kreep had already thought that one through and wouldn't go anywhere near her.

A tall white john with a Midwest accent misunderstood Wendy's presence here and suggested she might be interested in his Mighty Wurlitzer and some folding money. Without breaking either stride or concentration she swung a firm little fist into his solar plexus and carried along on her way, leaving him doubled-up and gasping behind her. A bunch of the actual hookers saw what happened and gave her a round of applause and a ragged cheer, but she paid them no more interest than she had the john.

Prospective john.

Well, not really prospective *anything* right now. He probably didn't require medical attention, but he might be best to find himself a cab back to his hotel and drown his sorrows up in his room watching something risqué on cable.

Wendy was a whole lot stronger than she looked.

She hadn't been joking when she told various cops that, despite appearances, she knew how to look after herself.

She had a map of New Amsterdam programmed into her brain, and she studied it now. Ideally she'd have come down here earlier in the day to sus out the area for herself, but the big cop – Moto – had pointed out to her that the Kreep might be doing something very similar, which would undermine the whole point of the exercise if he saw the same little girl come back again a few hours later. Wendy saw the logic of it, although it still irked her that the *terra* she was having to operate in was very much *incognita*.

Except for the map, of course.

Besides, she'd faced similar constraints in plenty of her other cases and they'd turned out okay, hadn't they?

Most of them.

According to her map, there was an alley somewhere just down here that most people didn't even notice as they walked past it – so narrow it was as if the wall had cracked open and no one had ever gotten around to filling up the gap with mortar.

It was, of course, full of crap: any pool of shadows in New Amsterdam immediately became fair game for anyone who had some condoms or needles to get rid of or a full bladder to empty. But the garbage wasn't much more than ankle deep – even on Wendy, whose ankles were lower than most – and she picked her way through it without too much difficulty.

The far end of the alley seemed a world away from the garish tumult of Sprigg Street.

The alley debouched into a sort of crucible of darkness, a place where the echoes howled. The walls surrounding the space were back ones, the rear walls of buildings in which all the life that was going on was going on on the far side. An occasional dim light showed at a window, as if in imitation of the stars that the perpetually smoggy skies over New Amsterdam forever hid from view.

Wendy's eyes adjusted immediately, confirming what the map had told her. At some stage in the forgotten past someone had cleared this area for redevelopment and then something had happened – the money ran out, the politicians whose palms had been greased had been jailed, somebody died. No one could remember now what it was, but work had ceased and ever since then there'd been nothing here but a gaping socket in the city's jaw, somewhere for winos and pushers to gather, for hookers and their johns to find their quick and soulless pleasures, for the rest of the world to forget.

There was a solitary fire in the midst of the gloom, and Wendy could see clumsily moving shapes around it, and hear a voice raised in cracked song, another in anger.

Wendy didn't head toward that distant warm glow.

If the Kreep Killer was out on the prowl tonight, he'd surely have spotted her earlier on Sprigg Street, and seen her head down the nameless alley.

He'd be coming after the little girl lost.

Hunting.

She waited.

~~~

Pincus smacked the radio box with his open hand. He and Moto could hear the sounds of Wendy's progress all right, but there was a lot of interference in the signal. There was a kind of rhythm to the crackling, a syncopation, and he suspected a faulty connection in one of the gazillion flashing lights up and down Sprigg Street.

"You wanting surround sound?" said Moto.

"Just good mono would suit."

"This is the NAPD. Count yourself lucky we haven't got two empty cans and a length of cord."

Below the box there was a little rectangular screen, which flickered at them as if enjoying a hidden joke. It showed Wendy's position as a little white dot that blinked at a different frequency from the rest of the screen. If you looked at it too long your eyes started going fuzzy and your brain began to hurt. The two cops had discovered the way to approach it was sidelong, glancing at it the way they would at a pretty woman, trying not to get caught staring.

They'd watched the little white dot go down Fleshraker Alley (see, the alley *did* have a name, whatever Wendy's map claimed, given to it in the days when there were meat-packing factories down here) and emerge into the vacant space where the new annex to the municipal library would have gone if the money hadn't gotten diverted to one of the mayor's pet projects, the enrichment of the mayor's pet people.

"I still think we should follow her," said Pincus.

Moto grunted. "She knows what she's doing."

"Lots of dead people thought they know what they were doing."

Moto turned to face him and emitted a sigh that smelled of hot dogs. "You want to blow this whole project?"

"'Course not."

"Then trust her. We'll get just the one chance. If the Kreep works out what's going on he's not going to fall for the same trap twice."

"I still don't like it." Pincus thought of that small figure again, looking like Little Red Riding Hood as she weaved her way down Sprigg Street.

"The Loo's not as stupid as he looks, you know," Moto was saying.

"Be difficult," Pincus responded automatically. It was an old joke, but all the new jokes sucked.

"He's got three of the bulls from the 19th playing winos around a campfire in there."

"How'd you know this?"

Moto tapped the side of his pudgy nose with a pudgy finger. "I got sources."

"Karen?"

For the past few years Moto had had this thing going with Karen Prestrantra, whom the two cops had first met when she was a SOCO back when they were working the Humor Guy case. Now she was climbing the forensics ladder. Pincus didn't know why she and Moto didn't just tie the knot, the way he and Laretta had, lo these many years ago, but the two of them still maintained the pretence of separate apartments. Pincus supposed it was an independence thing.

Moto nodded. "Karen," he confirmed. "There's always the

chance the Kreep's a cop, so the Loo's taking what he calls a modular approach. Each of us gets told just as much of his plan as we need. But Karen, well, you know how she is with computers and how she hates questions she doesn't have answers to. This whole area's stitched up tighter than a—"

Pincus never did find out what the whole area was stitched up tighter than, because at that moment the little black box on the dashboard started talking to them.

Well, it was Wendy doing the actual *talking*.

"I'm perfectly okay, thank you."

The cops could hear the other person now, too. A soft voice. An innocuous voice.

"But a child like you— It's not safe here."

Pincus was halfway out of the car, but Moto reached out a firm hand to stop him.

"You don't understand," Wendy said, sounding more like a child than ever. The crackling was getting worse.

"Does your mother know where you are?"

"You're getting in the way of something."

Someone started playing their trombone on the sidewalk directly outside the unmarked. By the time Moto had leaped out and folded the instrument into something that resembled an old-fashioned radiator, albeit in miniature, the two cops had lost quite a lot of the dialogue between Wendy and her unknown interlocutor.

"Please, lady, could you just—?"

And then, through the crackles and the pops of the ether, there came a piercing electronic screech.

Pincus had no recollection of how he got to be halfway down Fleshraker Alley, but he was there, his service revolver in one hand and a powerful long-necked flashlight in the other, trying not to trip on the underfoot garbage and take a flyer. The gap was barely wide enough for him to fit down without turning sideways. He could hear Moto crashing around somewhere behind him, and wondered how the big man was able to get through the alley at all.

He burst out the far end and paused for a split second, his arm up to shield his eyes. Powerful lights high up on two of the surrounding buildings were splitting the darkness. Another of the Loo's little secrets. Pincus had never been here during the day, so this was the first time he'd ever seen the vacant lot. The place looked like it had been transplanted from Gaza too late to escape the latest round of retaliation. Right in the middle of it there was a smoking fire. Closer to, three guys dressed like bums, but clearly not bums at all, were milling around the spot where a crumple of red cloth and a splash of yellow hair lay on the ground.

"Where'd he go?" Pincus yelled at the nearest fake hobo.

"He?"

"The guy who—" Pincus waved his gun around as if that would speak for him. "Whoever … the kid…"

Moto was dragging himself out of the alley's mouth. He looked as if he'd brought most of the garbage with him.

The cop from the 19th wiped some of the grime from his face with the back of his hand and then pointed down the length of the lot.

Pincus set off at a sprint, Moto close behind.

"But—" yelled the cop in their wake.

It looked to Pincus as if he were running straight toward a wall of blank stone but, as he got closer to it, he saw that the dark line of the corner between two buildings was actually another tiny alleyway, if anything even narrower than Fleshraker. The Kreep must have gone along it, unless he'd just thrown himself down among the debris of the abandoned site. If he'd done that, the cops who would soon be swarming here in their legions would find him, no doubt about that. Pincus had to assume the bastard was trying to escape through the cut.

He didn't have much time to think about this because moments later he was struggling through the alley himself. Ahead of him he saw a tall thin strip of brightness that he knew must be Chandler Street, at right angles to Sprigg and almost as busy. No chance to fire a warning shot. A stray bullet could easily plug someone.

At the bottom of the bright strip he saw a dark, moving obstruction.

Suddenly it vanished.

The Kreep had reached the thoroughfare at the end.

Pincus tried to bring up his memory of what he had just seen. Had the dark figure turned right or left? It was almost impossible to tell. One moment it had been there, the next it was gone. All he had was a hunch that the fleeing killer would have turned back up in the direction of Sprigg, which was where the greater throngs were. Easier to get lost there. The other way took you to Grantly Square (which was round) and the front of St. Bruno's Cathedral.

And then he was on Chandler himself.

The first thing he did was cannon into a white-painted street mime who lurched backward against a car and broke character by speaking, "What the fu—?"

"Sorry, friend," Pincus gasped. "Cop. Did you—?"

"Fascist bastard."

Pincus ignored him, looked up and down the street, bewildered by all the colours and the crowds. The Kreep could be anywhere, could be any one of these carousing people.

Moto was at his shoulder, panting like a punctured accordion.

"Which way did she go?" the big man wheezed.

"'She'?" said Pincus, reflexively dodging a kick that the mime had aimed at his shin.

"Didn't you hear?"

"'Hear'?"

"The nun."

Pincus bit back what he was about to say.

"It was a nun was the one who attacked Wendy," said Moto, still catching his breath. "That was what the bulls were trying to tell you. But you just set off like there was a wasp had got up your ass."

Moto plunged past him and began running as quickly as he could up toward Sprigg. That wasn't so very quick because of all the people.

"You see a nun?" Pincus asked the mime.

"What's it to you, you crypto—?"

Pincus stuck his gun right into the mime's groin.

The white-painted face managed somehow to go grey.

"That way."

The mime pointed in the direction of Grantly Square.

Pincus sucked in his breath. It figured. The place for a pimp or a hooker or a drunk or a pickpocket to be unobtrusive was in among the raucous hordes of Sprigg – easy enough to get lost there. The place for a nun to be unobtrusive was in the environs of a cathedral.

Pincus looked around desperately for Moto but his partner was gone.

"Thanks, citizen," he told the mime.

He snaked between two parked cars and into the road.

Chandler was one-way, which should have made life easier. Facing him was a solid line of vehicles whose drivers were either sticking their heads out of their windows and bawling curses or leaning on their horns. Tangled in among the cars and trucks were cyclists who weren't getting anywhere either but who were getting in everyone's way while doing it. It was as if someone had updated one of the more lurid visions of Hieronymus Bosch and then added a soundtrack.

On the other hand, if getting through this mess was going to be difficult for Pincus, it must be equally difficult for the nun.

And, sure enough, he could see the dark shape up there ahead of him, maybe fifty yards off. She was pushing her way along the sidewalk. Most of the people were stepping aside for her, the way people do for nuns, but she still wasn't making much speed.

Who in their right mind would suspect a nun? It was the perfect disguise.

Pincus kept his gun out but threw his standard-issue flashlight away from him. If this had been a movie he'd have jumped up onto the hood of the car in front of him and started running along the car roofs. Unfortunately, the vehicle directly behind that car was a towering supermarket delivery truck, and Pincus had neglected to bring his ropes and grappling hooks.

He made better progress than he'd anticipated, maybe because of the gun, maybe because of the expression on his face – the combination of the two probably made him look like a madman.

Truth be told, he more or less *was* a madman.

It was just beginning to hit him that Wendy was down, had maybe been killed by the bastard who'd killed all those other kids. He knew it was irrational to think of Wendy as a kid or even a person, but that didn't change the way his gut felt. The pain wasn't as big as if it had been Alex who'd been hurt, but it was the same *sort* of guilt- and rage-swamped pain. He and Moto and the other cops should have looked after her better. They'd let her down.

Who cared about Moto and the other cops?

It was *Pincus* who'd let her down.

A red mist descended. He heard himself growling.

Somehow he forced his way through to where the many-spired grey mask of St. Bruno's loomed.

~~~

Inside, there was a service in progress. A mass, Pincus supposed. He didn't know much about religious rituals in general. Laretta had tried to drag him along to church a few times "for the sake of the child", but Alex had sided with his father and soon she'd abandoned the project as futile.

The priest up at the front didn't so much as skip a beat at the sight of a cop staggering in through the door with a gun in his hand and a maniacal look on his face. Pincus had to admire the man's professionalism. The show must go on, what?

Slowly Pincus advanced up the aisle towards the altar. He had no real way of knowing if the fugitive "nun" had in fact come in here – the imposter could have run away around the building through the curtains of shadows that hung there – but his coppish instincts were telling him the Kreep would have headed for the light and the company of others. The Kreep wasn't unintelligent – the skill with which he'd pulled off his crimes was testament enough to that – so he'd have guessed, when the spots came on to light up the scene of his latest crime, that a trap had been laid and the streets would be full of cops. The best place a nun could become part of the scenery was here in the house of God.

Pincus found he couldn't force himself to interrupt the priest's spiel to ask if anyone had seen a fake nun come flying in here, looking the worse for wear and maybe covered in someone else's blood.

At this time of night the congregation was patchy, to be charitable to the drawing power of the still intoning priest. Perhaps a quarter of the pews were filled, perhaps not even that, and some of the flock weren't so much worshipers as folk seeking refuge and warmth; there was even a couple of teenagers necking at the back. At least a score of the congregants were nuns. Pincus wondered if they were bussed in to bolster the flagging numbers, or something.

As he stalked steadily down the aisle with his gun held loosely at his side, he felt as if he'd strayed into the wrong movie.

And then he saw it.

On the floor at the edge of the pew just to his right was a sensible black shoe. There was nothing of especial note about the shoe itself – all of the other nuns seemed to be wearing shoes from the very same store.

Pincus promised himself he'd never again cuss out people who threw their litter into Fleshraker Alley.

Stuck to the side of this particular sensible black shoe was a used condom.

~~~

"It wasn't just the used condom," Pincus explained to the squad room a couple of hours later, once everyone was back at the precinct house and the Kreep Killer was firmly in the slammer in the building's bowels. "It was the stubble."

The explanation did nothing to quell the mirth that filled the room. Pincus had vaguely hoped – well no, not *hoped*, exactly, because he was by nature a self-effacing sort of guy, but *anticipated* – Pincus had anticipated he might be treated as a hero of the hour, and indeed the Loo had shaken his hand gravely and muttered something vanilla about an eternally grateful city. As for the other cops, though – well, it wasn't every day one of their number half-killed himself running down a serial killer and ended up arresting himself a nun.

Even if the nun had been no normal nun.

The Kreep Killer must have noticed the condom at the same moment Pincus did, and recognised what it meant. By the time the cop had stopped and turned toward the pew, the Kreep had a knife out and was halfway to standing.

Pincus raised his gun quicker than thought, jamming it up under the Kreep's chin, wondering if he dared shoot an actual nun in an actual cathedral, bearing in mind he hadn't dared to do so much as interrupt the priest's peroration. With his other hand he chopped down savagely on the Kreep's wrist, sending the knife skittering across the cathedral's ornate mosaic-tiled floor to embed its point with a chunk at the base of the pew on the far side of the aisle.

There was another sound, which Pincus correctly interpreted as the Kreep's wrist shattering.

The Kreep howled in agony.

It was only then that Pincus realised that this *really* wasn't your orthodox variety of nun.

We all joke – except other nuns, presumably – about nuns having stubbly chins, but this one actually had a forest of the stuff.

That, and an Adam's apple.

The nun who'd been sitting in the pew just on the other side of the Kreep was beginning to notice exactly the same thing about her erstwhile neighbour. A practical woman whom Pincus grew to like a lot over the next few minutes, Sister Máire leaped to her feet and helped him get the Kreep face-down on the floor with his hands cuffed behind his back.

The cuffs must have been irksome to that broken wrist, but

Pincus didn't care.

By now the priest had finally stopped intoning and had dug a cellphone out of his cassock. Within minutes half-a-dozen uniformed bulls came charging through the door.

Pincus waited just long enough to make sure there was someone taking charge who knew it was their job to bring the Kreep Killer in to the 14th, and then he was setting off again as fast as he could go.

~~~

When he got there, he found that Moto must have had the same idea. The big man was among a little group of cops standing around the place where Wendy had fallen.

"There's a medevac copter on its way," Moto said in answer to Pincus's unspoken question.

"What's keeping them?"

Pincus had lost track of time but he knew it couldn't be less than a half-hour since he'd been here last.

Moto shrugged. "Bureaucracy, I guess. Or somebody's daughter needed it to take her to the ball."

He gave a sigh to indicate there was no end to the petty corruption of New Amsterdam's elected rulers. "You catch the guy?" Moto said, almost as an afterthought.

"On his way to the precinct, even as we speak." Pincus thought he ought to be feeling more satisfaction than he was. All he could make himself be concerned about, though, was the kid sprawled at their feet.

Not a kid, Pincus told himself angrily for the hundredth time. She just *looks* like a kid.

Despite what he was telling himself, he couldn't help feeling it was somebody's daughter he was looking at. Somebody's broken daughter.

One of the fake winos had rolled up a uniform jacket and put it under Wendy's head to make her more comfortable, but aside from that they were, like good cops, not moving her more than was strictly necessary.

Which was not at all.

"She going to live?" said Pincus, trying to make his voice sound matter of fact. It broke a little anyway.

"Depends what you mean by living," said Moto noncommittally.

"Where the *fuck's* that copter?" said Pincus after a few more seconds. He turned to look out over the wasteland.

As if it had heard his words, the bird suddenly appeared over the rooftops, bringing the ruckus of its rotors with it. It descended nervously, its pilot obviously unsure of the stability of the ground beneath.

At last it was settled and a pair of EMTs came sprinting toward the cops – well, not so much sprinting, the terrain being what it was, but hobbling pretty fast. The medics shoved the cops aside and got Wendy onto a stretcher as quickly as they could.

Pincus never knew why he said what he said next.

"Can I come with her?"

"Not a good idea, buddy," said one of the EMTs.

"But—"

"She's going to make it," the man said. "They're not like you and me. They can take far worse damage than this and be back on their feet, right as rain, within a week or two. It don't take that long for their flesh to regrow. It's not as if the bastard hit anything vital."

Pincus looked down at all the blood and torn skin across Wendy's torso, at the gash across her throat and the stab-wound in her left eye, and wondered where "anything vital" could possibly be located.

Just then she opened her good eye and looked directly at him with a piercing blue gaze.

"Don't worry, Detective Pincus," she said. "I've known worse. Like I said, I can look after myself."

"But you're hurt real bad."

"They don't feel pain," said the EMT. "Not the way you and I do. Her central processor's aware of all the physiological damage and disrupted circuitry, and no doubt it feels something equivalent to discomfort, but—"

The EMT broke off, suddenly aware that the direction of Wendy's gaze had shifted to him. Then the eye was looking at Pincus's face again.

"That's what it says in the manual, anyway," she told him.

~~~

The party in the squad room went on half the night, to the joy of who knows how many small-time crooks and lowlifes in and around the 14th, who were able to carry on their self-appointed tasks without the fear of untimely interruption from the boys and gals in blue.

Pincus phoned Laretta to explain he was going to be late, very late, and to tell her what had happened – not to mention murmuring a few sweet fatherly nothings into his son's sleepy ear – and she informed him that if he got home drunk she had the Bloody Marys already in the fridge and the strong black coffee already in the pot.

But Pincus didn't get drunk. He threw back a few just to show everyone he was one of them, but he soon realised he wasn't in the mood. He kept seeing that damaged little face, the blue eye watching him, the lips curling into a painful smile, and how the next thing he knew the EMTs were running back toward the copter with Wendy on the stretcher between them. He wanted to run after them but, as if he were trapped in a nightmare, the air had turned to glue and he couldn't move.

"I should have insisted," he'd said to Moto. "I should have insisted on going to the hospital with her."

"I know how you feel," said the big man, putting an arm around Pincus's shoulders. "But she's not going to any hospital. She's just going in for maintenance. Pretty drastic maintenance. The city's gonna have a big bill to pay."

Pincus shook his head, shaking away the words. "I should have gone with her," he said.

Now, while the squad room got noisier and noisier – things weren't helped by someone having had the bright idea of persuading a couple of the Sprigg Street hookers to come in and do a strip on top of a desk – Pincus sat with his chin in his cupped hand.

You can't take the moment with you, he thought. It soon becomes the past, and there's nothing you can do about that. She wasn't a child. She wasn't a woman. She was – she *is* – just a very clever machine. Manufactured nineteen years ago, going on twenty. A machine.

But the more he told himself this the more he couldn't make himself believe it.

PROMISES

Nancy Kilpatrick

Karl loved the freedom of the BMW R1200GS, had for the last two months he'd been touring, but today more than ever. He'd just spotted the rabbit or mole or whatever the hell that furry thing was darting across the A299. Hit the gas – great torque! Big tire at the back of the bike, anti-locking discs in the front, meant he could swerve and speed at the same time in this weather and miss the thing instead of having it squashed beneath his wheels. The R1200 was a major bike and he could have done with 460 pounds instead of 560 all equipped, plus him, but it's the one he and Jen had talked about so that's the one he used the money for. He had wanted to do it right. It was the only way.

He could ride half a day without the need to stop for anything, the foreign scenery enough to engage him, the feel of the wind on his face, the six speeds allowing ascent and descent with no trouble. And speed! He could speed from this present into a future that was far from the past.

The good part was that no one on this earth knew where he was. Or where he was going. He didn't know that himself, which was the best part. The worst part was the rain, cold, pitiless, relentless, wet and damp sliding down under the collar of his leather jacket like the icy fingers of death, the humidity building behind the visor until the road blurred to an altered reality. He flipped up the visor only to get pelted in the face by the onrushing torrent of moisture slamming him horizontally.

He pulled the visor down again and in that moment saw Jen's face. Her eyes, staring, seeing and not seeing him. It was enough to get his heart slamming against his ribs and in that split second he nearly lost control of the bike as he shoved the faceplate high again. Rain was better than that, way better!

As he caught his breath, he thought how he didn't care if he wasn't seeing so good. Riding without his full faculties might be dangerous for others. But he didn't really care about other people. We live, we die, he thought, and figured there was nothing anybody could do about that, or anything else. When your number is up, it's up. It was just some god's sick joke how some went out in pain.

Rain fell from the darkening sky in grey sheets. Many cars had pulled to the side of A299. Even his class-A German brakes probably wouldn't hold out for long – the highway was turning into a river. He pulled off at the next junction.

The exit led to a B road that went into yet another small sea-side town – he'd passed a sign that said Whitstable, or something like that. He hadn't heard of it, but he hadn't heard of any of these places in England. These were the spots he'd promised to take Jen to on their honeymoon, far from the congested cities and soulless suburbs she detested. "The world is different in England, in the small towns and villages," she'd told him. "It's old, older than North America. Odd. Not everything is what you think it will be." And while he didn't want reminders of the past, they came upon him often enough, like now, and he let the nostalgia roll off his back like water. Maybe if he hadn't embarked on this journey, crossed the ocean to fulfil their dream, *her* dream, maybe he wouldn't remember so much. But no. It was the remembering that drove him over here in an effort to finish remembering. He wanted this to end.

Once he reached the town proper, he found High Street and it eventually led to Harbour Street, one way, which contrary to its name wasn't at the water but after a few blocks curved to a different road with cottages on one side and the bay of the North Sea on the other. The gale knocked the boats in the tumultuous water wildly about, though he couldn't see either the houses or the water or the boats clearly in this downpour, just the overview.

The rain had increased, water gushing relentlessly from the sky, and he followed small streets and got as far as Harbour Street again before deciding he had to stop. Even the paved road here was too slippery now. The thought occurred to him that maybe he should turn around again, ride alongside the water until the bike skidded off the road and onto the sand, drive at full throttle letting the big bike soar into the estuary until the sea covered him, or until he was launched into the air, then plunging into the murky depths, letting the engine carry him along as far as it could into the icy cold bay, ending this bitter existence. He thought all this while he slowed the bike and perused the shops on Harbour Street. He hoped for a pub or cafe where he could get out of the wet, get one of those warm British beers he hated, or at least a coffee.

A shoe shop, an antique store, a café – and he'd spotted plenty of oyster shacks on his ride through town. He saw a large pub that looked possible, but every last shop, restaurant and even the pub was closed. He checked his watch, reading the time and the date and the day, remembering that they rolled up the streets early in small-town England, especially on a Sunday, but not this early. Maybe it was a holiday here or something. Maybe it was the storm.

He nudged the bike along at the lowest speed possible, barely able to even read the shop names. Lightning lit the sky beyond the buildings in the direction of the water that he couldn't see from here, and thunder crashed overhead. This was an unpleasant *déjà vu*, and his spirits sank. He could just imagine the BMW struck by lightning, knocking out the transmission, and him being stranded in – he didn't remember the name of this town – until the local garage could get replacement parts! Stranded and going crazy. Driving off a pier was looking better and better.

Lightning cracked overhead, the electricity zinging through the air, and he noticed a nearby shop with the sign turned to *Open*. It was in a narrow red-brick building, the door frame and those of the two bay windows on either side of it were painted white, the door itself a rich blue. The structure wedged tight against two other narrow buildings, a barbershop on one side, a bakery selling meat pies on the other, both closed. He figured whatever this shop was, they'd probably forgotten to flip the sign. Still, he pulled up to the curb and dismounted, not bothering to lock the bike since he was pretty sure the door wouldn't open so he'd be back out here in this devil of a storm any second.

But the door was not locked and opened easily. A small brass bell overhead jingling to announce his arrival. He pulled off his helmet but ducked his head back out the door to see what the lettering on the window glass said. Just before a ferocious wind drove him back inside he caught one word only: *Museum*.

Just his luck. A place with dusty crap from the past, a past that likely should be forgotten, as all pasts should be. He closed the door a bit too hard, dripping water onto the grassy mat with a picture of three black kittens just inside the doorway. Standing there, he felt awkward, as if this was the last place in the world he should have entered, and it was.

He'd never been into museums. Well, that wasn't completely true. He'd visited quite a few with Jen in Michigan, and one on a weekend trip they'd taken to New York. She'd grown up in England and retained fond memories of these pavilions that paid homage to former eras. And he had to admit that he'd become a little more interested as time went on, mainly because of her enthusiasm. But not now. Now, he never wanted to see another museum again. Not in this life, anyway!

He turned with a sigh, about to put his helmet back on and brave the elements. The street through the window glass had darkened even more from the hovering rain clouds, the precipitation still crashing to the pavement by the bucket load.

Suddenly, thunder boomed overhead and shook this building's foundation.

"May I help you?"

He glanced to the corner to find a thin woman with an erect posture whose face was wrinkled from what must have been at least eighty years on this earth. She wore a mid-calf, long-sleeved dress the colour of midnight, with small silvery stars sprinkled in the fabric's pattern, and over that a sand-coloured cardigan with black buttons. Her veiny hands were clasped one over the other at her waist, and he wondered if this was some sort of ex-nun's museum.

She tilted her grey-haired head slightly to the side and seemed to look past him, out the window, with pale rheumy eyes. "Inclement!" she remarked. Followed by a "Tsk". Then, "It's good you've come in out of the elements. You'd not want to catch your death, now, would you?"

He thought of saying *Ma'am, that would be a real blessing,* but decided on the more pragmatic, "Sorry. I didn't know this was a museum. I was looking for a café, or a pub, but they're all closed."

"Yes, well, Sundays in January are damp and chilly. And this weather," she said in her precise English, sweeping a bony hand towards the window with a flourish, as if he might have forgotten the heavy wind and rain, or as if she might be responsible for it. "The townsfolk tend to stay home and enjoy the roast." She paused and stared at him vacantly, then smiled. "We are not a café, but I can offer you a cup of tea."

"I don't want you to go to any trouble."

"Nonsense! It's no trouble at all. I've the kettle already on the hob. It will steam in a moment. In the meantime, I can show you our collection."

Great, he thought, she's going to bore me with all this old junk then sit and bore me with her life story for a couple of hours. The only part that sounded good was the tea, though generally, unlike Jen who grew up on it, he didn't much like tea. Still, anything liquid and warm would do. Besides, he didn't know how to get out of here without being rude, and this seemed to be the only game in town. The kettle couldn't be far from boiling and maybe he could just gulp down the tea and escape.

"Unlike other themed museums we do not have an enormous collection, but I must say that what we do have is unique. Come, have a look."

He glanced around and realised to his relief that there were only a few wood and glass cases of objects. A bust sat on a pedestal in one corner, and in another a uniform on a mannikin, complete with a plumbed helmet and sword, but he was never much for military history and had no idea what war it was from. There was also a bookcase with four shelves of volumes but he figured she wouldn't talk much about those, or at least he hoped not. Maybe he could convince her that as a North American native, he didn't know how to read English!

They started at the back and she went through the items fairly quickly, much to his relief. A medal for distinguished service for something or other, a small figurine "That he made," she said. It took him a while to figure out who she was talking about.

"And in this case is the locket Peter gave to his beloved wife Helen a decade before her death. You can see their pictures inside, and we've secured double mirrors behind so you can read the lovely inscription on the back."

The old woman paused, quietly staring at the locket. Her thin lips turned up a little at the corners. "They made a charming couple, and he adored her. Her passing left him devastated. Gone now, both, but they're together at last. Today's the anniversary of her death. Oh, there's the kettle!"

She turned and walked off, leaving him bent over the case, staring at an open round gold locket with images from the past, maybe from fifty or more years ago: a slim nearly cadaverous man and a pretty sweet-looking woman, the photographs hazy with time and the era in which they had been shot. On the back he could see reflected in the mirror words etched into the gold in a flowery script. As he peered closer to read it he heard a voice in his head that was not his own: *we will meet again, this is my promise.*

Jen's voice! Pain and fear radiated through his heart as if a thorn had gotten imbedded there. A date was inscribed on the locket: January 14th. Today's date. And also – the date Jen died.

What followed was what he knew to be his lifesaver: fury. He wanted to pound the glass case, shatter it, grab the locket and hurl it as far as he could. He snarled under his breath: "*We will meet again, this is my promise.* What bullshit!"

"I've a small table in back, if you'll join me there," the old woman said, and he snapped his head towards her. She didn't appear fazed by the hideously angry mask that his face must have become, or sense the despair and madness seeping from his pores, just stared at him with another small smile on her lips.

She turned and headed between the two panels of the dark fabric curtain, holding one side open for him to enter. For a moment he didn't want to follow, just get the hell out of here, out of this museum, this town, this country, this world! But he took a deep breath and stood upright, then moved towards the curtain, feeling the anger subside as if it was a boulder being eroded by the North Sea waves.

The back room was very small, a mini office really, with just enough room for an old-fashioned roll-top desk, a wooden desk chair, an extra chair, and a little table. On one wall-shelf sat a hotplate which held the heavy-looking iron kettle emitting steam through its spout. Next to the kettle were old-school boxes and tins of tea and cookies, and a mug holding cutlery. Beneath the shelf stood a bar-size refrigerator, and next to it an infrared heater glowing red-orange that barely warmed the room. Every other item was on the tea table: black porcelain tea pot with a silver moon and stars that rivalled the colour and pattern on the woman's dress, two matching cups and saucers, a solid black sugar bowl with silver tongs, a sand-coloured pitcher of milk, two teaspoons and a plate of what the British called *biscuits*, in this case the Walkers shortbread rectangles that Jen had loved.

"Please be seated, Mr … oh, we've not introduced ourselves! I'm Mrs Black. One of the infrequent curators of the museum."

"Harris. Bob Harris." He reached out a hand awkwardly and they shook, and he found her skin dry and cool, the bones beneath fragile and likely brittle enough that a firm handshake might break them. Harris wasn't his real name, Bob was. Harris was Jen's last name, and he didn't know why he'd said it but it was too late to retract now.

While he sat she went to the refrigerator slowly and took out a small plate, saying, "I'm afraid we don't keep supplies here but I imagine you're famished." She placed what looked to be an egg salad sandwich on brown bread on the table in front of him.

Before he could protest, or thank her, her hand fluttered to the silver broach of a full moon face pinned to the bodice of her dress. "I'm afraid I've no lemon. Do you take milk? Sugar?"

"Yes to both," he said, then, "thank you."

"Please, Mr. Harris, don't stand on ceremony. Do help yourself."

He realised that he hadn't eaten all day, nor most of yesterday. He picked up half the sandwich and took three quick bites, then two more, and that was the end of that half.

While she poured the old woman said, "I expect you're from North America."

"Detroit area," he mumbled, picking up the other sandwich half.

She handed him the cup of tea and then poured her own. "A lovely country, although I've not been in many decades. Do you miss your home?"

"No ma'am. I'm only here a short while."

"For business or pleasure?"

"Business, I guess you'd say."

"I expect that would be personal business, although I don't like to pry."

He looked at her, puzzled as to why she would think that.

"Because of the motorcycle." She smiled. "And your interest in the locket."

"I'm not interested in the locket."

That small smile turned her lips again. Lifting the plate, she said, "Biscuit?"

He helped himself to two, thinking that he would eat these then go, but she was already pouring more tea into his cup.

"Many are taken by the love between Peter and Helen. In our modern world, relationships frequently end abruptly."

He said nothing, just ate the shortbread, drank the new cup of tea quickly, and prepared to get out of here.

She kept talking as if she wasn't aware that he was about to depart. "I, myself, believe in an afterlife…"

Here it comes, he thought, *the religious spiel*. He placed his cup and saucer onto the table, about to stand up.

"Like Peter and Helen, I'm convinced of it. It's not unlikely. If we love someone deeply enough there's an expectation we will see them again."

"I don't believe that. I don't see any evidence of life beyond the grave."

"And me, I don't see at all!"

She stared at him with cataracted eyes, and it occurred to him that the woman was blind. Now that he thought about it, her movements, the way she gazed into space, how she had poured the tea, feeling the pot as if it were something she had to experience in a tactile manner… Knowing this made him feel more at ease and in control.

She placed her own cup and saucer on the table and said in a quiet voice, "Mr. Harris, I would not be surprised if you do see evidence yet refuse to acknowledge it. I sense you have lost someone dear."

It wasn't a question, but now that he knew she couldn't see him he didn't mind answering. "I have lost someone. My girlfriend. We were going to be married."

"What was her name?"

"Jennifer. Jen." For no reason he understood, he added, "She died a year ago today."

The old woman nodded in understanding. "And you see her everywhere, don't you?"

He closed his eyes. Yes, he saw Jen everywhere, all the time, twenty-four hours a day, and it was only by sheer willpower that he could block out images of her delicately beautiful face, the musical sound of her lilting voice, the sensual memory of her soft skin gently pressed against his…

"It's alright to cry, Mr. Harris. We all do. We've all lost someone."

When she said it he realised that a tear was trickling down his cheek. He looked up, unsure: maybe she *could* see him! But her blank gaze hadn't changed.

"Tell me how she died."

He didn't want to. He hadn't said these words to anyone and yet here he was, suddenly telling this stranger. "It was a heavy rain, like tonight. I picked her up from her bridal shower. I'd been out with the guys from work, both of us had been drinking, me more, I guess. Jen said we should catch a cab home but I didn't want to spend the money. In the car we argued, about something, about nothing. The truck came skidding out of nowhere and slammed into her side of —"

He stopped, listening to the silence in the room, the silence in his head. Somewhere a clock ticked as if time was passing quickly, too quickly, and he knew he had to get this out of him, he just had to!

"She didn't die right away. She lasted the night and most of the next morning. I was there, by her side, except for the OR. They put her into a coma, because of the head injuries, but she woke up once, just before she died. Jolted upright and turned to me, looked at me, looked *through* me, and…"

He stopped. He couldn't go on.

"What did she tell you, Mr. Harris? That you will meet again?"

He nodded, but of course the woman wouldn't see that. "She promised."

He bent forward, elbows on knees, face in his hands, sobbing like a child, his body racked with grief, the first tears he had been able to shed, and the old woman let him cry. Then, when the grief abated enough that he could hear her, she said, "Do you believe that she blames you?"

He shook his head. "No. Maybe. I don't know. I blame myself."

His mind was empty, as if every thought and image inside him had pulled away like a receding tide. Suddenly, he heard a voice. The old woman's? Jen's? He was unsure. *Whether or not we dead hold the living responsible for our condition, it is not your right to know. Only remember this, the promise: we will see one another again.*

The clock ticked and he felt a strange calm enshroud him, as if Jen's arms surrounded him, letting him know that she was all right, and that he would be as well. That she would keep her promise.

When he finally looked up, he was startled that the old woman was gone. He stood and went into the museum but she wasn't there either. A quick glance behind the curtain showed him that there was no washroom door, just a back door that must lead to a laneway, the security chain attached on the inside. Then he notice what was on the table or, more, what was *not* on the table. No tea service. No plates. Nothing.

A chill ran up his spine and he didn't want to think about what this meant. He just wanted to get out of this place, to keep moving, to be gone from here. As he hurried to the front door he thought, *I just want this over*. But he wasn't sure it would ever be over.

The rain had stopped. It was full night now, dark, this narrow street dimly lit, still devoid of life. The R1200 sat where he'd left it and he used his leather-jacketed forearm to brush rainwater off the seat and climb on. Just as the engine kicked in he noticed the sign in the window: *Closed*.

He thought about where to go: head back to the A299? Find another small town? Keep driving? For what? He had kept his promise to her; they saw her England together. It was over.

Instinctively, he drove along Harbour Street and turned towards the water. The full silvery moon lighted a carpet-like path along the sand to the black bay water aglitter with starshine. He pulled the visor down and then aimed the bike along this illuminated passage, picking up speed as he turned towards the darkness, letting Jen's enticing voice fill his emptiness with her promise.

THE SECRET PLACE

Samantha Lee

The baby in the guest wing,
Who crouches by the grate,
Was walled up in the west wing
In fourteen twenty-eight.
"The Stately Homes of England" – Noel Coward

The very first time Poppy saw Bertie he was standing on the first-floor landing peering down at her through the banisters. She'd come into the hall from the kitchen where she'd gone to get a drink, and suddenly there he was. A little boy in a sailor suit with curly blonde hair. Very solemn, very pale. Her heart gave a lurch and she spilled a few drops of milk onto the tiled floor.

"Who are you?" she said warily. "Where did you come from?"

"I'm Bertie", said the little boy, sidling along to the top of the flight. "I've come from upstairs."

Poppy took this information at face value, as any self-respecting five-year old would do. It was a big house. Lots of floors. Lots of rooms. Plenty of space for half-a-dozen little boys in sailor suits. Still, a bit more detail might come in handy.

"Whereabouts upstairs?" she asked.

Bertie waved a hand vaguely in the direction of the roof, as if the gesture explained all. "I'll show you sometime if you like," he said. "But you mustn't tell anybody I'm here. It's a secret."

Poppy knew all about secrets. Wasn't she a secret herself? Grandma said nobody knew where she came from. She was a present from Secret Santa. And she'd sniggered and Mummy had told her to "shut her face". And now she wasn't supposed to be here either. So yes, Poppy knew all about secrets. And about keeping quiet. And about hiding when things got "out of hand".

Bertie sat down on the top tread. He put his elbows on his knees and cocked his head to one side, staring down at her with his big blue eyes, eyes ringed with dark shadows, as though he hadn't slept in a while.

"Who are *you*?" he said. "Where did *you* come from?"

"My name's Poppy", said Poppy. "I've come from London. But I'm not staying long."

Bertie digested this, thoughtfully. Then his face brightened up as if he'd just had a wonderful idea.

"Would you like to come and play?" he said.

Poppy nodded. "I would, but I'm not allowed. It's against the rules. Mummy says that if I talk to anyone or go outside to play and anyone sees me, we'll be 'in the shit and no mistake'."

"Oh, I can't go outside either," said Bertie enigmatically. "But we can play indoors, can't we? If we're very quiet." His lips contorted into a conspiratorial smile and his voice dropped to a whisper. "I won't tell anyone if you won't."

Poppy glanced guiltily in the direction of the study where her mother was hammering out her thesis. They'd only come down to Wales so she could "get it finished in peace". After that they'd be going back to Grandma Johnston's flat and Poppy would be going to school. She didn't know whether to be excited or terrified at the prospect. There weren't many other children in the block where they lived. None that her mother thought were "suitable" company for her, anyway. If anyone came to the door and asked whether Poppy wanted to come out, Mummy sent them away "with a flea in their ear". So she didn't have any friends and she didn't really know how to play. Except by herself. But Bertie seemed nice. And anyway she liked the idea of having a secret of her own. So she smiled back at him and said "Okay."'

~~~

Brenda Johnson had won a bursary from a foundation that supported "people in strained circumstances" who might not otherwise have had the wherewithal to finish their studies. The grant came with a three-month tenure of a house down in the wilds of Wales where the charity ran self-improvement courses during the summer. It was a draughty old place full of shadows and strange creakings after the sun went down, which it did pretty early in the bleak midwinter. But it was a God send for Brenda. It got her away from her dipsomaniac mother and the buildings. The only fly in the ointment was Poppy. The rules said no children and she'd had to smuggle her daughter into the old manse under cover of darkness. She'd actually hidden her in the boot of her old banger when Mrs Evans, the caretaker, met her with the keys. Luckily the place was in the middle of nowhere. The ideal writer's retreat. And she was damned if she was going to leave Poppy with that drunken old sot. It wasn't ideal. But needs must. And it was only for three months.

The thesis was Brenda's passport to a new life. She thought she might even move out of London when she qualified. Wales seemed a safe sort of place, at least what she'd seen of it so far. It was certainly a world away from East Acton. She could change her name, maybe apply for a job at Aberystwyth University once the thesis had been accepted. Or Cardiff even? Somewhere a bit less isolated, where Poppy could go to a decent school. Make some friends. Stop having nightmares. She'd always had them, poor kid. Small wonder. But they seemed to be getting worse. When Brenda woke her up these days, the only thing Poppy would say was that it was dark and it was a secret. It was a bit of a worry to be honest. The child shouldn't be on her own so much. But it wasn't for long. And in this case, the end justified the means.

~~~

Poppy woke in the middle of the night. Bertie was standing by her bed, a dark shadow backlit by the night-light that her mother always left by her bed "to keep the goblins away". He looked so fragile she could almost see through him.

"I'm very cold," he said. "Can I come into your bed?"

Poppy peeled back the bedclothes wordlessly and he slipped in beside her, snuggling down under the eiderdown with a sigh. Cold wasn't the word for it. His skin was like ice. Poppy put her arms round him and hugged him close.

"Where's your mummy?" she asked. "When I'm cold my mummy lets me come into bed with her."

"I don't know where Mama is. I can't find her. I can't find anybody. They've all gone away."

"Away where?"

"Papa's gone away to the war. Fighting the Hun, Alice says. That's all I know. I've tried calling for Alice and for James and for Mama. I've even tried calling for Thomas, though he can't manage the stairs because of his bad leg. And I've told James I'm sorry. I've promised I'll never do it again. I've called and called. And it's cold and dark. But nobody comes."

The small body began to shake, racked with the despair of silent tears. Poppy hugged him tighter.

"Shh," she said. The last thing she needed was for Bertie to start crying in earnest. Somehow she didn't think her mother would approve if she came in and found them in bed together. Better she kept the whole thing a secret. That way nobody would get into trouble.

"I'll help you look for them tomorrow," she whispered. "They must be round here somewhere. They wouldn't just leave you on your own. Maybe they've gone to visit your Daddy at the war?" She sighed. "You're very lucky to have a Daddy. There's only Mummy and me. And Grandma of course. But Mummy says she doesn't count."

Bertie gave a little hiccup. Then he sniffed and wiped his eyes with a grubby fist. His fingernails were ragged and torn, as though he'd been scrabbling desperately at something and broken them in the process. Seeing Poppy's expression he tucked his hands away under the bed covers. "Do you have any brothers or sisters?" he asked, deflecting her question with a question.

"No. And I don't suppose I will have. Mummy says, 'never again'. Is Alice your sister?"

"No. Alice is my nurse. Her boyfriend is at the war too. She misses him dreadfully. James is my brother. James is a pig. It's warm in here. I haven't been warm for so long. Thank you, Poppy."

"That's okay," said Poppy. "It's nice to have company."

~~~

Brenda was in the middle of a particularly tricky paragraph when the doorbell rang. She was tempted to ignore it. Her head was in another time, another place. The Battle of the Somme to be precise. She knew if she left it now, the sentence she'd been constructing would disappear into the ether, never to be found again. But the damage had already been done, the thought was broken, so when the bell sounded a second time she gave a frustrated sigh, put the laptop on hold and moved out into the hall.

Poppy was sitting at the top of the stairs talking to herself. She stopped, looking slightly shifty, when her mother appeared. Brenda waved her off to her room, putting a finger to her lips in warning. Then she opened the door.

It was Irving Thomas, clutching an overflowing box of groceries. Brenda's heart sank. She'd forgotten a delivery was due. She reached out to take the box but he pushed past her with scant ceremony, a middle-aged Neanderthal in a dun grocer's coat. The red van with the family logo "Thomas and Son. Grocery and Dry Goods to the Gentry since 1915." throbbed and shuddered behind him in the drive. A trail of black smoke leaked from the exhaust; Mr Thomas was obviously of the school of thought that global warming was "a load of old tripe". The window was wound down on the driver's side. The ear-shattering blare of a rock anthem punctured the normally peaceful silence of the surrounding hills, the vehicle thus polluting the atmosphere on many levels.

Brenda stood back to allow the grocer to pass, picking up her purse from the hall table as she followed him into the kitchen. Irving Thomas gave her the creeps. The way he looked at her made her feel naked. That and his habit of using every excuse to make physical contact without actually giving offence. His big hands, pink as uncooked hams, had lingered too long against hers the last time she'd counted the money into his clammy palms. Normally she wouldn't have given the man house room but the nearest town was miles away and she couldn't leave Poppy alone to go shopping. So there was no alternative but to have her order delivered.

Unfortunately, Irving Thomas seemed to be labouring under the impression that this was an excuse on her part to strike up an acquaintance with him. Perish the thought. Each successive visit was becoming more of a trial. Despite her every effort to discourage him his looks were becoming more suggestive, his suggestions closer to the mark. She should have complained to the Foundation but then how could she explain why she didn't go and collect her groceries herself? So she suffered his intrusions in silence and tried to get shot of him as fast as possible.

"Keep the change," she said, scarcely glancing at the invoice, plonking some bills onto the kitchen counter in an attempt to avoid touching him.

Thomas raised his eyebrows.

"For your trouble," said Brenda lamely.

"No trouble at all, Miss Johnston. Pleasure to be of service."

He shoved the notes into his coat pocket with a leer, moving a bit closer than was strictly necessary as he squeezed past her, allowing a rogue hand to brush against her breast, "accidentally on purpose, like". His expression said it all. A woman on her own. Obviously gagging for it. Be doing her a favour really.

Brenda, sensing the insinuation, stepped back, flattening herself against the knife drawer, sweat starting to form in her hairline. She closed her eyes, disallowing a memory. Above all she mustn't make a noise. Mustn't frighten Poppy into showing herself. She needed this bursary. She needed this degree. A new life would mean her daughter never had to put up with this kind of shit.

"Any other little service I can help you with, you only have to ask." Thomas' breath, close to her cheek, smelled of boiled cabbage and tobacco. And something else. A hint of spirits. At three in the afternoon. Deja vu.

Brenda pulled herself together and opened her eyes. The grocer's face was a scant inch away, his eyes narrowed into feral slits. She remembered Poppy hiding upstairs, and a sudden fury surged into her veins. Fight – not flight then. She had someone other than herself to protect now. The thought gave her courage and, taking a deep breath, she stared her visitor down as though he were a rabid dog. Surprised at the sudden change of atmosphere, Thomas stepped away from her and headed for the door with a smirk.

"See you next week then," he said.

Not if I see you first, Brenda thought, scurrying down the hall after him to slam the door on his retreating back.

But Irving Thomas had not finished with her yet. As she heaved a sigh of relief, the flap on the postal slot snapped open and he peered into the hallway. "You must get lonely out here all on your own," he said. "Good looking woman like you. Any time you need some company, you know who to ask." Then he dropped the flap and moved away to the van, chortling under his breath.

Brenda leant her forehead against the door until the sound of the engine faded into the distance. Her knees were shaking and she was afraid if she moved she might fall flat on her face. She took a deep breath and went into the kitchen to make herself a cup of tea. She had a horrible feeling that Poppy wouldn't be the only one having nightmares tonight.

~~~

Poppy and Bertie were up in the attic, playing noughts and crosses in the dust on the floor. They'd been all over the house looking for James. Looking for any one of Bertie's relatives. But there was neither hide nor hair. Eventually they'd repaired to this space under the eaves, to what Bertie called "the nursery".

"I win again," he said, gleefully, drawing a line through three crosses. "You're not very good at this game, are you?"

"I've never played it before," said Poppy in her defence and then, changing the subject, "why did you say James was a pig?"

Bertie's face took on a bleak expression.

"Because he *is* a pig. You wouldn't want a brother like him. If I annoy him, he puts me down in the secret place."

"What's the secret place?"

"It's over there," Bertie inclined his head towards the fireplace. "It's a sort of hole. Behind the wall. We found it one day when we were playing hide and seek. None of the grownups know about it."

"Can I see it?"

"No."

"Why not?"

"Because."

"That's no answer," said Poppy. But Bertie just closed his lips very tight and shook his head, so she tried another tack. "What do you mean he puts you down the secret place if you annoy him? How do you annoy him?"

"Oh, you know. If I play with his toys without permission. If I beat him at noughts and crosses. He's not very good at it, either. Mamma says I'm the clever one in the family. James doesn't like that. If I do anything at all to make him cross he puts me down in the secret place. It's dark and cold and scary. I hate it."

Poppy was scandalised. "That's horrible," she said. "Why don't you tell someone?"

"James says if I do, he'll put me in the secret place forever and never let me out. He says he'll tell Mamma that I've run away. He says they'll never find me. They'll think the man with the sack has taken me."

"The man with the sack?"

"Yes. You know. The one who comes and takes naughty

children away. He puts them in a sack and takes them to his cave in the hills. And eats them."

"There's no such person." said Poppy, her voice trembling.

"Yes there is. Alice told me. Anyway I think James may have done that this time. I was playing with his favourite train and he caught me. He was absolutely furious. And he put me in the secret place. And he hasn't come back. And it's been a very long time. I'm hungry and I want my tea. I've called and called. But the walls are very thick and I don't suppose anyone heard me. I'm afraid Mamma will think the man with the sack has taken me. I'm afraid I'll never get out."

"What do you mean, never get out? You're out now, aren't you?"

Bertie brightened up. "Yes. Of course I am. And so are you," he said. "Maybe I just dreamed it? I like you Poppy. You won't go away, will you?"

"Not for a while anyway."

"I'd like it if you stayed here always," said Bertie. "Shall we have another game of noughts and crosses?"

~~~

Brenda looked up from her research papers. Through the study window she could see Mrs Evans coming up over the rise. The long-overgrown garden led down to the canal so she must have come along the towpath and in through the back gate. The Evans farm lay in the valley about a mile-and-a-half away, and the caretaker popped in now and again, usually around tea-time, just to make sure everything was "tickety boo".

"Not that I need to," she had said on her first visit. "You're as good as gold. Wish I could say the same for some of that lot what comes down in the summer for the workshops. Up to all sorts." She raised her eyes to heaven as though she hoped the Almighty might be her witness.

Brenda looked forward to Mrs Evans' visits. She sometimes brought fresh eggs and always home-made Welsh cakes. It was good to have a cup of tea and a "bit of a chat". Much as she loved Poppy, five-year old conversation wasn't the most stimulating thing in the world. She just had time to check that her daughter was upstairs before the older woman rapped on the door and let herself in with her own key.

The farmer's wife was everybody's image of the prefect grandmother. Cheery, kindly, homely. Normal. The total antithesis of the miserable gin-swilling old biddy back in East Acton with her fags and dubious hygiene and her filthy temper. Poppy would have loved Mrs Evans, and Brenda felt that if she'd taken the woman into her confidence in the first place she might have turned a blind eye. Too late now though. And at least Poppy would have a home-made Welsh cake for her tea.

"Yoo hoo. Anybody in?" Mrs Evans trotted down the hallway, divesting herself of scarf and coat. "Time for a cuppa?"

Brenda followed her through to the kitchen, reaching into the cupboards over the sink, transferring cups and saucers and plates and sugar and milk onto the big wooden table that commandeered the room, while her visitor put on the kettle. "Just a quick one," she said, pulling out a chair and sitting down.

"All work and no play," said Mrs Evans. "Bit of a break'll do you good." She warmed the pot, swirling the boiling water round and throwing it down the sink before ladling three spoonfuls of tea out of the caddy. "One for each person and one for the pot". Hot water added, she gave it a stir, put the lid on the teapot and poured the resultant brew into the cups through a battered wire strainer. The liquid was dark and strong. "The cup that cheers," she said, popping a knitted cosy over the pot and sitting down. Mrs Evans had brought the tea (and the pot) the first time she'd come over. "Proper Welsh tea," she'd said. "Not that coloured water you get from bags," and she'd shuddered as if she was talking about arsenic.

Brenda loved the ritual and though she still used bags herself, she had to admit the result was nothing like Mrs Evans' offering. She took a grateful sip and felt it flow into her veins like hot lava.

"Have a Welsh cake," said Mrs Evans, pushing across the plate. "Have two. You look peaky, child. You should get out more. I can't understand why you don't go into town now and again? Not healthy to be stuck in the house all the time. Especially this house."

"What do you mean, this house?"

"Big draughty rambling place," said Mrs Evans evasively. "And you all on your own, rattling around like a pea."

"It breaks the concentration if I leave." Brenda used the usual excuse. "I need to get this thesis done before the tenure is up. I can't afford to go gallivanting into town."

"What's it about then? This thesis of yours?"

"It's about the Great War."

Mrs Evans looked at her over the rim of her teacup.

"My Grandfather fought in the Great War," she said. "Never came back. Buried in Belgium somewhere. The Scott-Archers owned this place then. Well-to-do family. Owned most of the surrounding land too. Or did until the tragedy happened."

Brenda pricked up her ears. "Tragedy? What tragedy?" she said

Mrs Evans looked uncomfortable. She shifted in her seat. "Never mind," she said. "I shouldn't have mentioned it."

"Too late now. You *have* mentioned it. So come on. Tell me. What tragedy?"

Mrs Evans shook her head. "It's not a pretty story. I had it from my mother and I have to say the thought of it has haunted me ever since. Better you stay in blissful ignorance."

"I'm a city chick, Mrs Evans," said Brenda. "Not much spooks me. Tell me. Otherwise I'll be imagining all sorts of horrors. Don't leave me hanging on."

Mrs Evans shuddered. "Hanging's the word," she said. "They hanged the nurse, you know? Even though they never found the body."

Brenda's bravado slipped a little. She took another sip of tea to conceal her unease. "What nurse? What body?"

"The little boy's body. There was talk about him being snatched by the man with the sack."

"Sorry?"

"It's an old wives' tale," Mrs Evans went on. "Country folk

used to believe that if you took the fat from round the vital organs of a child and smeared it on your body and ate the heart it would give you eternal life. There was supposed to be a man with a sack who would kidnap children and sell them on for just such a purpose."

"That's preposterous," said Brenda, scornfully. "Who would believe such a thing in the twentieth century?"

"You'd be surprised. Especially in the winter when the dark nights start drawing in. There wasn't the education back then. A lot of ignorance. No television. These stories got handed down from generation to generation. Embellished. Like Chinese whispers. Might have been some basis in it in the dim dead days beyond recall. We're Celts, you know? The old religions performed human sacrifices."

"That apart, you and I both know there's no man with a sack. So what happened to the little boy?"

"Nobody knows. That's the problem. The whole episode started with an accident. Colonel Scott-Archer was an Army Chaplain. He was away at the front at the time, so there was only Mrs Scott-Archer and the two boys and the nurse living in the house. Oh, and there was Irving Thomas. He worked as a sort of odds-body. Driver. Gardner. He had a gammy leg so he couldn't be drafted. Lived out but came in every day in a horse and buggy. His son was engaged to the nurse by all accounts."

"Anyway, one day the oldest boy, James, tripped on a toy train that had been left at the top of the stairs and fell down the whole flight. His mother and the man, Thomas, drove him to the doctor but he'd broken his spine. The state of the roads didn't help and he died later that night. Needless to say his mother was distraught. But there was worse to come. They'd been in such a rush they hadn't had time to locate Bertie, the youngest, before they left so the nurse was instructed to find him and give him his tea. But when they came back, Alice – that was the girl's name – swore the child wasn't in the house. She said she assumed he'd jumped on the cart at the last minute and gone with them. Whatever, the child was missing. They searched the place from top to bottom to no avail. That's when the rumours started about the man in the sack."

"But surely the police didn't believe that?"

"No. Good sense prevailed with the authorities, at least. But in the absence of any other evidence the nurse got blamed. Even though they never found the body she was found guilty of doing away with the child."

"Why? Why on earth would she do such a terrible thing?"

"Why indeed? There was talk of witchcraft and all sorts. Nonsense of course. But the Colonel was well thought of and people were baying for blood, anybody's blood. They might have put it down to accidental death but on the day of the Assizes word came through that the Colonel had been killed in action. It tipped Mrs Scott-Archer over the edge. She drowned herself in the canal. That sealed the Alice's fate."

Brenda drew a deep breath. Despite having said she wasn't easily spooked, she could feel goose bumps rising on her forearms. The ensuing silence was punctured by the sound of a sheep calling down in the valley. "My God," she said. "What a catalogue of disasters."

Mrs Evans nodded in agreement. "The only one that got anything out of it was Irving Thomas. Colonel Scott-Archer left him some money in his will and he used it to start the Grocery business. It's still a mystery what happened to little Bertie. The nurse went to her death protesting her innocence. But if Alice didn't kill him and dispose of the body, then where is he? There hasn't been a sign of the child since."

Brenda shuddered. "Maybe he's buried in the garden?" she said.

"No, the police dug that up. But his poor mother's there. They wouldn't bury her in hallowed ground. Suicide, you see? She's under the pear tree, down by the wall."

"That's awful. There isn't even a headstone."

"Different times," said Mr Evans. "The house lay empty for years. Nobody local would touch it with a bargepole. It's was in a terrible state of disrepair by the time the Foundation bought it.

Needless to say, they got it for a song. There's always been a rumour about it being haunted. You haven't felt anything yourself, have you? Not seen anything … unusual?"

"You mean like a ghost?" Brenda snorted. "I'm from East Acton, Mrs E. We don't believe in ghosts."

Mrs Evans gave her a long look. "You're not in East Acton now," she said.

A sudden image of Poppy sitting at the top of the stairs talking to herself floated into Brenda's mind. She blanked the thought out before it could take hold. Just an invisible friend. Kids invented them all the time. Known fact. Nothing to worry about.

Mrs Evans reached across the table and took Brenda's hand. "Don't look so concerned, dear," she said. "It was a long time ago and I shouldn't even have mentioned it. I'm sorry."

"Was Irving Thomas related to the man who delivers my groceries?" said Brenda, changing the subject.

Mrs Evans screwed up her face. "His grandfather was the one as was engaged to Alice. Survived the war. Married a girl from Swansea. They've always been an honest family. But you want to watch the current Irving. Bad lot. Too fond of the drink. Handy with his fists as well. His wife's my second cousin. Poor Oinwen has walked into more doors than I've had hot dinners, if you get my drift? Never mind things that go bump in the night," she said. "I wouldn't trust Irving Thomas as far as I could throw him."

~~~

Poppy, squashed against her chest, could feel her mother's heart thumping beneath her jumper.

She'd been sitting on an old cabin trunk, drawing a picture, when Brenda had burst in like a whirlwind in jeans. "What are you doing up here?" she scolded. Her voice had a strange shake to it. "I've been looking all over the house for you. I thought you'd run away."

Poppy disengaged herself and smoothed out her artwork, which had been crumpled under the force of the attack.

"I like it up here," she said. "This is the nursery. And I'm only drawing."

"Who told you it was the nursery?"

"Nobody," said Poppy, the same guilty look sliding across her face. "I just guessed."

"Well, come downstairs now. Mrs Evans has left some Welsh cakes." Brenda reached over to take the piece of paper from Poppy's hand. "Can I see?"

The sketch was crude. No more than a doodle really. But it was obviously supposed to be a little boy. A little boy with a shock of curly hair and a big smile on his face. He was wearing some sort of sailor outfit. Brenda felt a cold shiver run up her spine.

"Who's this?" she asked, not really wanting to know the answer.

Poppy's head swivelled towards the fireplace. "It's a secret," she said.

Brenda followed her gaze. The outline of a child hung for the merest instant, superimposed against the wallpaper. Then, like a fading firefly or a guttering candle the image was snuffed out. She shook herself. Then she took Poppy by the shoulders and shook her too. "I don't want you to come up here again, Poppy," she said fiercely. "Do you understand me? Not now. Not ever."

"Why not?" Poppy protested.

"Because I say so, that why not," said Brenda pushing her daughter out of the room. Her voice floated up into the nursery as they clattered down the stairs. "We'll be going home soon, and until we do I want you to stay on the ground floor, close to me."

~~~

It was four in the morning when Brenda heard the noise. It didn't wake her up. She hadn't been asleep. She'd asked Poppy to come and sleep with her, more for her own sake than anything else. But Poppy was adamant. She wanted to stay in her own bed. In her own room. It was just down the hall and Brenda had been there three times already during the course of the night, just to check. But Poppy was sleeping peacefully. Dead to the world.

The noise came out of the blue, a sudden sharp sound like shattering glass followed, after a short interval, by the sound of someone or something moving around furtively downstairs. Brenda held her breath. Dear God, was the place really haunted? The vision in the nursery had really unhinged her. For the first time since she'd moved here, the isolation of the old house impressed itself on her. At least in East Acton you could rush out in the street and shout for help. Who would hear her in this neck of the woods if a man with a sack came to snatch her Poppy?

Came an ominous creak from the stairwell.

Brenda sat bolt upright in bed. Get a grip. Ghosts didn't break windows. And there was no man with a sack. If it had just been herself, she might have stayed shivering under the covers. But there was Poppy to think of. Who or whatever was in the house, she was going to have to confront it.

She swung her feet out of bed and picked up the poker she'd brought up from the study earlier on. Why had she done that? Could you hit a ghost with a poker? The thought made her smile despite herself. It was probably the janitor in a mask. Like in Scooby Doo.

She turned on the bedside light and was shrugging into her dressing gown when the door swung open and Irving Thomas tip toed into the room, undoing the belt on his trousers.

~~~

Poppy was deep in a dream when the scream brought her back to reality. A happy dream for a change, not a bad one. In her dream it was a sunny day and she and Bertie were out playing in the garden. His mummy was there too, sitting on a deckchair under the pear tree. For a minute when she woke up she didn't know where she was. Then came another scream, louder, more piercing. She sat up and rubbed her eyes. There were voices coming from the next-door bedroom. Voices raised in anger. The same sort of voices she used to hear when Mummy and Grandma were going at it "hammer and tongs". But Grandma wasn't here. And anyway one of the voices was deeper, darker. A man's voice.

She slid out of bed and padded out into the hall in her bare feet. It was cold but she didn't want to go back for her slippers. Now that she was closer she could hear what the voices were saying. First her mother...

"Get off me, you bastard."

And then the other voice, the man's, wheedling. "Come on girl. You know you want it."

Then her mother screaming that he should "fuck off" and sounds of a struggle and the tone of the man's voice changing suddenly to fury—

"Come at me with a poker, would you, you bitch? Well I'll show you who's master here—" Followed by another scream.

Then a loud thunk.

Then silence...

Poppy scurried to the bedroom door, her heart in her mouth, afraid of what she might see. And what she saw was like something out of a nightmare. Except that in this case, she wasn't dreaming.

Her mother was lying on her back on the floor. A trickle of liquid, seeping from her left ear, was slowly surrounding her head in a dark puddle. Her pyjama top was torn open. A man was leaning over her, a bloody poker in his hand.

Poppy screamed at the top of her voice and the man turned, his face a monstrous mask in the light. His eyes opened in surprise when he saw her. Then his mouth contorted into the semblance of a grin and he made a sound, half-snarl, half-chuckle. For all the world like the wolf in Little Red Riding Hood.

He should have said "all the better to eat you with, my dear". Instead he said, "Any port in a storm." He dropped the poker and took a step towards her, his trousers concertinaing round his ankle as he did so.

Poppy stood transfixed, her mouth dry, her heart racing. She knew she needed to get away from the danger but her feet wouldn't move. Wake up. Wake up. But she couldn't wake up. And then Bertie was there beside her.

"Run, Poppy. Run." he said. "It's the man with the sack."

And Poppy fled following after the wraith-like figure as Bertie flitted along the dark corridor and up the stairs towards the nursery. Behind her she could hear the man cursing as he tried to pull up his trousers. His voice filled her with unimagined terror and she started to shriek, the sound of her howls giving her whereabouts away so that he knew which direction she'd taken.

She ran like a headless chicken, bumping into walls, her bare feet skidding on the dusty floorboards. She could hear the man grunting, gaining on her, his strides longer than hers, his footsteps thudding on the uneven floor. She could smell him now too. He smelled like Grandma when she'd been "at the sauce".

She hurtled up the stairs in Bertie's wake. Into the nursery. Mummy had told her not to come up here. Mummy would be cross. Mummy. Poppy looked round for somewhere to conceal herself. The nursery was a dead end. Nowhere to go. Nowhere to hide. She could hear the sound of the man with the sack lumbering up the final flight. He was taking the stairs two at a time. Her pyjamas bottoms were sticking to her legs where she'd wet herself.

Bertie turned to face her. A sliver of moonlight shining through the dormer window haloed his blonde curls, outlining his translucent body in light.

"Over here," he said, gliding over to the fireplace, insinuating himself into a space between the chimney and the wall, beckoning Poppy across, pointing to an uneven spot in plaster. "Press that," he said, and when Poppy hesitated, "press it. *Now!*"

Poppy did as she was bid and a small section of the wall slid away revealing an empty space in the darkness. A sort of large cupboard leading back and down. A kind of pit. Empty. Or was it? As her eyes adjusted to the gloom she could just make out something like a bundle of old clothes huddled in the lower far corner.

"Get in," whispered Bertie.

"I don't want to," said Poppy. She was trembling all over. "I don't like it in there. It's dark and it smells funny."

She could hear panting from the direction of the stairwell and then a voice, filled with a kind of maniacal glee. The scariest voice she'd ever heard in her life. Scarier even than her grandmother when she was in one of her drunken rages.

"Come out, come out, wherever you are," said the voice.

"Get in," said Bertie, getting in himself and turning towards her, holding out his hands. "Come on. Jump down. I'll catch you. Get in, Poppy, or the man with the sack will get you."

Poppy jumped. And as her feet hit the floor, the section of wall slid closed behind her, trapping her in the dark.

She began to cry in earnest then, her voice coming in great hiccups between the sobs. "I'm afraid, Bertie," she said. "I'm afraid. The man with the sack has killed Mummy. Don't let him get me. Don't let him eat me."

A small cold hand snaked out to take hers in the darkness.

"It's all right, Poppy," said Bertie. "Don't be afraid. You're safe now. You're with me. I'll look after you. I'm your friend. Don't worry about the man in the sack. He'll never find you here. This is a secret place. The walls are so thick nobody can hear. Nobody. Lie down beside me for a while, Poppy. James will be coming to let us out soon."

HYDROPHOBIA

John Llewellyn Probert

When she wakes the world is water.

Tamara is dreaming. She must be. How else can she account for the fact she doesn't need to breathe? Neither does she need to pull back the bedclothes because she is lying, or rather floating, five inches above them. Her first thought is of the mundane. She must have gone to sleep outside the covers last night, but she doesn't remember. Had she really had that much to drink?

She doesn't remember drinking either. Not alcohol, anyway.

The water reaches to her bedroom ceiling. Perhaps it extends beyond it, for all she knows. The room is lit by a dull glow. It's not from her bedside lamp, nor from the ceiling light. She stifles a giggle and notes two tiny bubbles escape her lips as she does so. Maybe she has been asleep for so long those deep-sea creatures that can phosphoresce have taken up residence, creating the eerie blue-green light that allows her to see what little she can.

The bedside lamp is on its side, but the metal canopy that houses the bulb doesn't look rusty. She can't have been down here that long, then.

Down here?

Now her eyes are adjusting she can see more, but that's not necessarily a good thing. Because now she can see the shapeless shadows above her, the ones twisting in sinuous movement around one another.

She has to wait for her heart to calm down (how is it still beating, anyway?) before she realises these creatures of darkness are her clothes.

The wardrobe door is opening and closing, opening and closing, pushed and pulled by the gentle rhythm of the water's movement. With each pull another garment sneaks its way out to add to the growing population.

As a red flat-heeled shoe floats past (she bought the pair on sale at M&S and is sorry to see how much the water has already ruined the leather) she realises that the ongoing accumulation of such items is going to trap her here as surely as the thickest underwater weed.

Movement is surprisingly easy.

Waving her right arm moves her to the left, and vice versa. She reaches behind her and grips the horizontal bar of the headboard (thank God it has a metal frame). Once she has pulled herself as close to the wall as she can she places both palms flat on the crumbling plaster and pushes with all her might.

Her foot gets knotted in a nightgown as she is propelled towards the door, but otherwise she makes it out of the room without incident.

The current picks up as she enters the hall. Her children's bedroom doors are wide open but she scarcely has time to glance within (there is no sign of them) before she is swept onwards and downwards, down the stairs to the living room.

Which is where the children are.

Jake is five. He is by the television set in the corner. Or rather he is over it, floating above the black blank screen. His further progress upward has been impeded by the lounge ceiling and now he is stuck there, eyes closed, chin tight on his chest, back of his neck pressed against the plaster. Is his tongue poking out? Is he even alive?

Ellie's foot is trapped beneath the sofa which means Tamara's thirteen-year-old daughter is at ground level. Her eyes are open but that just makes it worse than with Jake, because now she is regarding her mother with blank, white, sightless eyes as her stiffened upright form bobs before her, her left arm extended and buffeted by the current in a horrible semblance of beckoning.

Tamara wants to call out to her children, to cry for help for all of them, but she can't take a breath, is incapable of doing so. All she can do is float, helpless, drifting beside the lounge door as the current refuses to take her any further and her efforts have little more effect that than of a butterfly trying to move in a hurricane.

And so she floats and bobs, her little boy to her right, her daughter straight ahead, and behind her the broad expanse of the lounge window with the stillness of the blue-black darkness beyond.

No, not quite darkness, and not quite still, either.

Something is moving out there, beyond the house.

Something that's getting closer.

She looks from her son, to her daughter, to the beyond. The beyond where the shadow of something starts tapping at the glass.

~~~

Tamara woke, for real this time (she hoped). A glance at the alarm clock confirmed that either it had failed to go off, or the dream had prevented her from hearing the alarm. Either way she was late.

Shit.

She got dressed and brushed her hair, all at the same time. She pulled on shoes as she exited the bedroom.

"Come on kids! Mummy's late! Time to get going!"

Jake had wet the bed again.

Tamara knew it wasn't his fault, and she knew the doctor had said he would likely grow out of it, but it was the last thing she needed to have to sort out.

"By the age of ten he has a ninety-five per cent chance of being dry," the doctor had said. She had even shown Tamara a graph, pointing out where a boy of Jake's age lay on the curve. While it had reassured her to a degree, the thought of having to deal with this for another five years felt like just another little atom bomb in the constant ongoing war someone was waging to destroy her soul.

"Sorry mum."

"That's okay." She bundled up the sheet and threw it into the laundry basket. They would have to wait for later. "Let's get you dressed."

Ellie had already left, making the most of her newly asserted teenaged independence. That and the fact that walking to school with her friends held a lot more street cred (did kids even say that anymore?) than her mum dropping her off or, even worse, walking to school with her.

She got Jake dry and dressed and ready in record time, pausing only to pick up the post from where it lay on the blue hall carpet.

Spam, spam, spam, and a bill. Oh, crap.

There was no time to deal with it now. She left the lot on the hallway table by the phone, then shuffled Jake out of the house and into the drizzling rain of the grim morning.

~~~

Her shift at the shop lasted four hours and once it was over Tamara came straight home to get on with the laundry. As she unravelled the sheet prior to putting it in the wash she couldn't help examining it.

The stain was small, lending barely a spot of discoloration to the otherwise pristine whiteness. Maybe that meant he was getting better, she thought. Maybe it even meant they were closer to the point where she could remove the rubber under-sheet from Jake's bed. The thought of it drew her into her son's bedroom where her gaze fell to the currently exposed mattress.

The rubber sheet was nowhere to be seen.

Hang on, there it was, curled up at the foot of the bed where his feet must have somehow pushed it, one side lolling over the edge like an obscene and very flat tongue.

The mattress was exposed, and wet.

Tamara laid a hand on the dark patch just to prove to herself it was actually what she thought. The dampness on her fingertips confirmed it. How this patch was larger, and quite considerably so, compared to the sheet awaiting a good dose of Persil and a thirty-minute spin at forty degrees, made no sense at all. The sheet should have taken the brunt of his accident, shouldn't it?

And if the top side of the mattress was this damp then what about...

It took some effort to flip the mattress up, but no effort at all to take in the wide, wet stain Tamara found herself looking at, nor to appreciate that this side of the surface was so soaked drops were now forming. As she watched they trickled down, passed between two of the darkened slats of the bed base, and added to the little pool on the floor.

Out of everything she had examined, Jake's bedsheet was the driest and the floor was the wettest.

Which made no sense at all.

Unless Jake had flipped the mattress over himself in a bid to disguise what had happened. Even so, the sheet should have been far more soaked than it was now, and the mattress was heavy enough that if she had trouble lifting it there was no way a five-year-old boy could have.

But how else could this have happened?

Never mind, she thought. She took the fan heater from its place on the wardrobe floor, set it at a safe distance, and aimed the hot air at the worst of the moisture. Then the sheet went into the wash and she was free to look at what the postman had pushed through the letterbox.

Most of it was exactly as she had thought. There was an offer for home-delivered vegetarian food, free socks that were far too big for her from a company plugging their bamboo clothing line, and something about winning a matching set of blue plastic luggage. It all went in the recycling.

The fourth letter, however, was the water bill.

Tamara's heart began to race once she had unfolded the white piece of paper with the blue stripe across it. The amount couldn't possibly be right. There had to be some kind of mistake. The bill was five times what it had been previously, despite her attempts to reduce their water use (the flat was on a meter) and her strict instructions to the kids not to leave taps on and only spend as short a time as possible in the shower.

No, there had to be a mistake.

Her heart beat faster as she realised what she had to do now. It still took her a little while to gather sufficient courage to pick up the telephone receiver and dial the number.

Her call was answered almost immediately.

"It's about my bill," she stammered. "My bill you've just sent me." God what had been the point of rehearsing what she was going to say if it was still going to sound as if she hadn't a clue what she was talking about? "It's too much. The bill. Way too much."

The voice on the other end of the phone sounded muffled, as if whoever was talking had a scarf around their mouth, or perhaps were talking from the other side of reinforced glass. It reassured her, in the kind of I'm-better-than-you tones that sounded like the headmistress of Tamara's old school, that if she was having difficulty paying then there were various instalment plans they could send her details of, or why not look them up on the water board's website?

"No." The blood in her ears was now pounding to the extent that she was starting to panic she wouldn't be able to hear what the woman said next. "You don't understand. There's no way I – we – could have used that much."

"Are you on a meter, Mrs Chescott?"

"It's Miss and yes we are but—"

"Sorry, *Miss* Chescott – well, the advantages of a meter are, as we always say, that you get a far more accurate record of your water usage, so—"

"But it's not accurate! It's wrong! Wrong! Wrong! Wrong!" She was losing it but she didn't care. Sometimes you had to scream until you were blue in the face before anyone actually listened to you.

"Well, have you noticed a leak from anywhere?"

Only from her son and she certainly wasn't going to mention that.

"If there's a constant drip these things can build up, you know."

"No I haven't spotted a leak." But Jake's carpet was wet. She had just seen that it was. "Except … er … maybe I have. I'm not sure."

"I see." The pause probably lasted less than a second but to Tamara it felt like an age. "Would you like us to send someone out?"

"Oh, could you? Would you?" She wished she didn't sound so desperately grateful, but the truth was she was.

"I'm not sure if it's possible today, but we'll see what we can do."

Tamara was in the process of thanking her when she realised the receiver must have been put down at the other end. She replaced her own and jumped when it instantly began to ring.

Had the water board forgotten something? "Hello?"

"Tamara Chescott?"

"Yes. Are you able to come round today after all?"

"I beg your pardon?"

"To check for leaks. You said you were going to send someone."

"I'm not sure who you think I am but it's Roberta Sherwell here, Mrs Chescott. Ellie's head teacher."

What? Who? "It's Miss. Miss Chescott."

"Sorry, Miss Chescott. I've been trying to get hold of you for the past ten minutes but you've been engaged."

"Yes." Why was this woman who sounded like the water board woman telling her something she already knew? "Yes I've been on to the water board."

"Never mind that now." The voice was muffled. Maybe there was something wrong with the phone line. "Are you able to come to the school? Now?"

It wasn't a question, Tamara could tell that much. She put a finger in her left ear in the hope it would help her concentrate. "Is everything all right?"

"You'd best come to the school. Miss Chescott." The voice seemed to be getting more distant all the time, as if the person in question was slowly moving away from the receiver.

Or as if she, Tamara, had her head under water.

"We can discuss everything once you're here."

It was only after Tamara had put the phone down and assured herself that it wasn't going to ring for a second time that it hit her.

Something must have happened to Ellie.

~~~

Her daughter was looking very sorry for herself. She was also looking very wet. Her soaked hair looked even blacker than usual, the snaking curls worming their way over her collar resembled glistening sea creatures come to rest in the glare of the school nurse's examination lamp. Ellie was currently sitting on the couch. Tamara could tell the girl's clothes had been pulled on hastily.

"Wednesday morning is swimming lesson," Mrs Sherwell explained as the nurse regarded all three of them with concern.

"I know." Tamara had got Ellie's kit ready, after all. "Did she have an accident?" She looked at the headmistress, then at the nurse, then finally at Ellie. Silence. "She wasn't being bullied again, was she?" That had been a problem last year but she thought everything had been resolved with that other girl being excluded.

"No." The school nurse's name was Parsons and her soft Scottish burr added to her general demeanour of calm, which was good because right now Tamara didn't feel calm at all. "In fact it was two of the other girls who pulled her out."

"Pulled her out?" Tamara gripped Ellie by the shoulders. Her daughter still refused to meet her gaze. "Did somebody push you in?"

Ellie shook her head.

"Did you get in a fight in the showers?"

No.

"Did somebody—"

"It's nothing like that, Mrs Chescott." The headmistress was looking at the girl. "We were rather hoping, now that you're here, that Ellie would open up a little more about what actually did happen."

Tamara resisted the urge to remind them she was now single. "You mean you don't know?" She looked again at her daughter, took her daughter's chin in her hand and made the girl look at her. "What are they talking about?"

Still no words, still eyes averted. Tamara could feel anger starting to build. She turned back to the two women who were looking at her and her daughter. If Ellie wasn't talking it was certainly time for the adults in the room to.

"Well?"

Mrs Sherwell exchanged a glance with Nurse Parsons. They both looked uneasy. "Perhaps you'd like to take a seat, Mrs Chescott."

"No I wouldn't!" It was too much, it really was. "And for the last time it is Miss! Miss! I haven't been married now for ages! Can't you amend your records or whatever it is you people do to avoid making mistakes like this?"

Nurse Parsons dragged up a chair. It was horrible and blue and plastic and the metal legs made a scraping sound on the floor tiles that set Tamara's teeth on edge.

"Please," said the nurse. "Sit down."

"And I'm very sorry about getting your title wrong," said the headmistress. "Of course we are aware of what happened before. I promise we won't make the same mistake again."

Tamara found that hard to believe.

The chair was rigid and uncomfortable and she didn't like it because now she was at a lower level than the other two women, who towered over her. She made to stand but Nurse Parsons' gentle (was it gentle?) hand on her shoulder insisted she stay there.

Mrs Sherwell dragged out a swivel chair from behind the

desk in the corner. She sat in that while her colleague took a few steps back, presumably to diminish her own presence. When the nurse leaned against the desk the cheap plywood gave an ominous creak.

For a moment this tableau seemed frozen. Nurse Parsons in the corner, Roberta Sherwell and Tamara facing each other – Mrs Sherwell in the posh chair, Tamara in the shitty one. Between them, sitting on the couch, still silent, still not making eye contact with anyone, was the reason why they all were there.

Eventually, the headmistress broke the silence.

"Ellie was found in the swimming pool."

"So? I thought you said it was a swimming lesson."

"Yes that's right. But she was found in the pool at the end of the lesson."

"You mean after all the other girls had got out? What's so strange about that? She likes swimming, she always has. She was probably just dreading the thought of maths or physics or some other subject she hates."

As if to compensate for the stillness of the headmistress's tongue, the woman's hands were going into overdrive, clasping and unclasping, fingers knotting and unknotting. What was she finding so hard to put into words?

"Miss Chescott, at the end of the swimming lesson, when everyone should have been out and showered and dressed, your daughter was found in the pool, at the bottom of the pool. Not moving. Not doing anything. In fact she gave Jemima Marston – the games teacher – quite a fright."

Tamara's heart was racing so fast it decided to just skip a few beats. "You mean she was drowning?"

"Not exactly. Miss Marston dived in to get her out and apparently…" Tamara couldn't help notice that Ellie was staring at Mrs Sherwell now, the kind of blank cold stare a shark gives something just before it devours it. "Apparently Ellie kept fighting her off. When they finally broke the surface of the deep end, all your daughter could say was that she wanted to stay down there, that she was … happier down there."

Tamara looked at Ellie for confirmation but the girl's eyes were still on her headmistress. Tamara had never seen her daughter glare like that.

Meanwhile Mrs Sherwell seemed to have run out of words. Finally it was Nurse Parsons who broke the agonising silence.

"We were thinking that ... perhaps ... after what happened before..."

Good God what was she trying to say? Weren't these people trained for this sort of thing?

"We know that her father is gone, and that it was under tragic circumstances. We are also aware that once it transpired what had been going on it was felt to be a merciful release for all of you. But children can react in strange ways to the absence of a parent, and that reaction isn't always—"

"We're going home." Tamara didn't remember getting to her feet but suddenly she was standing up. She extended a hand and Ellie took it. Well at least that was something. Her daughter's hand certainly felt as if it had been in water for too long, and very cold water at that.

"Of course." The nurse stepped back. Tamara felt as if she was being given permission to leave. Not that she needed it.

"And we understand if Ellie might need a couple of days off," the headmistress added. "It might be for the best."

"I'll decide what's for the best, if you don't mind." Tamara had to pull her daughter off the couch. The girl's feet hit the floor with an almost imperceptible squelch and Tamara couldn't help but notice the faint outline of moisture on the grey plastic where Ellie had been sitting. "Jesus Christ, couldn't you have even made sure she was properly dry before she got dressed?"

She ignored the perplexed looks she got as she made her way out of the nurse's office, Ellie in tow.

The corridor outside was empty, the only sound the rain hammering insistently against the wall of sheer glass to their left.

"It wasn't so bad on the way here." Tamara hadn't brought an umbrella. "We'll just have to run."

~~~

They still ended up soaked through by the time they got home. Tamara sent an even more sullen and silent-than-usual Ellie upstairs to change. Then she noticed the time.

"Ellie?" No answer. "I've got to pick Jake up from school!" Nothing. "Will you be okay?"

The muffled blast of water from the shower being turned on was all Tamara got as a reply. Well she'd only be twenty minutes and the girl seemed too dazed to get herself into any trouble. The fact that Tamara found herself already halfway down the street as these thoughts entered her head meant the decision had already been made anyway.

She ran so fast she got to Jake's school out of breath and a few minutes early. The pouring rain and her obvious state of exhaustion caused the school caretaker to take pity on her. The old man in the dripping brown overall unlocked the school gates and ushered her into a small office just inside the main doors where she could wait. Tamara didn't sit down. She didn't want to soak the grey cushions of either of the two chairs. Her throat was dry from her exertions and even though she would have killed for a hot drink right now, the water cooler in the corner would have to do.

One sip suggested to her why the office wasn't currently occupied. The water tasted foul, like rotten meat. Presumably whoever usually used the room had gone elsewhere while the matter could be attended to. Tamara spat the fluid back into the cup and put it down. The taste remained and she found herself running her tongue between her teeth in a bid to get rid of it. God, and now her ears were ringing. At least, she assumed that distant rushing sound was inside her head, a noise like a fast stream over a bed of loose pebbles, rattling and jostling them so they clicked and clunked together. Tamara held her nose and blew hard in case it was catarrh.

When she relaxed the sound was louder.

Her anxiety was just on the verge of developing into full blown panic when the noise began to resolve itself into voices.

Children's voices.

They must have let the classes out.

Tamara exhaled a breath of relief. The awful taste was still there but it didn't seem quite so bad now. She opened the office door to behold a tidal flood of children sweeping past her, one so great in force and numbers she had trouble picking Jake out, and even greater trouble gaining his attention. Eventually she had to enter the flow and was swept along until she found herself outside in the wet, where an already distraught Jake was searching for her.

"I thought you'd forgotten about me again!" He said, the rain mixing with his tears. "Like before!"

That was so long ago she was surprised he could remember it. "Of course not, darling. Mummy told you that would never happen again and it hasn't, has it?" Jake didn't answer. "Has it?"

Jake nodded, eventually. Either that or it was just his head bobbing from the force with which she was now dragging her little boy along the road in the rain. Jesus Christ, she hoped he didn't catch pneumonia again. When she felt him slowing she gathered him into her arms.

"I'll carry you if you're tired, all right?"

Nod. Bob.

"We'll get home quicker. Mummy doesn't want you catching another cold."

Bob. Nod.

"Good boy."

Tamara started to run, Jake so light in her arms she could move almost as fast as she had getting there. When she got them into the house she sensed immediately that something was wrong. Closing the door should have shut the hammering sound of the rain out. It should have been quieter in here.

Instead it was louder.

"Stay by the door, Jake, until Mummy's made sure it's safe."

She put her son down and went into the kitchen.

Both taps were on and the sink, filled to the brim with filthy crockery, was already overflowing. Water was pooling on the floor and making its way towards the hall.

"Ellie!"

Tamara ran upstairs. The crimson carpet squelched beneath her feet. The sound of roaring water was even louder now. She was finding it difficult to tell how much of it was inside her head and how much was coming from the bathroom.

Both taps were on in there too, and the sink was overflowing. Behind the shower curtain it sounded as if the shower was on and the bath taps were running all at the same time.

"Ellie?"

No answer.

"Ellie, I need to check you're okay."

Tamara gripped the stained mildewed curtain and drew it back.

There was something in the bath. The overflowing filth-encrusted bath.

Tamara backed away, biting the urge to vomit as the thing raised a pale, bloated, swollen arm.

She ran back down the stairs, her descent made all the more difficult by the water now cascading over the steps, her only thought to save Jake from whatever it was that had invaded her home.

Jake wasn't where she had left him.

But something was.

A tiny something that bared perfect tiny white teeth in the wet papier-mâché mass of what remained of its face as it reached out to her.

She didn't know where Jake had gone. She had no idea what this was. But as she ran into the lounge to look for him, all she knew was that neither it nor the thing upstairs were as awful as the thing of water and rotted flesh that was hammering on the window, bones protruding through ragged fingertips as it seethed with lust for a violent revenge.

WHAT DID YOU SEE?

Paul Finch

"Excuse me," the old woman said, leaning across the table, "I hope you ladies don't think I'm intruding, but I couldn't help overhearing that you're on your way to Norwood Lee?"

Kay and Marsha were a little surprised. Not least because they'd been speaking together quietly while the old woman had apparently been asleep, but also because, while it might be impossible *not* to eavesdrop in the close confines of a crowed train compartment, it wasn't the sort of thing you'd readily admit to.

As if reading their thoughts, the old woman gave an apologetic smile and raised a shrivelled, jewel-encrusted hand. "It's just that I live close to Norwood Lee. I know it well, and…" Her words tailed off as she pondered the best way to continue.

She was in her late seventies and though wizened, with a mop of unruly white hair and far too much make-up, some degree of feminine allure remained. She'd once been a beauty, that much was evident, though as time had taken her looks, perhaps it had taken her wits also. It was warm and cosy inside the carriage, but an overlarge fur coat, a woolly hat and a many-times wrapped-around muffler engulfed the old dear in dramatic and preposterous fashion.

"Forgive me … you must think me a silly meddlesome old thing. But, and I'm sorry to ask you this … you ladies weren't by any chance thinking about going to the parish church tonight?"

The two young women glanced at each other.

"No ... erm." Kay shrugged. "We ... we don't go to church."

"Oh..."

The old woman seemed a little bemused by that, which perhaps was understandable. By her accent she was local to this region, the Cotswolds, which was largely rural – as the snow-clad landscape rolling by outside, shimmering with moonlight, attested – while, from her age, she belonged to a generation for whom church-going, especially on Christmas Eve, was more or less obligatory. But what she said next surprised them.

"I fear we misunderstand each other. Looking to attend the Nine Lessons at Norwood Lee tonight would be futile. It's only a hamlet really, and the church reflects this. We call it a 'parish church' but it's actually rather small, with an even smaller congregation these days, I'm sad to admit. The vicar, Reverend Donaldson, has four other village churches in his care ... so tonight the Christmas service will be held at St Margaret's in Long Hanborough. But that wasn't what I was referring to anyway."

Kay, who, with her honey-blonde hair, schoolgirl looks and petite frame, was always the more approachable of the twosome, leaned forward. "I'm sorry," she said in her soft Manchester accent, "but you've *really* lost us."

"Ah, well ... yes." The old woman sighed. "That will certainly be the case shortly, I fear..."

"Hey, I hope you don't mind," Marsha interrupted, her puzzlement finally giving way to aggravation. "But we're making our plans for Christmas and we're kind of busy..."

The old woman gave her a strange strained look, as if something about *this* particularly concerned her. "Just so long as those plans don't involve the Wilcote crypt, my dear."

Marsha pulled a face. "I'm sorry?"

The woman dug under her fur, producing a pair of glasses on a chain, placed them on the end of her nose, and drew a sleeve back to glance at a delicate little watch. "We are ten minutes from

Bladon, which is my stop. I may just have enough time to tell you a story…" She arched an inquisitive eyebrow. "If you'll permit me?"

Marsha was a tall Brummie, older than Kay by two years, and much more athletic thanks to her hockey and netball. She had a shock of dark hair and attractive feline features, which made her a striking individual to look at, but she was also inclined to surliness when denied her own way. She now looked increasingly disgruntled, only a covert squeeze of the thigh from Kay, which translated into "let's not make a scene" preventing her giving voice to this.

"It's just that you remind me of me and my friend, Miriam," the old woman said. "We made this exact same journey to Norwood Lee on Christmas Eve some sixty years ago…"

"I don't think you quite understand," Marsha replied tersely. "We're *not* going to this parish church of yours. We don't believe in God."

That arched eyebrow again. "And yet you're making plans for His birthday?"

Marsha looked flustered at that. "It's a holiday, okay? We're going to Norwood Lee for a break … to get away from it all."

The woman sat back, her lips pressed together in a curious half-smile. Kay thought she looked sad rather than offended and couldn't help but feel embarrassed by Marsha's abruptness. At the same time there'd been something about the urgency with which the old dear had suddenly tried to speak to them that left her uneasy. She and her friend had come this same way sixty years ago? It would have been nice to know what the exact circumstances of that long-ago trip were that made her feel it necessary to pass on a warning.

On top of that, it could be awkward travelling for the next ten minutes in total silence, face-to-face with someone they'd just reprimanded.

"What happened sixty years ago?" Kay asked.

Marsha tensed, sucking in a tight breath.

"It can't hurt to know," Kay said quickly. "After all, we're strangers in Norwood Lee. We don't know anything about the place."

"Whatever it is, I've just made it quite clear that we won't be going near the parish church," Marsha retorted.

"My dear, my dear…" The old woman shook her head gently as if chiding a recalcitrant child. "Norwood Lee is a speck on a map. You can't go anywhere in the village without being close to the parish church."

"And is there a problem with that?" Kay asked. "You mentioned a crypt. Is it dangerous?"

The woman leaned forward, gazing birdlike from one to the other. Irritably, Marsha scrunched up the plastic cellophane from the packet of sandwiches she'd eaten earlier but couldn't throw it anywhere and so had to keep it screwed into her fist.

"The crypt houses the tomb of a knight, Sir Henry Wilcote, and his wife, the Lady Abigail," the woman said. "It's fifteenth century but safe enough to visit as it's been well maintained – at least, that's my understanding. Personally, I haven't been down there since December 24, 1958."

If nothing else, *that* impressed Kay.

The old woman remembered the exact date and had clearly crossed off all the days that had passed since. Whatever had happened, it had obviously been significant.

"The crypt is easily accessible … or it was," the woman said. "There are two doors on the church's south side. The one on the left leads to the vestry, but that one is kept locked when the church is closed as there are some items of value inside. But the one on the right, the old one … that leads down to the crypt. That one is not locked, or it never was in our day. No one went down there, you see. During the Wars of the Roses, Sir Henry fought for the House of Lancaster. It was a bitter struggle, and when it was over he was fortunate to return to his wife, who he was very much in love with. They remained together for the rest of their lives, but later on developed a reputation for dabbling in the dark arts."

Marsha muttered under her breath, "For Heaven's sake…"

"It was a dangerous time, and this, it was said, was the only thing that spared them the vengeance of Richard III."

Kay continued to listen, intrigued despite herself.

"I'm not saying that people believed it, of course," the woman added. "Most likely, the dark arts story was untrue, a fable that grew up in later centuries. Otherwise, how could the Wilcotes have been laid to rest on hallowed ground?"

Marsha muttered again, something about her not being able to care less. Anything relating to religion was of zero interest to her. She tried not to consciously hate it. Hating stuff was no good for you. She just considered it silly and irrelevant.

"That rumour alone created sinister atmosphere in the crypt," the woman said. "The effigies of the knight and his lady were badly eroded. Little more than lumpen monstrosities back in 1958, so Heaven knows what they look like now. After nightfall, no one, not even the most rational man, would wish to go down there."

"So how come *you* went down?" Marsha asked. "I'm assuming that's what you're going to tell us? That you and this Miriam went down into the crypt that Christmas Eve."

"Yes, it's true." The old woman removed her glasses, digging a tissue from her sleeve to clean the lenses. "We both lived in Oxford then. But we'd heard all about the church at Norwood Lee, and the Wilcote crypt. We were children. Grammar schoolgirls. We didn't believe there was anything particularly ominous about the place but one particular superstition had ... well, it'd rather captivated us."

She carefully replaced her glasses. They awaited her explanation.

"It was claimed," she finally said, "that if one visited the crypt on Christmas Eve one might perform a love divination."

"A what?" Marsha said.

"A simple ritual." The old woman considered. "These old country ways ... they were always simple at heart. I suppose so that simple folk could practise them."

"A love divination?" Kay said. "I don't understand?"

"On the stroke of midnight, at the very moment of Christmas, one stood at the foot of the slab on which the knight and his lady rested, threw a handful of hemp-seeds over one's left shoulder, and uttered these words: *Hemp-seed I scatter, hemp-seed I sew, He that's my true love, come after me and mow.*" She paused briefly, looking breathless, as if mere recollection of the rhyme had taken something out of her. "The belief was that on completion of this ritual one glanced over one's shoulder and one would see the image of one's future spouse. *Ahhh...*" She registered their bemused expressions. "You look at me as if I'm mad. I can't blame you. Even *we* didn't think it would work. We scoffed at the folly of it, but it would be a lie to say that we weren't intrigued and ... maybe a little hopeful. You must understand, being the era it was, we girls were first and foremost raised to seek out solid dependable husbands..."

"And you seriously thought *we* were going to Norwood Lee to do this?" Marsha interrupted, almost openly scornful.

"In truth, my dear, no." The old woman removed her glasses again, staring from the train window. "I can see, having spoken to you, that you are spirited, intelligent and independent-minded ladies, who no doubt will make marvellous futures for yourselves without the assistance of any men."

You don't know the half of it, Kay thought, but she kept this to herself.

The old woman now seemed embarrassed by the story she'd told. "Doubtless, you have no truck with folk tales or other such childish beliefs."

"As I say," Marsha said, "we're not religious."

But then the old woman turned again, unexpectedly, and reaching sharply across the table, seized Kay's wrists in both her hands.

"Hey!" Marsha protested, reaching out, herself, to intervene. However, the woman released Kay almost as quickly as she'd grabbed her.

"Please understand..." The rheumy gaze roved frantically from one to the other. "I made no assumptions about your character or intellect. But when I heard you were headed for Norwood Lee, old memories were stirred. And I couldn't … well, I couldn't allow it. Not without warning you first."

"Well, so far you haven't warned us about anything," Kay said, a little shaken. "What happened in the crypt, Mrs…?"

"*Miss* Jenkins. Gertrude Jenkins."

"What happened in the crypt, Miss Jenkins?"

The woman fidgeted with her tissue, shrugging. "We performed the ritual. Obviously we did. When we actually got there it was almost midnight and terribly cold. I wasn't so sure about it but Miriam was adamant. And very excited. Even as a youngster at school her head had been in the clouds about men and boys. From earliest girlhood she'd dreamed that somewhere a handsome beau was awaiting her. So … after we'd performed the divination, which as I say was very simple, she was the first to look over her shoulder. She was so eager, her eyes bright with candle-fire, cheeks flushed, mouth wide open…"

She paused, as though struggling to remember, or at least to understand.

All around them the swaying carriage was crowded with noisier-than-usual folk heading home, having finally finished their last day's work before Christmas commenced. That good-natured uproar now dwindled to a dull distant monotony as Kay and Marsha waited.

"And then she screamed," Gertrude Jenkins said in a distant voice. "Just that. Gave a short, rather terrible scream."

"Okay," Kay said, vaguely alarmed. "So … what did she see?"

The woman's expression remained blank as if she'd mulled this matter over many times and had never yet found a satisfactory answer. "A wraith-like figure, apparently. Of a much older heavier-set man than she'd hoped for. A man with a sour face, and an air about of him of violence and cruelty."

Kay's skin prickled. "And did she go on to marry such a person?"

"I honestly don't know." The woman sniffled into her tissue.

"I lost contact with Miriam after we left school. And in the half-year before that happened she never spoke about the incident again. Or about very much in fact. All the life seemed to have been sucked out of her, all the gaiety, the hopes, the dreams…"

"Oh, that's ridiculous," Marsha cut in. "Total nonsense. Your friend could have married anyone she wanted. She didn't have to fall in with a brutish idiot just because of some stupid spell in a church cellar…"

The woman eyed her with something akin to pity. "My dear, if only it were that simple. I'm sure that, even at your tender years, the pair of you already know many a poor girl who'd never have entertained the man in her life had she known his true nature."

"And what did *you* see?" Kay asked, sensing that there was more to come.

"Me, my dear?" The woman gave a wintry smile. "Why … I didn't look. When I saw Miriam's reaction, I couldn't bring myself to. And I've never looked over my shoulder since. For any reason at all."

"Sorry?" Marsha sounded even more sceptical. "You've never glanced over your shoulder once in the last sixty years?"

"I can't afford to take the chance."

The train decelerated as they slid into a station. There was a stirring and shuffling as passengers collected baggage and fastened coats.

"Ah … this is me," Gertrude Jenkins said. "Bladon."

She pulled a pair of woollen gloves over her thin beringed hands and produced two bags, a shopping bag and a handbag from the small space on the seat beside her.

The younger women watched her askance. She noted this.

"I hope I haven't unduly frightened you?" she said.

"You've never once looked over your shoulder?" Kay was fascinated by the mere thought.

The train came to a standstill and there was noisy movement all along the carriage. The woman stood up, making to join the slow-moving queue forming in the aisle.

"It's not as difficult as it may sound," she said. "I *hear* him, you see. From time to time. When it's quiet. Always close behind, just waiting for me to look." She regarded them dully. "It's a terrible sound. Quite horrific. I know just from that noise that I'd be appalled at what I'd behold —"

Kay couldn't help herself. "Wait, Miss Jenkins. I mean … not looking? That keeps this *thing* at bay?"

"I've no idea, child. It has so far, but I'm only seventy-seven next February, and some would say there is still time." With a weak smile directed at no one in particular she stepped into the aisle and edged towards the doors. "Just heed my advice, ladies. I beg you."

Several seconds passed before either of the twosome could speak. Inevitably, it was Marsha.

"My dad always says that one advantage of rail travel being so expensive these days is that you don't get as many loonies on trains. Wait till I tell him about this one."

Kay stared out onto the platform, which was crowded with people heading for the exits. Gertrude Jenkins was among them, her short distinctive figure still buried in that overlarge fur coat. More by instinct than design, Kay glanced down at the old woman's booted feet and the tracks they left in the snow, and then at the snow behind her, to see if any other tracks were appearing there. But there were too many other people and it was already churned to slush. So there was no way to tell.

~~~

Kay Letwin and Marsha Finnegan had met on the very first day of Freshers' Week at Balliol College, Oxford, when by happy fortune they casually chatted in the Student Bar only to find that they'd both enrolled on the same course to study geography. It was well into that first year of study, during a very drunken Christmas party, when they learned that they'd come to be more to each other than mere friends. But it was almost twelve months after that before their lives and emotions had become so interwoven that they'd begun tentatively to discuss tying some kind of knot.

Initially, both were hesitant, Marsha wondering if they were getting their priorities wrong and if it would distract from their coursework and interfere with their exams; Kay suspecting that they'd allowed themselves to be seduced by the relative novelty of gay marriage and that they might be rushing into something they hadn't thought about sufficiently. In addition, neither of their families, with the sole exception of Tom, Kay's older brother, were aware of their daughters' sexual orientation, and while neither bunch were especially conservative in their views it would likely come as a shock if the first they heard of it was the day they were invited to a wedding. In light of all this the two friends had taken what they considered to be the very adult decision of isolating themselves for a few days, over the next Christmas period in fact, in a relatively luxurious environment – Tom's weekend cottage – where they would discuss every aspect of their relationship, weighing up the pros and cons and hopefully reaching the most sensible decision possible.

Even so, despite the seriousness of this – it was a weighty matter which could impinge on both their lives for decades to come – when they disembarked from the GWR train at Norwood Halt that very chilly Christmas Eve, with backpacks hoisted, scarves, gloves and hats in place, and unbroken snow crunching underfoot, it was impossible not to feel a tingle of holiday excitement.

Unlike at Bladon, where plenty of people had got off the train, Kay and Marsha were the only ones at Norwood Halt, and it was eerily beautiful. After descending the staircase alone (hanging onto each other for dear life) and passing out through the unmanned entrance hall, they found themselves on high ground overlooking the silent village. As Miss Jenkins had said, it was no more than a hamlet, the narrow lane from the station descending amid wintry trees to a small green, now completely white of course, with what remained of a Saxon cross in the centre and a clutter of thatch-roofed buildings around the edges. For the most part, these were cottages built from Cotswold stone, though there was also a pub, The Countryman, with a black-and-white Jacobean exterior, and a post office/corner shop. Under pristine snow, with warm lamplight leaking from a scatter of curtained windows, and yet all of it cast in a silver hue by a sky now cleared of cloud and ablaze with moon and stars, it looked fantastically festive but also snug and peaceful.

In most British towns and cities, nine o'clock on Christmas Eve would be riotous, the streets chaotic with drunken revellers. There'd be shouting and fighting, and copious amounts of vomiting. Even Marsha, though she didn't consider Christmas a holy feast, held the whole irreverent display with total distaste. This place, however, Norwood Lee, was entirely the opposite. As the women came down to the bottom of the lane, again keeping a tight grip on each other's arms because of the treacherous surface, there were none of those garish outdoor decorations that turned so many suburbs into neon nightmares, though fairy lights and the occasional Christmas tree did sparkle from behind half-drawn curtains. Likewise, there was no rowdy caterwaul from overcrowded bars, their windows fogged with sweat. Music and laughter *could* be heard from inside The Countryman but it was harmonious and low-key.

"This is perfect," Kay said, delighted. "Wouldn't surprise me if a horse came clopping through, pulling a sleigh."

"Yeah, it's also damn cold," Marsha replied. "Let's get indoors, eh? See if your lovely brother's come through for us."

Tom Letwin, who was ten years older than Kay, was an investment banker in the City, but all their lives he'd been her closest buddy and confidante. His cottage in Norwood Lee, "a crash-pad in the sticks", as he referred to it, was only one of several properties he owned. His pride and joy was a villa in the foothills of the Gascon Pyrenees, which he used in summer for the sun and in winter for the skiing. Kay and Marsha had been invited to join him there now with his wife, Tamara, and their two children, but when she'd said that she wanted some privacy he'd happily handed over the keys to the crash-pad.

They found it in a narrow mews just behind the post office, one of a row of three. Tom had already warned them that it was small, comprising a single room downstairs with a kitchenette, and a single bedroom upstairs. But they had a real fire, for which there was lots of firewood and kindling stored in the outhouse, and once they lit that, he'd promised that it would be very comfortable. It also boasted a plethora of *olde worlde* fixtures, including a large stone hearth carved with ancient characters, exposed wooden beams on both floors, and a staircase so steep that it was more like a loft-ladder ascending through a hatch.

They built up the fire until it was roaring, and when they checked in the kitchenette and the ice-box of a scullery attached to it, they found all the consumables they'd need, from six-packs of lager to boxes of wine, from packets of biscuits and cereal, bread, butter, milk, sugar and eggs, all the basics, to sacks of potatoes, carrots, onions and the like. There were also a few extras, provided generously and unexpectedly by Tom, such as an oven-ready prize turkey, several strings of sausages, a box of mince pies and a tinned Christmas pudding.

"Good as it gets," Marsha said a couple of hours later, when they were unpacked and settled. She wriggled her sock-clad toes in front of the fire while using the remote for the big hi-def telly to channel-hop through a procession of atmospheric but for the most part empty-headed festive entertainments.

Kay muttered a vague response as she wandered – for the third time now – to the window overlooking the back garden. There wasn't much out there. Again, it was small and blanketed with snow, but beyond the frosty hedge, wooded hills rose into view against the hanging orb of the moon. Silhouetted on its bluish lunar face, amid black tangles of leafless boughs, was the castellated tower of a country church.

"You really want to go up there, don't you?" Marsha said, joining her.

Kay, who'd first spotted the religious edifice outside and had immediately been entranced by it, was taken aback by the question.

"No," she said, rather too quickly. "Well … look, I know it's silly. It's just … I keep thinking … you know, we're here to make a big decision. And if we go up there and perform this crazy ritual and when we look over our shoulders, we see each other … well, then we'll know, won't we?" She gave a sheepish shrug. "It'll make everything a lot easier. We can relax and enjoy Christmas without any heavy conversation."

"Are you actually serious, babes?" Marsha looked astounded. "It's an old wife's tale."

"In which case it can't hurt, can it?"

Marsha had never been relaxed with that argument: if you didn't believe in something, where was the harm in indulging it? So often it had been used by religious types in conflict with irreligious types. "If you don't believe in God you've no problem with me going to church, have you, because it doesn't mean anything anyway?" What that point of view didn't allow for was the fact you were still being asked to give credibility to something that simply wasn't real, which was basically asking you to be dishonest. But then again, you also had to consider the give-and-take so essential to successful relationships, and in their particular case, the fact that Kay had long been interested in the odd, the unusual and the uncanny. She had a pile of ghost books back in her room at college, was fascinated by folklore and the occult, and even posted about stuff like that on her blog from time to time.

"I just thought it would be cool to check it out." Kay shrugged. "Don't you think that was an interesting story about the crypt?"

"I think it was a horrible story, and a load of guff as well, no disrespect to batty old Miss Jenkins. But … as I don't believe it'll do anything at all, let alone do any harm, I don't suppose I mind a late-evening walk. Should be quite invigorating."

Kay beamed. "And on a clear night we can see all the Christmas stars."

"They're the same stars as usual, Kay."

"Don't be boring."

"I'll try not to be." However, as she sat on the sofa pulling her walking-boots back on, Marsha had a thought. "There is one thing. If you genuinely want to perform this ritual, or something similar to it – and frankly, I can't believe we're even contemplating such a nonsensical game – you've not got everything you need."

Kay looked puzzled. "We don't really need anything."

"Hemp-seed," Marsha said. "Whatever that actually is."

"Oh, dear." Kay looked worried. Before a sly smile crept over her face and she produced from behind her back a sack of "healthy option" granola. "Would you believe, there's hemp-seed in this?"

Marsha tried not to laugh. "So ... we're going up that hill to chuck a handful of breakfast cereal over our shoulders and that will confirm the hopes and fears of all our years?"

Kay's impish smile faded, as if such mockery was hurtful but perhaps not entirely unjustified. "Like you said, it's game. We don't *have* to do it. I just wanted to check out this spooky crypt at a time when it's supposed to be at its spookiest."

Marsha sighed obligingly. "Well, it's not far off midnight. If we're going, we should go now."

~~~

They couldn't initially find the way. There were no signs to it and no one was around to ask. But fortunately the parish church was visible from just about everywhere thanks to its lofty perch, and after circling the green a couple of times they chanced on a narrow passage between two cottages, which initially they'd thought a private entry, and this led to a road on the village outskirts. Evidently the road was used very little because only one or two pairs of runnels from passing vehicles marked the carpet of snow lying across it, but they followed it for thirty yards to a finger-posted junction, and from here another minor road lead uphill in roughly the right direction.

Breath smoking and backs bent, they trudged up the slippery incline, following a pavement that was all but indistinguishable from the road itself. To either side, thickets of frozen trees crowded against the low, stone walls.

"Getting spooky," Marsha observed.

"Thought you didn't believe in that stuff," Kay said.

"I don't. And neither do you, remember. It's just a bit of fun."

Some fun, Kay thought, squeezing her gloved hands into fists to prevent the fingers turning numb, grunting as she struggled to keep her footing.

A short time later, a lychgate appeared on the left. No doubt it would normally stand as an icon of elaborate rusticity, a simple latched gate hung between two wooden posts wound with rose bushes and supporting a tiled roof, the lintel of which was inscribed with Latin lettering. But now that roof was buried under snow and the lintel dangling with icicles.

"With any luck this'll be locked, and we can go back to the cottage," Marsha said.

But the gate wasn't locked. They had to force it open, the hinges stiff with frost, but a sufficient gap had soon been made and they sidled quickly through, hoping to avoid precipitating an avalanche from overhead.

Beyond the lychgate a path that was just about visible meandered through the trees towards a dark distant structure. When they passed a large noticeboard on the right, it was so plastered with flakes that they couldn't read it.

"Everyone loves a white Christmas," Marsha said. "Until one comes along and the sheer impracticality of it kicks in ... like, when you can't even find out what time you're supposed to go to church."

Kay didn't comment, her eyes fixed on the gaunt building looming ahead.

The truth was, and she'd only partially admitted this to herself, she really wasn't sure the route they were currently contemplating was one she wanted; okay, they were both uncertain about it but her fears, she suspected, went much deeper than Marsha's. She'd never had any partner before coming to university, girl or boy. Oh, there'd been the usual kissing and fumbling at school parties, but none of that had carried an emotional price-tag. In contrast, it had been very different with Marsha. Kay had been strongly attracted to the older student from the moment she'd met her, and now felt deeply connected to her. If there was such a thing as spiritual love then perhaps this was how Kay felt. But increasingly she had reservations. Marsha was taller and sturdier than she was, which gave her a protective aura. Kay couldn't help wondering if she'd fallen for someone like this because she'd been unconsciously seeking a parent-type ally during those difficult early days at university, when fear and loneliness were issues.

She wasn't saying there was anything false about her feelings, but on reflection it still seemed very early – she'd only recently turned twenty – for a commitment like marriage. By modern standards that was astonishingly young.

And will the parish church of Norwood Lee really help with any of this?

It now stood directly in front of her and didn't look much different from other rural churches, except for being older and more weathered than most, and for the snow overhanging its roofs and the spears of ice descending from its eaves. As the leafless trees parted, and they emerged onto flat ground where ancient headstones jutted from the snow like black badly-angled teeth, Kay forcibly reminded herself that this was just a silly old tradition, that her curiosity about it sprang from her interests in the odd and esoteric, that she wasn't taking it seriously.

Marsha gazed at the leaning gravestones and then up the towering edifice, its tall stained-glass windows blacked out by the icy darkness behind them. "Where's a Hammer Horror film crew when you need one?"

"Didn't think it was going to be this big," Kay admitted. "Didn't Miss Jennings say it was small."

"I think she meant it was small by parish church standards, which it probably is."

"Why have something like this in a village the size of Norwood Lee?"

"It was probably paid for by that character who's lying in the vault ... what's his name?"

"Henry Wilcote."

"Yeah. Speaking of which —" Marsha looked at her phone " — it's ten to midnight, so if we're going to do this daft thing we'd better get on with it."

A small part of Kay felt a twinge of unease. Perhaps, now that they were actually here, she'd been subconsciously hoping they'd have run out of time, but she nodded all the same.

They didn't have a compass but circumnavigated the building on the basis it would have been built facing east, which meant that the main entry doors would be at the western end. From there, it was easy to deduce which side was south, and indeed when they crunched their way around there along a side-path shin-deep in banked-up snow they encountered two doors standing ten yards apart. The one on the left looked like a relatively recent addition, but the one on the right was made from older semi-perished wood filled with flattened nail-heads. What was more, that one stood ajar by a couple of inches.

"There's an invitation if ever I've seen one," Marsha said in a voice that was more cheerful than Kay thought the circumstances warranted.

For some reason, a dead chill now ran through Kay that had nothing to do with the temperature.

"Five minutes left," Marsha said. "Are we going down?"

"Erm, yeah ... sure."

"Before we do, there is, perhaps ... *something*."

Kay glanced up, surprised at the querulous note in Marsha's voice, and even more surprised to see the moonlight reflecting from a face suddenly taut with foreboding.

"Supposing," Marsha said. "Just supposing ... well, imagine that this ritual works. And we look round, and each of us ... we see someone else? I mean not each other?"

"Oh." Kay didn't want to give away that this was precisely her own fear, but at the same time she didn't want to dismiss it either, because maybe if they both felt this way it would be easier now to just turn around and walk in the other direction.

"I'm joking, you dipstick!" Marsha cackled.

"Oh, right. Yeah ... sure." Kay tried to smile. "What a shock it'd be."

Marsha pushed at the door which swung open on silent hinges. Beyond it, when she turned her phone-light on, they saw a stone stairway falling into blackness. "After you," she said.

"You know…" Unavoidably, Kay hesitated. "Maybe this wasn't such a good idea."

Marsha frowned. "You marched me all the way up here and now you want to march me all the way back without us at least setting eyes on this mysterious medieval warlock?"

"If you just want to look at his tomb we can come back tomorrow."

"We're here *now*. And it's nothing to do with what *I* want. So, after you."

Teeth gritted, Kay commenced a slow cautious descent. It was a narrow stairway, very much something she'd have expected from the Middle Ages, the rugged ceiling arching just above her head, the stone walls to either side crumbling and covered with moss. Her vaporous breath filled the tight space, white phantasms curling in the bright glow of her phone-light. When they reached the bottom, Kay at the front, Marsha behind, a gate stood in front of them set with corroded iron bars. And it appeared to be closed.

"Looks like we can't go any further," Kay said.

Marsha leaned past her, gripped one of the bars and pushed. With a grating and groaning, the gate opened. "That old biddy was right about one thing. This place is completely insecure."

With no option, Kay ventured forward, phone held rigidly in front. The floor was paved and dry, but the actual dimensions of the place difficult to judge. Her light didn't travel far, just sufficiently to show pillars and vaulted arches, but also, some ten yards ahead, a flat slab elevated to about three feet, with two colourless figures lying side-by-side on top of it.

Kay slithered to a halt. And flinched when Marsha's hand landed on her shoulder.

"Bloody hell," Marsha chuckled. "You're really jumpy."

"I'm just cold…"

"It's only another of those crusader tomb-type things. You've probably seen one in every cathedral you've ever visited."

"Yes, but Marsha … we were told not to come here."

"By someone who's three sheets to the wind. Look, babe, *you're* the one who wanted…"

"I know, but isn't it…?"

"Hey, we don't have to do it." Somewhat belatedly, Marsha had latched onto the fact that Kay was quite nervous. She held up to two flat palms to indicate that they didn't need to proceed, though the gesture was underscored with amusement implying that she still thought it a load of hogwash. "Won't it give you a great blogpost, though? Your very own Christmas ghost experience?"

As if to illustrate, she strode along the left side of the tomb, phone clicking as she took photographs. Encouraged a little by this, and agreeing that yes, it would be an excellent post for her blog on Christmas morning, Kay shuffled closer, though even that slight movement echoed eerily, the mobile-light sources playing visual tricks in the deeper recesses of the undercroft.

Now that she was right up to him, Sir Henry Wilcote and his wife, Abigail, were much as Miss Jenkins had described them: smooth, featureless travesties of the detailed sculptures they'd once been.

"Wonder if their actual bones are lying under here?" Kay said, peering at the timeworn faces, only vaguely definable bumps and contours hinting at the eyes, mouths and noses.

"Presume so," Marsha replied. "Otherwise, why would this place have any alleged magical power? They kind of lucked in, don't you think?" She walked around the stone effigies until she was back where she'd started. "They weren't just together all their lives, they've been together ever since. What was it … the Wars of the Roses? That's nearly five-hundred years, yeah? These two were right for each other at least, even if they mucked about in the black arts to ensure it lasted. Anyway—" she checked the time "—we've got one minute, babe. Are we doing this thing, or what?"

"Suppose so." Kay tugged off her left glove and stuck her hand into her anorak pocket where she'd stored a fistful of the high-health granola.

The Wilcotes' long-lasting fidelity was surely some kind of indication that it was possible for people to remain loyal life-partners from an early age. Even in turbulent times. How old would Abigail Wilcote have been? Back in the Middle Ages didn't girls get married as young as twelve or thirteen? And yet here she was in 2018, still lying alongside her husband.

"Let's just do it," she said, suddenly feeling energized by that. "After all, it's better to know than not to know."

Marsha held out her gloved palm so that Kay could sprinkle some grains into it, but arched a curious eyebrow. "You're not *really* buying into this, are you? I mean, not *seriously*?"

"Like you say, let's just do it." Kay positioned herself so that they faced each other directly. "Now, do as I do…" And she threw the handful of grain over her left shoulder.

"Babe, whoa." If you're … look, maybe this isn't such a good…"

"Please, Marsha!" Now that they'd started Kay was eager to see it through.

Defeated but bemused, Marsha tossed her own seeds backward.

Kay remained focussed. "Now repeat after me…"

"Whoa, you've memorised those lines? The old bat only said them once."

"I only remember vaguely but I'm sure it's the thought that counts…"

"Kay, listen…"

"'Hemp-seed I scatter' – come on, Marsha, you've got to say it."

Reluctantly, Marsha said, "'Hemp-seed I scatter.'"

"'Hemp-seed I sew'—"

"Kay, this is—"

"Come on, please!"

Marsha shrugged exasperatedly. "'Hemp-seed I sew.'"

"'Let my true love come after me and mow.'"

"For Christ's sake!"

"Marsha!"

"'Let my true love come after me and mow.'"

Kay nodded, compressing her lips into a tight tense smile. Briefly, the silence in the crypt seemed to thunder in their ears. The friends regarded each other fixedly. And then Marsha jolted, her head jerking part-way around as though in surprise.

"What is it?" Kay asked, her pulse immediately racing. Almost as an afterthought she turned to glance over her own shoulder.

Marsha had heard something: a hollow wooden *thud*. Initially it had sounded like a door closing. As she'd glanced around she'd expected to see a priest or vicar, or some other custodian of the church who'd just emerged from another part of the cellar. That would have been difficult enough.

But *this*...

Her mouth slackened open, her eyes bugging in a face rapidly draining white.

"This ... it's a trick..." she said hoarsely, backing away until she collided with Kay, half-knocking her sideways. Kay turned and tried to grapple with her to prevent them both falling over but Marsha was rigid, a virtual stone. "It's a damn trick!" she hissed again, staring at what to Kay looked like empty darkness.

"What is it?" Kay attempted to put arms around her. "What did you see?"

Marsha tore loose and backed frothy-lipped towards the iron gate. She pointed a shaking finger. "You ... *you* had something to do with this. You *must* have. No one else could've—"

Kay held her hands out. "What is it? Just tell me."

"It's a damn trick! That's all it can be! And a bloody nasty one!"

Marsha turned and blundered up the stairway.

"Wait!" Kay yelled, more confused than frightened, though that confusion lent wings to her heels as she stumbled up the steps in pursuit.

Marsha was the athlete, of course. When Kay reached the surface world there was already no sign of her friend, but there was only one way she could have run. Increasingly bewildered, Kay hastened along the side of the church. When she reached the end of the building she halted, lungs heaving, sweat chilling on her brow. From the chopped-up snow it appeared that Marsha had descended the hill the same way they'd come up here: down through the graveyard and along the lychgate path.

As Kay went that way too she spotted her partner's lurching shape some fifty yards ahead.

"What in God's name?" she stuttered as she ran. "Marsha! *Marsha, wait!*"

She finally got to the sloping road, sliding out through the gate and falling full-length on the pavement. The snow cushioned the impact but from here it was much more difficult: downhill and a smoother surface, her feet repeatedly skating from under her. Marsha was having similar problems and was now only thirty yards ahead. She too fell repeatedly and heavily until by the time she was at the bottom of the hill she was limping.

"Marsha!" Kay called again. "Wait, please!"

Marsha at last came down to the little-used road on the outskirts of the village. This area was street-lit, and perhaps feeling she'd returned to some version of civilisation and sanity, she turned around, her face flushed and soaked with sweat, though perhaps soaked with something else too – tears?

Kay was incredulous, never having once known Marsha to cry.

"What happened?" she asked, approaching with arms outspread. "For Heaven's sake!"

"Don't come near me, Kay." Marsha retreated steadily. "If you didn't know about that ... well, it doesn't matter because I *know* you didn't. I know it couldn't have been you. And if that's the case I don't like to think ... I can't even imagine…"

She stumbled off a kerb that was hidden in snow but continued to backtrack.

"So, you *did* see something?" Involuntarily, Kay's own advance faltered.

Marsha shook her head, perplexed, baffled, tormented. "I just … I can't believe it. I turned my head … and it was there. Right behind me. Only for a second, but—"

"*What* was there?"

"It was standing upright. Like a joke, like someone had put it there…" Fresh tears brimmed from Marsha's eyes. "But I know that nobody did."

"What? What was it?"

"For God's sake, Kay … I saw a coffin."

Kay's blood iced over as she stopped in her tracks. She was still on the pavement, of course. But Marsha, unwittingly, had retreated into the very middle of that little-used road.

Little used, but not *unused* – as a sudden screech of brakes and squealing of tyres attested. The van, which had come around the corner at reckless speed, went careering out of control, its wheels locking on the frozen surface.

Kay shouted hysterically but it was too late.

The impact was shattering, the detonation reverberating across the sleeping village.

Within a couple of minutes people were emerging from the nearest houses, wearing coats over their pyjamas and wellingtons instead of slippers. A short time later an ambulance arrived, followed almost immediately by a Thames Valley police car. Questions were fired around as people stood dumbfounded in the cold.

Kay watched it all from a sitting position on the kerbstone, through a bur of tears and clawed fingers. She barely spoke, scarcely aware of the hot tea and blankets offered by concerned villagers. She voiced no opinion, as the van driver, who was incoherent – whether that was through shock or drink or both was unclear – was taken away in handcuffs. She literally lost track of time as the haze of spinning blue lights slowly mesmerised her.

"Excuse me but I must ask you this … what happened?"

Kay could barely respond though she was aware the question had come from a police officer, a sergeant by the stripes on the epaulettes on her hi-vis, waterproof overcoat.

"I'm sorry, I don't know who you are yet," the policewoman persisted. "But perhaps you can tell me ... did you *see* anything?"

Kay looked up at that, the policewoman blanching at the depths of horror and misery etched into her face.

"I'm sorry," the officer said. "But I need to know ... what did you see?"

Kay directed her gaze back across the road, thoughts straying to that frigid pit beneath the church – but her eyes fixed on the large black bag, heavy and cumbersome and zipped securely up one side, that the undertakers were manhandling into the back of their hearse.

"Nothing," she said in a voice of utter bleakness. "I saw nothing at all."

LIRPALOOF ISLAND

Garry Kilworth

When I was a mere operative in OCC, working on an island in the Pacific Ocean, the company laid a communications cable between Japan and Hong Kong under the South China Sea. A unit containing a microphone was installed every hundred miles along the cable. These units were there to detect any interference with the cable, such as deep-sea fishermen accidentally damaging our equipment. However, we were astonished to discover that the microphones were picking up the sounds of WW2 sea battles between Japan and the Allies; battles apparently recorded by deep cold-water currents that acted in the same way as magnetic tapes. I tell you about this astonishing phenomenon in order to prepare you for the following story, which may on the surface appear fantastic, but which I assure you is a true account of one of those strange warps or kinks in the laws of the universe which we believe to be immutable.

~~~

There's always a fall guy in any office. A gullible member of staff: the brunt of all the jokes. At the time all this took place, I was the CEO for the Overseas Communications Company, a firm which supplies and runs the telecommunications systems for small island groups which did not have the technological ability to establish and operate their own telephone and telex systems.

Now, getting back to fall guys, the man who had that role in our Head Office was William Mcleod. The first thing our Chairman, Abe Hamber, said when Bill joined the company was, "I hope you haven't got your head in the clouds, Bill, because we need sharp minds around here." We all laughed at that, Abe being the boss.

When April the first came around I got the call from Abe and went to his office, to find Clara there already. Clara was the Vice Chair of the company, so I knew this was going to be a hush-hush meeting. I was on my guard because Abe was famous throughout the business world for his April Fool jokes.

His most famous joke, a legend now, was when he had one of our telephone engineers go into Head Office the night before the first to take the phones apart. The engineer rewired the number buttons so that if someone pressed, say, 0202 348732 they would actually be dialling 6868 573418 or whatever. Then the next morning Abe watched as chaos ensued amongst his bewildered staff. It all went as he had planned until old Joe Keppling – who could never take chaos without getting over-stressed – Joe had a heart attack and the people who were dialling 999 were getting nowhere until some bright spark thought to use a mobile.

"In a few days' time," Abe said to the two of us, "it'll be the first of April."

I nodded and smiled. "What have you got up your sleeve this year?"

He leaned forward, elbows on his huge oak desktop.

"Elaborate ain't the word for it," he said, grinning.

Clara said, "I hope it's not too cruel."

"Don't be a party pooper, Clara," replied Abe. "He'll come to no harm. In fact he might enjoy it, once he knows."

"So," I said, surprised. "Just one victim?"

"Bill Mcleod. He's the only one who would fall for it. Any of the others would see through it. It's a real doozie, this one."

"So tell," I said.

Abe chuckled to himself for a few moments, then told us: "I'm sending Mcleod to Lirpaloof Island. The station there seems to have got itself in an operational mess. If Mcleod does a good job I'll tell him, there might be a promotion in the offing."

"Lurpa what?" I said. "Where the hell is that?"

"In some ocean somewhere," cried Abe, nodding at Clara who had cast her eyes to heaven. "Ha! Ha! He'll have a whale of a time drinking piña coladas and sunning himself on the sands. Of course—" he winked at us "—there's a few dangerous creatures there. Snakes and scorpions, that kind of thing. But the beach parties will make up for that – barbecues under the palms – and the girls. Yes, I know Clara, but I'm sorry this is no time to spoil a good joke with PC. The girls there are buxom and willing, Polynesians naturally, or similar dusky maiden types. Can you imagine Bill Mcleod, glasses slipping down that narrow nose of his in a sweaty climate, getting down and dirty with a hula girl? I have to wonder if the guy has ever had a hard on. Yes, yes, all right Clara, I'll shut up. Well Jack, waddya think?"

"I still don't understand," I said, feeling uncomfortable under Clara's hard stare. "Where's the joke in sending him to an island in the sun?"

Abe snorted. "Shall I send you instead, Jack?"

Clara let out a huge sigh. "Oh for fuck's sake, Jack, Lirpaloof is April Fool backwards. There's no such island. It's a fiction."

"Brilliant, eh?" cried Abe, slapping the desktop with a heavy palm. "My PA will fix him an electronic air ticket which will take him to Auckland and on arrival there he's expected to book his own flight to Lirpaloof Island using Turtle Airways—" he winked again "—a small airline dealing with offshore destinations."

"Won't Mcleod see through this before he even gets on the long-haul flight? Clara did."

"But you didn't," Abe pointed out, "and the man is not as bright as we hoped, we know that now. In fact he's pretty short on initiative. I should have sacked him a month after he arrived, but hell, he's fun to have around. Someone's got to take the flak, otherwise it might be me."

I said, "I don't think anyone would dare…"

"No, neither do I—" cut in Abe "—I'm just spouting. Anyway, what do you think? Think the rest of the staff will have a laugh?"

I nodded enthusiastically, Clara less so. Abe was Abe and anything we said would have no effect on deterring him. This hoax would go ahead and neither Clara nor me would have the courage to tell Bill Mcleod what the company Chairman was up to. I persuaded myself it might even be fun for the victim. After all, he was going to get a free flight to New Zealand and back, and would probably get a nice hotel, meal and drinks on expenses while he was there.

Abe was going to tell Mcleod two hours before his flight that he needed to go immediately to the island. It was an emergency. This would give him no time to ponder over the destination. Abe was going to hand him sealed instructions on what to do and when. Even if he unravelled the name on the flight over, I was convinced Bill would not dare to open the envelope until he arrived in Auckland. He was a man trapped by his character. He took the office jokes against him solemnly, but without complaint. It was as if he knew his role in life and had accepted it long ago. At school he must have been bullied mercilessly. At least in the office he was held somewhat in affection.

And so the day came. He was called to the Abe's office and given strict, hasty instructions. Abe personally imposed the importance of the mission on him, and Abe's PA and Human Resources swiftly arranged the paperwork needed. The firm's car chauffeured him to his flat to collect his passport and pack a small bag. I accompanied him to flat and airport, talking to him the whole time about everything and nothing, to keep his mind occupied. Poor Mcleod was whirled this way and that in order to get him on that flight to Auckland. Indeed, he seemed delighted with all the attention, which made me feel bad on seeing the recrimination in Clara's eyes. I don't think he had time to even consider decoding the name of the place to which he had been sent or to contemplate the nature of his destination.

The morning after his departure I hurried to Head Office and went straight to Abe Hamber. When I knocked and entered, he was reading something on his laptop. I sat down without being asked. His seniority was only marginally above my own.

"Fuck!" he said, looking up at me with a puzzled expression. "Email from Mcleod: *I have lost envelope containing instructions —*"

"He would do that," I said, nodding. "He loses everything."

"*—however, will proceed to Lirpaloof to ascertain problems and hopefully to solve them. Will report back once I have arrived. W Mcleod.*"

"Proceeding? But is there a real Lirpaloof?"

Abe shook his head. "I've already made several calls, to the Foreign Office, to the British Library and even the Royal Geographical Society. There is no and never has been a Lirpaloof Island."

"You think the Kiwis are taking the piss out of him too, then?"

"Maybe. Or maybe Mcleod is cleverer than we think – what about if he's turning the whole joke on us?"

"It wouldn't be in character, Abe. You know what he's like. He absorbs the fun poked at him. He just gives you that watery smile and says, 'You got me there, fellah.' That's all he ever does. I've never known him to take umbrage or say anything else. He's a sponge and sponges don't turn jokes on the jokers. No, especially one as elaborate and costly as this one. Not Mcleod. No way."

"You're right. He's too wet. But you would have thought by now he'd have worked out the back-to-front name?"

"Abe," I said, "there's an Easter Island. There's a Christmas Island. The Whitsundays. Hawaii was once called the Sandwich Islands. Captain Cook even named a town 1770 when he'd run out of names. Maybe Mcleod really believes there's an April Fool Island, the name of which was reversed for the sake of humour?"

At that moment Clara entered the office with an envelope in her hand.

"He did leave it behind," she said. "His landlady brought it in."

"His sealed instructions," Abe said. "The note that would

have told him it was all an April Fool's joke."

"Still," I said, "he could have worked it out anyway." I paused, shook my head and added, "but not to call in and say, 'You got me there, sir!'."

Clara said, "He might be in trouble. Perhaps his state of mind? You know? You must make enquiries, Abe."

Abe took her seriously.

He made calls to the long-haul airline, to Auckland Airport authorities, to the New Zealand police, the hospitals and to Immigration Services. No one knew where this W Mcleod was. He had indeed entered the country but no one was sure where he'd gone after he left the airport and whether he was still on New Zealand soil. An enquiry had now been set up and any member or members of staff responsible for dereliction of duty would be reprimanded. New Zealand took its administrative duties seriously.

Everyone, it seemed, was taking things seriously but no one was coming up with answers.

~~~

A month later we received a call from a New Zealand fisherman. He had netted a bottle containing a message. The sender had indicated that the finder should contact Sir Abraham Hamber of the Overseas Communications Company, London. However, before the fisherman would read it to us over the telephone he wanted assurance that there would be a reward, since the call was costing him "an orm and a lig". Kiwis do this funny thing with their vowels, exchanging the phonetics, so that a "e" becomes an "i" and "pen" becomes "pin" and the "i" becomes a "u" and you get "fush and chups". Not easy for a Brit to follow, especially taking it down on a keyboard as it's spoken. The fisherman was told the amount would be more than adequate. I typed the letter with difficulty on Abe's computer as it was read to us in a twangy Kiwi accent.

Dear Sir Abraham,
I am not quite sure why I've been sent to Lirpaloof, but I would

appreciate it, sir, if you could manage to arrange for me to leave as soon as possible. On arrival at Auckland Airport I enquired about Turtle Airways. No one had heard of it. So, using my initiative I took a taxi to the nearest yacht marina and asked everyone I met if they knew how to get to Lirpaloof Island. I wasn't successful until around midnight when a man stepped out of the shadows – I remember his hair was as white as salt and his skin like tree bark – and he said he would take me to there. He had amongst his tattoos one of an island group which covered his chest. He pointed to it, saying, "This is the archipelago, the atoll, my friend. This one at the bottom, is the island you need." I recall climbing into his canoe with some reservations, but by this time I was desperate and also exhausted with jet lag. I fell asleep in the bottom of the pahi.

I next really only became fully conscious of my surroundings on finding myself on the beach of this godforsaken place. I thought at first to acquaint myself with the procedures used in the local station, but have so far been unable to locate anything that resembles a communications centre. Also, conditions are not what I expected, even though you warned me of certain dangers. There are various creatures on this island to be avoided. Indeed, even the locals are less than friendly and treat me as an interloper. They are of a rather savage nature and if it is not unacceptable to say so, of a primitive mind. There are ugly pagan rituals the details of which I will not go into here, but I honestly believe they practise bestial sacrifice, perhaps even worse.

Please, sir, find a way to get a loyal and faithful employee passage away from here, I beg you. I am sleeping rough on the beach and finding food where it drops from the trees. The local fishermen ignore my pleas for transport and there is no ferry. I am at a loss to know where to turn to next.

Yours sincerely,
W Mcleod

PS. Of one thing I am absolutely certain. This is Lirpaloof Island. The name is up on the shack that serves as a store and whenever I ask a local, he or she always confirms the fact. I am happy to report, sir, that I carried out the first part of my instructions, to reach my destination, though without one of our comcens I am unable to perform the rest of *my duties.*

"We have to get him home," whispered Clara. "The poor boy."

"Get him home? Get him home? For fuck's sake, Clara," I cried, "he's on a fictitious island!"

Abe said, "We have to send someone else, someone with a few brains, to find him and bring him back."

"Does no one listen to me?" I said. "He's told us where he is and it doesn't exist. Abe has confirmed that with every living authority."

I knew with both Clara and Abe that I was dealing with unimaginative people. They were pragmatists who dealt in scientific fact, but I had to persuade them that what we were dealing with here was the preternatural world. It was not going to be easy.

"Look," I began, "you have to develop a little imaginative elasticity. It may be hard to accept standing here in this office, but space, time and dimensions are not set in stone. There are those scientists who truly believe in time travel. There are those who believe in the flexibility of space. And more relevant to our problem, there are those who believe in more than three dimensions. Abe, Clara, have you ever heard of the theory of parallel worlds, where the earth that we live on is only one of many similar earths?"

"Heard of it," replied Abe, grudgingly. "Films and stories."

"Well, I believe that what's happened here is that Bill Mcleod has slipped into another dimension."

"How would he manage to do that?" asked Clara. "Accepting that there is such a place."

"Because he really believes that Lirpaloof exists. He's been told so by the chairman of the company he works for, a man he looks up to as a god. He's found his way to Lirpaloof because he's convinced it's there, just as those who believe you get to Heaven if you have faith in its existence probably get there too."

Abe said, "Shit, this is too far-fetched for me, Jack."

"Look," I replied, sighing deeply, "I know it sounds unbelievable, but I'm simply trying to cover all bases here. Mcleod has been missing for several weeks now and all we have is a bottle with a message in it. We can still keep exploring the idea that he's been stranded on a real island that the locals have decided to call Lirpaloof, but probably has another name on the charts—"

"I really do like that idea," murmured Abe, firmly.

"—but we can also open our minds to the possibility—" I held up my hands "—the very remote possibility, that we're dealing with the otherworldly here. You know I spent several years in the Pacific as the manager of one of our comcens—"

"Kula Mahi Islands," said Clara. "You came home a little strange from that place, Jack."

"—well, those isolated volcanic islands do things to your heart and your head. They retain some of the mystical elements of their early histories. There are tremendous electric storms that come sweeping in out of the sea, the like of which we never see in this safe land of ours. The scenery is uncanny: high escarpments with weird shapes to them which do eerie things with the sound of the wind. Deep impenetrable jungled interiors where men live without contact with the modern world. The retention of ancient rituals, even though the islanders may follow a modern religion on the surface."

I realised I was in danger of sounding like an ex-colonial here and I could see Clara was beginning to purse her lips.

"Oh, I'm not saying all the Pacific islands are like this, just one or two forgotten ones, away from the shipping lanes, out in the blue isolated darkness of the largest ocean on the earth. I just know that on the Kula Mahis I learned to let go of reality once in a while, to open myself to experience the numinous of an ancient landscape, and the barely concealed beliefs of its inhabitants. It was actually enlightening, rather than upsetting. I came home feeling I had expanded my mind and my spirit."

"All this is very well," broke in Abe and I knew I hadn't changed his scepticism one jot, "but what about the bottle with the message in it. Did it float across dimensions? How does it get from one world to another? Tell me that, Merlin."

"Well, of course I can't give you a definite answer, Abe. But what I will say, that if there is a passage between dimensions, between parallel worlds, it would be on an open stretch of water with no land in sight and no sign of the now. Just the winds, the sea and the sky. Eddies, tides, deep water currents, the ocean swells, they do strange things and find and reach unusual places. They find hidden caves and unknown shoals. They reach the depths of our world, places which have never been seen by the eyes of Man. They enter the narrowest cracks, the tightest fissures in the skull of the earth. They curl, they rip, they tear away the landscape to reveal lost wonders. And if there is a way to cross time and space, people, it's out on those watery wastes, unseen by you or me. A bottle drifting aimlessly, caught and carried by currents and waves? I would say that might be the way to cross from one parallel world to another."

"We need to send someone to investigate," stated Abe, firmly. "Someone who doesn't know I invented the name of the island. If Mcleod can get there then maybe someone else can too. Two heads may be able to find a way off that place, where one is left dithering, especially as that one head is stuck on the shoulders of Bill Mcleod."

"Well it can't be me or Clara because we are two people who believe that the island is fictitious. Can I suggest it should be someone who is open to the idea of the paranormal? You don't need to tell them that there's the possibility the island doesn't exist. Just send them out with unencumbered information, but with a mind able to accept the fantastical as well as the reality of this world or any other."

"Bates," said Clara, quickly.

"Bates?" Abe and echoed in unison and I added, "Who's he?"

"She. Alison Bates. She works in the mailroom."

Abe frowned. "How do you know she believes in – what is it? The supernatural?"

Clara looked a little defiant. "Because we were once an item."

"Oh," I said, "so you know her pretty well."

"Very well. She'll jump at the chance of an adventure that's paid for by the firm."

Abe wasn't thoroughly convinced by the idea but as he said later, what else was there? Mcleod was festering on some hostile landscape, probably nearing starvation or being treated like an animal by unfriendly locals and we had no real plan for getting him back. Indeed, he was a poor lost soul unless we could find some way to reach him, whether the island was real or fabricated.

Abe still believed that the island was real and some local sailor had taken advantage of Bill and dumped him on a place with a name close enough to Lirpaloof to fool his passenger. It would take a lot to stretch the mind of Abe Hamber, Chairman of the Overseas Communications Corporation, a man who dealt solely in paperwork and board meetings. Abe wasn't even a comms man. He hadn't come up from operations like Clara and me. He was one of those businessmen who move from company to company, acutely aware of finances, personnel and global planning, but no engineer or communications operator.

Clara was right about Alison Bates though. She was tremendously enthusiastic about the project we'd given her. She was a small woman, around twenty-five, with dark hair and dark flashing eyes. Not once during the telling of the tale did she look as if she was going to laugh at us. Her expression was intent. She asked some serious and pertinent questions after the briefing, then told us she would bring William Mcleod back or die trying.

"I'll bring your boy home," said Alison, as I drove her to the airport. "Don't you worry for second, sir."

Foolishly, I believed her.

~~~

We heard nothing for several more weeks, then we received the second bottle message from Bill Mcleod. The "Dear Sir Abraham" had been thrown to the winds. It seemed we had crossed William's anger threshold at last.

Listen, you bastards at home, safe in your bloody comfortable offices in the middle of London. Alison Bates arrived on the island just a week ago. Unlike me, soft-treading Mcleod, she waded into the tribal elders and made demands. Last night they sacrificed her, live and naked, to some rock they worship. Her intestines were hung on an ancient tree and they dangle over a river. Fish with razor teeth leap out of the water to snap mouthfuls of her blood-dripping colon. Her torso was eventually thrown to some huge reptiles. Oh, and they hung her head on a string outside the village so that it would attract the flies and keep them from the huts. For fuck's sake get your fingers out and get me out of this hell hole. I know they're coming for me next. I have built a palm hut on the beach and I hear them outside, whispering and laughing. I'm terrified. What happened to Alison is nothing to what they'll do to me. Women are despatched quickly because they are held in some reverence. Men are toyed with just as cats play with mice. I've seen them take three days over killing a marooned sailor, whose screams seemed to delight the audience as they skinned him alive with scallop shells, and then fried his genitals while still attached to his body. There is no grave for the victims. Any pieces of their body left over is tossed to those giant lizards I told you about They have such strong jaws, they can crush and even swallow bones – skull, pelvis and everything else.

GET ME OFF THIS ISLAND, YOU ARSEHOLES!

PS. I've run out of the paper I brought with me in my briefcase now and the ink in my ballpoint pen is hardening. This is my last message. Tell Louise I love her desperately and will always love her. She is the brightest star in the firmament of my life. WM.

We were devastated of course. One of the worst aspects of it was, we had no idea who Louise was or where to find her. We went through Bill's desk drawers but there were no clues there. His landlady was not helpful, saying she had never heard of a Louise and that Mr Mcleod's letters were all bills or junk mail. No one tried to contact the company, as might be expected when someone goes missing, and Bill's only surviving relative, an

Aunt Rosimund, had not heard from him since he sent her a thankyou note for a birthday present when he was ten years of age. After that time, she said, she got no thanks and so stopped sending gifts altogether.

~~~

Poor Alison too! Clara wept for several hours and Abe kept repeating, "I'm never going to do another April Fool's joke. Never." For my part, I couldn't get the picture of that lovely energetic young woman as fierce in her determination to find and bring home Bill Mcleod mirrored Stanley's quest for Livingstone.

"She was such a gutsy girl," I said.

A tearstained Clara retorted, "I don't think that's appropriate, do you, considering what they did to her." And I realised what I'd said and apologised to everyone in the room.

~~~

Abe went burning into action now and mobilised politicians, the military and life-saving services. He did not mention that the island might be fictional. He merely reported Bill missing and said that the young man had gone in search of a place which was not on any known map and had not been heard from since. We said Bill was supposed to be somewhere in the region of Tasmanian Sea. Ships, boats, yachts and other seafaring vessels were sent messages and asked to be on the look-out for any suspicious craft or uncharted atoll. Abe even hired aircraft to scour the area, but not only did they find no Lirpaloof archipelago, they found no island whatsoever. Bill Mcleod was lost on a small kink in time and space.

After six months the whole episode was put on the archive shelves of Head Office, with a note to say that no OCC employee should ever be sent to a foreign station alone. Of course rumours circulated amongst the staff. One bad-taste joker wrote on the toilet wall "OCCult" which I was glad was in the Men's and out of Clara's view.

Just a week after the Bill Mcleod incident was shelved we received the final letter in a bottle, this time apparently from the

Lirpaloof elders.

Ew terger ot mrofni uoy taht ruoy tnavres doelcM W saw dellik dna netae yb a odomok nogard. Lirpaloof Licnuoc.

THE HATE WHISPERER

Thana Niveau

There are faces that live inside of other faces. Only rarely do we see them on others, and never on ourselves. We can't know what's hiding beneath our own skin. But there are those who can coax it to the surface.

It should have been an ordinary photograph. But it wasn't. The girl glared out from what was an otherwise conventional family portrait. She sat between an older man and woman, presumably her parents, with a younger boy at her feet. The other subjects were smiling, the mother's eyes bright and delighted, the father's full of pride. The boy was laughing, gap-toothed and unselfconscious.

But the girl…

Although her mouth had the shape of a smile, there was something off about her expression. Her eyes were filled with loathing, a threatening, visceral fury. It was too intimate, as though she were transmitting some awful secret through the picture. Marta quickly turned the page, her skin crawling with unease.

The rest of the portfolio was unremarkable. There were the usual formal portraits – weddings, head shots, the obligatory pregnant nudes – along with a variety of creative compositions. Like artists, photographers had their own unique styles and it wasn't difficult to identify similar themes running through each person's work.

But there was only one photo by *him*. Marta didn't need to read the copyright notice to know it was Volmer's work.

She could still see the look of barely suppressed rage in the girl's piercing eyes as though it were burned into her own retinas. After a moment's hesitation she flicked back to the picture and stared at it. The girl stared back.

The image made Marta feel watched, stalked, preyed upon. And yet here it was nestled in amongst all these other perfectly ordinary and unremarkable photos. Sickeningly sweet "new baby" pics, clichéd "wise old grandma" portraits, obviously staged "candid" engagement photos. And then this girl, like a malevolent presence in the middle of her family's portrait. Had no one ever remarked on it?

"See anything you like?"

Marta glanced up at the receptionist's voice. The receptionist looked to be about the same age as the one in the picture. A crooked name tag read ASHLEIGH.

"I'm not sure," Marta said. She got to her feet and took the photo album to the front desk. "What do you think of this shot?"

Ashleigh peered at it through enormous false lashes, her mouth set in a bored little frown. "Hmm. Just a family, innit? Nothing special."

"You don't think it's … strange?"

The receptionist looked at it again, then shrugged. "Dunno. Mum's jumper is ugly as fuck, though." And she laughed.

It was obvious that she couldn't see it, couldn't feel it, the seething anger in the daughter. Marta forced a smile. "Yeah it is," she said.

She was satisfied now that it was no coincidence, that she alone was able to see the secret horror in certain photographs. She had visited every freelance studio within fifty miles, occasionally finding a single image by *him* in a portfolio, more often finding none. A bride with the eyes of a serial killer. An old man whose hatred for his wife was horribly apparent, at least to

Marta. Once she'd even seen a baby whose face was all wrong. Its expression hadn't sparkled with the usual curiosity and wonder that talented photographers were able to evoke in children. There was no other word for it: this one had looked evil.

Ashleigh was watching her, looking expectant.

Marta almost didn't trust herself to speak. The words, when they came, sounded forced, like a confession obtained under torture. She touched the family portrait. "This photographer," she said, not wanting to say his name aloud. "How can I contact him?"

"Clients reach the photographers through us. Or you can use the studio's email address. Have you already looked at our website?"

Marta nodded. She had, but this photo hadn't been part of the gallery there. She had never found any trace of Volmer or his work online.

Ashleigh frowned as she peered at the watermark at the bottom of the photo. "Hmm, I don't recognise that name," she said. "Hang on." She began pecking at her computer keyboard, typing far more letters than were in the single name.

The few seconds it took felt like an eternity to Marta, whose heart was already pounding at the prospect of what she was doing, what she might be setting in motion.

"No luck, I'm afraid," Ashleigh said, shaking her head. "That's weird. It doesn't even look like our studio. That background is way retro. Must be someone's front room. Maybe he worked for us once and that picture just never got taken out of the book." She dug inside the plastic sleeve and yanked the photo out. "Sorry about that. But we have over thirty photographers registered with us who can—"

"No!" Marta's shout halted Ashleigh as she was about to crumple up the photograph. The girl stared at her, eyes wide. Marta lowered her voice. "Sorry. But can I have that? I mean, if you're just going to throw it out?"

Ashleigh's brow furrowed and she looked at the photo as though contemplating some great ethical dilemma.

"It's just," Marta said, with some desperation, "I know the family. And I was hoping I could hire the same photographer for … for mine."

The lame story was good enough for Ashleigh, who smiled and handed her the photo. "Sure, no problem!" Then she winced. "Erm, sorry about the jumper comment."

"Don't worry about it," Marta said, manufacturing another smile. The photo paper was unpleasantly smooth and cold in her hand and she longed to shove it out of sight inside her handbag. "I'll have another look at your website in case this guy doesn't work out."

"Cool." Ashleigh gestured to a colourful printout behind her. "There's a special on right now so don't wait too long to book. The studio gets crazy busy this time of year."

"Sure thing," Marta said as she headed back out into the street. The door banged shut behind her.

Clouds churned in the sky, rumbling with distant thunder. A breeze threatened to tear the photograph from her hand and she tightened her grip on it. She was getting close. So close. Soon the secret would burst open like a storm, raining down violence on an unsuspecting world.

She dared a final glance at the image. Perhaps she just hadn't noticed it before, but now there seemed to be something conspiratorial in the girl's expression. As though she and Marta were connected.

As though they shared a secret.

~~~

Marta couldn't stop looking at the photo. She had stared at it for hours until she knew every detail of it. If she closed her eyes, she could reproduce the image exactly in her mind. But the intensity in the girl's eyes never seemed to lose any of its power. The loathing was as ferocious as the first time Marta had seen it.

Marta's own eyes had been unable to find any clues, so it was time to try something else. She scanned the picture into her computer and opened it in three separate photo editing programs. In each one she magnified the image, scrolling over it millimetre by millimetre. She tweaked the contrast, saturation, brightness and colour, playing with every available setting. She didn't know what she was looking for, but she was certain she'd know when she found it.

Perhaps it was only her intense scrutiny, but the family began to seem even more peculiar to her. Their clothes and hair were curiously nondescript, giving no hint as to when the photo was taken. It might have been done yesterday or forty years ago. Likewise, the background was a plain wash of olive green, offering no information of its own.

Marta slumped back in her desk chair, rubbing her eyes. They were burning and unfocused after so much time staring at the computer screen. She supposed she could go door to door in town, asking shopkeepers if they knew the family. But that could take weeks. And besides, the family could have been from anywhere. They could have moved. Or died.

A chilly little shiver tickled Marta's bare arms, as if spiders had run over them. She looked back at the screen. The girl's eyes bored right into her own.

"Who are you?" Marta asked. "How do I find him?"

But the image of the girl remained silent. Silent and sinister.

And Marta finally saw it.

She sat forward and clicked the icon for the magnifying glass until the girl's left eye filled the screen. Despite the pixellation something was reflected in the pupil. A few adjustments to the exposure revealed a shape deep within. Marta fine-tuned the highlights and shadows to bring it into view. It was dark and murky, but she could just make out the silhouette of a camera on a tripod. And beside it – the figure of a man.

She felt lightheaded as she stared at the shape. It was him. Volmer.

She dragged the magnification window to the side, locating the same image in the girl's other eye. Only now there was a little more clarity. One final adjustment to the contrast revealed the glint of an eye. It was like spotting a predator lurking in the shadows.

She didn't even know what half the tools in the program were for, but with random experimentation she managed to bring the background into sharper focus. There was a window behind the man's silhouette. Marta's stomach swooped as she peered closer, deeper, as though she were moving through physical space.

She could see letters through the window, the fragment of a shopfront. At first she thought they spelled "A2A" until she realised she was looking into a mirror.

"Gotcha," Marta whispered.

~~~

The Azalea Café had closed down years ago, shutting its doors along with most of the surrounding shops. But its painted sign still arched above the entrance. At least some of it did. "AZA AF" was all that remained. Just enough to identify it.

Marta stood gazing up it. Chipped and flaking blossoms faded alongside the letters of the sign, their colour leached away by time and neglect. She remembered coming here as a child, back when she still used to wish her parents would pay more attention to her. Back before she learned that being invisible was actually a blessing.

With a shudder at the unwelcome memory, she turned away. Across the street from the café was another derelict building. She couldn't remember what shop had been here but it was obvious no one could be living in the flat above it now. The first floor was a charred and blackened ruin. All the windows were smashed and the roof was open to the sky. Was this where the picture had been taken?

Marta darted a quick glance up and down the empty street. The winter sun was low in the sky, spilling sickly yellow light across the rubbish and debris. A plastic bag chattered at her, trapped by a lamppost, but otherwise the area was silent. Deserted.

She strode towards the building with purpose, pushing aside her unease. The stairwell to the left of the shop presumably led to the flat above, and Marta edged past the splintered boards of the broken doorframe. It was dark inside the stairwell, reeking of mould and rot. She didn't want to imagine what might be crunching beneath her shoes. Soon enough she was at the top of the stairs. She was spared having to open the door to the flat. It hung askew from its half-melted hinges.

Her brain struggled to unpack the layers of smell. It was an assault on her senses and she had to wind her scarf around her mouth and nose to muffle the stench. Her entrance disturbed a flock of fat pigeons that flapped noisily up through the burnt roof, stirring clouds of ash.

The fire had obviously happened a long time ago but the wood smelled as though it had been doused recently. There was an overpowering wet-charcoal stink and Marta was convinced she could see wisps of smoke still rising from the boards.

She faced the window that looked out over the Azalea Café. This was where Volmer had stood to photograph the family. The wall was too burnt to see what colour it might have been, but Marta was sure they had stood just to the left of the window.

Her hands were unsteady as she fished the photograph from her handbag. She held it up to the room, positioning the family and trying to imagine the room as it had been. In the photo, the wall behind them was a putrid dark green. Had it really looked like that? Or, like the girl's hatred, had Volmer somehow brought out the hidden ugliness in the room as well?

But there was no epiphany, no flash of insight or understanding. No solution to the riddle that had obsessed her. Marta's shoulders slumped as she gazed at the ruins of the flat. Just what had she expected to find here?

Something scuttled in the blackened debris behind her but Marta didn't turn to look. Instead she closed her eyes and lowered her scarf from her face. She braced herself and then inhaled deeply. Nausea rose in her throat at the stench. Damp, decaying wood. Burnt plastic and fabric. Rotting food. Putrefaction.

But behind all that, there was something else. A bright, sharp smell. It only took her a moment to place it. Petrol.

The girl's face surfaced in Marta's mind, the expression of

venomous hatred becoming even more pronounced as the realisation set in.

"Did you burn them alive?" Marta whispered. "Or did you kill them and set the fire after?"

Silence swelled in the empty room, roaring like waves in her ears. The voice, when it came, made her jump.

"Oh, she burned them alive."

Marta whirled round, her eyes wide. A man stood in the doorway, watching her. He was tall and lanky, his face obscured by shadows. He seemed made of shadow himself.

For long moments Marta couldn't speak. Her panting breaths were making her giddy and she pressed the scarf back against her face to lessen the smell of death.

She was afraid to speak his name, to voice it aloud. Her actions had already brought him to her and now she feared what else he was capable of. She could only stare, wide-eyed, as she waited to see what he would do.

His silhouette shifted slightly as he crossed his arms, leaning against the doorframe. The casual pose seemed to mock their surroundings, like laughter at a funeral.

"No one has ever sought me out before," he said, a note of amusement in his soft voice. A smile glinted in the swarming darkness of his face. He let the unspoken question hover in the air between them.

Marta swallowed. "I just… I wanted…" She looked down at the photograph in her hand, not knowing what to say. What *did* she want?

Volmer didn't offer her any help. He stood silently in the doorway, waiting.

A sharp pressure was taking hold behind Marta's eyes, pulsing deep inside her skull. She hadn't noticed it before. It must have started when she entered the derelict flat. She pressed the fingers of her left hand against her temple, massaging it gently. The faces in the photograph began to swim and she shut her eyes to block them out.

But behind her eyelids she saw even more. She saw the girl,

fury in her eyes, grim determination in the set of her jaw. Marta saw her grabbing the petrol can and splashing it on the walls and floor. She moved with calm deliberation, going from room to room, soaking the entire flat. From time to time other glimpses came: the curl of someone's lip, a cruel laugh, clutching hands. Marta's own hands drifted up in a warding-off gesture, but there was nothing here to escape. Not any more. The girl had seen to that.

Marta watched as the match flared, reflected in the girl's eyes. She held it up, admiring the little flickering flame, in awe of the power she possessed. Such a tiny thing, filled with such devastating potential. Just like her. She took a step back and let the match fall. The fire caught, flashed, and within seconds it was roaring along the path she had laid for it. Even if she wanted to change her mind, it was too late now. The flames raced for the back bedrooms like wild animals unleashed. She need do nothing more, just let the violence of nature run its course.

The girl stood in the doorway, just where Volmer stood now, impervious to the screams as her family woke to the horror of the inferno. They ran into the lounge but a wall of flame raged there, cutting them off from the door, and the girl. The expression in her eyes was the same one Marta had seen in the portrait. Remorseless, pitiless hate. It was the last thing they would ever see.

The flames licked the walls and furniture, consuming everything in its path. Smoke filled the room as her father, mother and brother succumbed. Their screams gradually gave way to choking gasps as they collapsed one by one. The girl was feeling dizzy now as well. She sank to her knees on the threshold as the windows exploded outward, showering the street below with shards of glass.

Whispers followed, teasing words that danced in the girl's mind. The same words of encouragement that had led her to this point. They had never been spoken aloud. He had never said a thing. But he had known, had seen the potential within her. Somehow he had coaxed it out. The idea had scurried through her brain like rats in a maze, suggesting, compelling her. And she had acted.

The girl crumpled to the floor outside the burning room. In the distance she heard sirens, shouting, pounding, and finally she felt strong arms pulling her away from the scene. Later she would claim to remember nothing.

Marta's eyes fluttered open and she found she was lying on the floor. Splintered boards jabbed at her and she winced as she pushed herself away from them and struggled to her feet again. Her clothes were stained with soot. Flames crackled, a distant echo in her mind, and she became aware of a new smell. It reminded her of the time her mother had burned the roast. The connection made her stomach lurch.

"How…" she murmured, "how did you…"

The glint of Volmer's smile was a little wider now. "I only showed her what was already there."

"And the others?"

Volmer cocked his head, lending his silhouette a mocking aspect. "Others?"

Marta took a few steps closer. She was keen to get out of the derelict flat, but she had to know more. She had to know everything.

"The people you photograph," she said, recalling all the images she had seen. "There was a bride. An old man. Other families. I even saw a baby once. It looked … savage. What did you do to them?"

"I didn't do anything to them." A warning note had crept into his voice. "If they later acted on their own impulses, that's nothing to do with me."

Marta lowered her head. "I'm sorry. I didn't mean to accuse you. But – if these people did do … things…" She swallowed. The smell of burnt rotting meat was threatening to make her sick. "Whatever they did – or might have done… How did you…"

He seemed to be enjoying her discomfort, her inability to voice what was in her mind.

"If you are able to recognise what I can bring to the surface," he said, "why do you need me at all?"

Marta was close enough now to see his face. His eyes were bright, dancing with an obscenely playful light. He was toying with her. He wasn't going to tell her anything unless she came right out with it.

"I want them dead," she said, forcing the words out. "But the desire isn't enough."

"Not enough to make it happen by some magic that absolves you of blame?" Volmer shook his head. "That's not how it works, my dear."

"No, no, I don't mean that!" Tears stung her eyes as she recalled standing in the doorway of her parents' house with a knife, frozen and unable to act. "I mean, how do I find it? The hate. How do I release it?"

Volmer's eyes gleamed. "It's as simple as crossing a bridge," he said. "When you reach the other side, it will consume you."

Her heart was pounding. She could feel the desire within her, swelling, pulsing. But it was still not enough to make her act.

"I can't," she whimpered. Her mind was replaying the events she had witnessed in the flat. The girl's uncompromising vengeance. The release she had longed for all her life.

"If you *can't*," Volmer said with icy contempt, "then perhaps it's something else you're looking for. And I am not the one to give it to you."

Marta gritted her teeth, glaring at him. "Just tell me how! What did the others do afterwards? The baby! How could it hurt anyone? What did you do to it?"

Volmer laughed. "As I've already explained, I didn't do anything to them. I only made them aware of what was already there." He watched her for a few moments, enjoying her torment before speaking again. "Sometimes the hate is seeded by people or events. Like Lila here." He nodded at their surroundings. "You saw her memories, yes? You know what she was avenging."

Marta nodded.

"The baby you saw is a different story. Some people are made to hate. Others are born with it inside. That baby will grow up to be a cold-blooded adult, one capable of astonishingly brutal acts."

"But it wouldn't be, if you hadn't – done what you do."

He smiled, a strange, cryptic expression. "I have other plans for that one."

Marta shook her head. The stench was making her dizzy and she was losing patience with his games. "I need your help," she pleaded. "I can't take that final step without you."

"Perhaps you aren't actually a killer," Volmer said. "Perhaps you only want to be. If so, you're wasting my time."

Marta's hand tightened into a fist, her fingers crumpling the photograph. She was surprised to find it still in her hand. Looking down at it, she reconnected with the fury in the girl's eyes, the fury that had led to so much destruction.

"I only want…" But as she raised her head again to address Volmer, she saw that she was alone.

~~~

It had been weeks. Weeks of simmering anger and resentment. Weeks of searching. Weeks of frustration.

Marta retraced her steps until she had identified all of Volmer's subjects. All the ones she'd found photos of, anyway. She knew there must be others she hadn't discovered yet.

Lila Barrow had been convicted of arson and three counts of premeditated murder. She was sent to a psychiatric hospital and later transferred to prison, to rot there until she died. The scant information Marta was able to dig up online suggested that the girl hadn't spoken a single word since her arrest, not even in her own defence.

The bride's name was Hannah Kelso née Chappell, and she had killed her husband while on their honeymoon in New Zealand. The resort staff had come to investigate when the couple didn't check out at the end of their stay. They found Andrew Kelso in pieces, his limbs scattered throughout the suite of rooms. His head was enshrined on the bed, propped up with hotel towels folded into swans. They found Hannah dozing in a lounger on the beach. She offered no resistance to the police and she remembered nothing about her wedding or anything that happened after it. There was no evidence that Andrew had ever mistreated her, and by all accounts they had been typical newlyweds – madly in love and looking forward to their future together.

Hugh Simmons, the old man, had gone beyond simply killing his wife. He had rigged a homemade bomb that took out the coffee shop where she'd been meeting an old friend from university. Six other people died in the explosion, including Hugh. His body was found in the alley behind the coffee shop, his hands clenched around the detonator. No one had really known the couple, and no motive was ever unearthed.

There were other people, other crimes, but these were the most lurid, the most gruesome. Marta was a little disturbed to realise she thought of them as her favourites.

She hadn't bothered asking the studios for the photos; she'd simply stolen them from their portfolios. Running the images through the computer programs produced the same result as with Lila's family portrait. In each one Marta was able to find Volmer's silhouette and the glinting shard of a smile.

The baby was the final piece of the puzzle. What had Volmer meant, that he had "other plans" for it? Did he hope it would grow up to be a killer? Looking at the photo again, Marta could easily believe it.

The baby was cradled in the arms of a young woman whose smiling face couldn't hide her weariness. But while the mother's eyes shone with love, the baby's were like chips of ice. It had no soul.

The mother's name was Ruth Coates and the baby was Ian. They hadn't been at all difficult to find. Like the other photos, this one had been taken in the subjects' home. The window behind Ruth afforded a view of a familiar church only a few miles away. Its largest stained-glass window had shattered in a recent storm, and the boarded-up cavity was just visible in the edge of the photo.

Everyone in town knew Ruth, and Marta soon grew bored with hearing about how her shifty boyfriend had dumped her once he'd found out Ruth was pregnant. Maybe he'd have left anyway once he saw his son's evil eyes in that portrait.

All of Volmer's subjects were dead. All except Ian Coates. And Marta skulked around the grim little village for days until she finally found him, contriving to run into Ruth in the high street.

"Oh, what a beautiful baby!" Marta cried, bending down over the pram. "What's his name?"

If Ruth was startled by her presumption, she didn't show it. She smiled wanly and answered Marta's insipid prepared questions. His name was Ian. He was seven months old. He was her greatest joy.

Marta suspected that wasn't true. And she suspected that Ian knew it too. As she met his eyes, she recognised the malevolent expression. There was no other way of putting it: the baby *glared* at her.

"I expect he can be a little devil though, right?" Marta asked, forcing a laugh to hide her unease.

The creature's mother forced a laugh of her own at that, and didn't reply.

Marta stepped back, smiling. "Well, I'll let you two go. Sorry to barge in. I just can't walk past a baby without saying hi!"

For a moment Marta wondered if Ruth was on to her too. The words couldn't be further from the truth. But instead, she simply returned Marta's smile and wished her a pleasant day.

Marta watched as Ruth shuffled away. Under her breath she said, "Bet if I offered to take him off your hands you'd give it serious thought before pretending to be outraged."

She waited until Ruth was at the end of the road, then followed at a distance. Ruth made one final stop at the chemist's before turning down a side street and trudging up a steep drive into a row of terraced houses that had seen better days. Hers was the end house on the far right. Marta made a note of the address and slipped away.

Sleep didn't come easily, especially not when Marta knew her alarm would only be going off again at 2.00 am. She didn't imagine Ruth kept anything like normal hours with a baby in the house but it still seemed a safe time of night for what she had planned. At least the neighbours should be asleep.

The street was dark, and Marta could hear no sounds from inside the house. She crept into the back garden and found a kitchen window. Dead and dying herbs were lined up along the inner sill in tiny plastic pots. Ruth might once have loved to cook but those days were over.

The sash was old and the lock gave way with minimal effort from Marta's screwdriver. She slid the window open and gently moved the pots down onto the worktop. Then she clambered through and a rush of adrenaline hit her as she realised she was actually inside the house. She had never done anything like this before. It was exhilarating.

She crept silently through the kitchen, pausing only to pull a knife from the butcher block next to the cooker. Not the largest; that wasn't necessary. It only needed to be sharp. As she made her way up the stairs a sudden flash of panic froze her. She pictured the baby sleeping with his mother. Then she calmed herself. No. Something with eyes like that wouldn't be welcome in the same bedroom, let alone the same bed.

Ian's room was just as Marta had imagined: blue wallpaper decorated with boyish teddy bears and aeroplanes. Not that any of it would make those dead eyes twinkle. How disappointed Ruth must have been the first time she tried and failed to make him laugh. And later how horrified.

The baby was watching her. And not with the normal dazed but animated interest of pre-verbal children. He was sitting up in the crib, staring frankly. Expectantly. In the darkness his eyes were little more than a predatory gleam. Gooseflesh rose on Marta's arms and she almost dropped the knife. A normal baby shouldn't even be able to sit up by itself, let alone stare daggers at her.

Volmer's words echoed in her mind, telling her of the baby's future potential. Marta shook her head to silence the voice.

"Not if I have anything to do with it," she whispered.

The baby cocked its head, a gesture so unnatural it made her stomach lurch.

This wasn't right. She wanted hatred. What she felt instead was revulsion. Horror. Fear.

She kept her eyes locked on the baby's, trying to stare it down. But it held her gaze, its expression full of menace. Marta forced herself to move, to take one step closer. Then another. The baby didn't even blink.

When she finally stood only inches away, she raised the knife and positioned it just beneath the baby's chin. Then, with one quick slice, she opened its throat.

Blood leapt from the wound in shockingly huge gouts, splashing across the blankets and wooden slats of the crib. The baby made no sound as it bled. It sat still, gradually lowering its head until the chin rested on its chest. Its eyes never left Marta, though. They continued to gleam with unearthly luminescence.

As Marta backed away, the eyes remained locked on hers. She became aware of a strange low whine, like a blade scraping the wires inside a piano. The whine rose in pitch, becoming acutely painful. The sound reached its peak and exploded in a harsh burst that filled with room with blinding light.

A camera flash.

Marta stumbled in the doorway, dropping the knife. It fell with a soft *thunk* onto the carpet. Dizzy and disorientated, she turned to go, but she didn't recognise her surroundings.

"What's happening?" she murmured. "Where am I?"

The whine began to build again, and this time the accompanying flash was even louder, brighter. Blinding.

Marta cried out, shielding her eyes. But shapes and tracers continued to dance behind her lids. Twin pinpoints of light shone mercilessly, piercing her mind. The baby's eyes.

"He was not yours to take."

The voice was low and menacing. Volmer.

"But I found it," Marta said, "the hate. The fury. I did it!"

She felt for the doorway, trying to orientate herself. She could see nothing but blazing garish white.

"He was *not yours*," Volmer repeated.

Another burst of light exploded behind her eyes, magnifying the excruciating glare. She cried out and fell to her knees. The hot sharp reek of blood filled her nostrils and when she reached up to touch her face, her hands came away wet. Blood was streaming from her eyes.

From somewhere behind her came the sound of a woman screaming. Ruth. And Marta realised what she'd done, the plan she'd derailed.

I have other plans for that one.

Ruth was meant to kill her own baby.

Light flashed again, increasing in frequency until it became a ceaseless strobing. Marta couldn't escape it. She could feel it invading every cell of her body, every spark of energy in her mind. But instead of hate, all it found was fear.

Muscle memory caused her hands to clench around the knife she no longer held, and she flailed desperately at the air around her. Through the endless popping bursts she heard the scuffle of feet on the carpet, drawing nearer. There was the impression of a frail female presence close by. A curse hissed through gritted teeth. And then the bright jolt of pain as Ruth plunged the blade into Marta's belly and wrenched it sideways. A hot writhing knot of wetness came slithering out.

As the blaring light began to dim at last, Marta heard one final pop of the camera flash. She had just enough awareness left to wonder if her portrait would be found someday, and what her sightless staring eyes would transmit.

I REMEMBER EVERYTHING

Debbie Bennett

I remember everything.

I remember every little thing as if it happened yesterday, this morning, *right now*. I can see them with their hands all over me, hear the whispers and the cries. I've never understood why nobody else can see them or hear them – why I seem to be the only one who watches them as much as they watch me. Somebody has to, don't they? Somebody has to keep check on what they do. I write it all down in my notebook, just like I've always done.

I was sixteen the first time. I'd been in my room, doing my homework. Mathematics, it was – trigonometry to be precise. I like to be precise. It avoids any ambiguity and there's a lot of ambiguity in my life. But mathematics is black and white, right or wrong, just like computers. Imagine all those little ones and zeroes scurrying around inside the computer – adding up and taking away, until the right answer comes squirting out the end like icing from the piping bag. I've always thought I'd be good with computers, but I've never been allowed to have one. I have to make do with cake decorating instead, although I think I'm quite good at that too. Cupcakes in particular.

So I am sixteen and alone on a Saturday night, doing mathematics homework in my bedroom. I'd stopped being invited out years earlier. I was the weird kid, the freak, the one person in the class you didn't invite to your birthday party in case – you know – somehow the weirdness was catching and I might infect my classmates. So I did homework, convinced that education was the way out of this life. Education would get me a job and a job would get me money and money would get me everything. Wouldn't it? And anyway, I just like mathematics.

And the voice told me this was good.

It did, really. An actual voice. *This is good*, accompanied by a little pat on the head, as if I were a small dog performing a trick. *Trick or treat*? And I went for the treat of course – doesn't everybody? Trick are scary things. Why would anybody want a trick?

~~~

I'm scared of everything.

Waking up in the mornings, I worry that I've maybe died in the night. Is this heaven or hell I find myself in? Is the new day real at all? I used to check every morning – read a page of a book or newspaper to see if it made sense. If it wasn't real, the words would be backwards or sideways or upside down, I know. I've practised these things.

They read books out to me when I ask them to – they're very good like that, very *literate*. I wonder whether they'd do French if I asked them. Or how about Russian or Arabic? Something with a different alphabet, but then I'd never know if they were tricking or treating, would I? It's not like I actually know any Russian or Arabic myself, although I did some French at school.

I don't know why I'm scared. Heaven or hell might be better than reality, anyway. I often think it must be – after all, reality is very overrated most of the time. I think they know this. When I wake in the mornings and I'm all alone and wondering if I'm still alive, they tell me I am. Will they tell me I'm dead one day and will I notice?

Mid-morning and I'm always scared that today will be the day that Helen doesn't come. Helen comes every day – she's another one who makes sure I'm still alive. Actually, she's the only other person I see. I did tell her once that it wasn't necessary, that they let me know these things, but she looked at me in a funny way. I think they scare her too because she doesn't like me to talk about them. At all. Which seems a little odd to me, but each to their own. And I do worry that she won't come anymore and then who would help me make my lunch and clean my flat? They are good at talking, but useless at everything else. They are not practical – not at all. Helen takes me shopping once a week and we go to Tesco in her red car and eat lunch in the little café. I have beans on toast, with no butter on the toast. And hot chocolate. Helen has lots of different things, but I like to be consistent. I think consistency is important. Thursdays is Tesco and beans and hot chocolate.

In the afternoons, I'm mostly scared that it might rain forever and I'll drown. I mean, what if the rain never stopped? The water would just keep coming and the world would fill up. And I can't swim. I tried to learn once, but water scares me too and I'd really rather just have a wash than get in a bath.

And they tell me this is good. Baths can be dangerous. What if the radio fell I and I got electrocuted? Far better to stand on a rubber mat and have a light wash. No tricks there.

~~~

I write down everything.

I start a new notebook every month. On the first day, from the minute – the *very second* – I wake up. My notebooks are labelled and stored chronologically in crates in the loft. I'm sure somebody will find them entertaining reading in the years after my death and I wonder if one day they will make a film of my life, with the script based on the contents of my notebooks. Really, they wouldn't have to do very much – I have made it easy for them with the amount of detail I include.

The time and the weather are always the first things to be recorded. Who I can see from my bedroom window; whether my neighbour has any workmen starting early. I think they must arrive very early or even work through the night because they are always leaving first thing in the morning – but she's very quiet and they never make any noise.

After breakfast, I watch the school children walk through the park opposite. Sometimes I watch the watchers too. Often there are men in the bushes who watch the older girls and I wonder why they are hiding. It all goes down in my notebooks. Sometimes I pretend the watchers are taking notes too and maybe we could compare what we have each written. But they don't like that – that's a trick – and so I never have. How would I contact the watchers anyway? It's not like I'm going to run down the stairs and across the street. That would be wrong. I don't ever go out my own. It's not allowed.

In the afternoons, before the children come home from school, the park is the home of the lurkers. Little more than children, sitting on benches or waiting in the undergrowth to meet other lurkers, to shake hands and smack each other on the back. I imagine *Hello, how are you, I'm fine thank you and what about you,* but the lurkers are often alone and talking to themselves and I wonder if lurkers can hear the voices too and I am not alone after all.

I think perhaps I should buy a camera. Maybe I should take some photographs and add them to my notebooks – would that make it easier for the filmmakers of the future? They disagree and I wince as they pinch me hard on the legs with their little fingers. I think I may have bruises but I'm too scared to look. Shrill chitterings in my ears tell me how angry they are, and I say sorry, sorry, sorry over and over again and I promise to be good. My heart flutters but a pat on the head calms me and all is well.

Helen arrives at exactly eleven o'clock. She knows to arrive at that time and she knows it upsets me if she is early or late, so sometimes she waits outside in her car. I want to ask her why she has to wait. She must know how long it takes to get to my flat by now, so why doesn't she just leave at the right time? Sometimes I see her checking her watch and tapping the steering wheel impatiently as if she is in a hurry to be somewhere. They laugh at me as I worry, because they don't like Helen. They think she interferes too much and she encourages me to leave the flat. I think they might be jealous of Helen, but I can't say that or they will bite me.

~~~

I feel everything.

The bed sheets are smooth against my naked body at night, except where the fabric has bobbled slightly with wear. Helen says I need to use special conditioner in my washing machine, but the machine is old and noisy and there is so much *water* sloshing around in there – sometimes I sit on the kitchen floor and watch the washing going round and round and it sucks me in and I feel like I might vanish into a pinprick of nothing. They laugh at that too. They are always laughing at me.

The air is cool as I don't like to have central heating on. The pipes make weird clunking sounds and there's a whistle that sounds like they might be trapped inside and that makes me sad, so I keep the temperature as low as I can and I watch the ice make frosty patterns on the windows in the winter. It's pretty. Helen gasps when she walks in and immediately turns the dial up. She thinks it's because of money and tells me to stop worrying, that I have plenty of money for such things and I'm well provided-for. I can't tell her it's because they are trapped in the pipes – she'd think I was mad – so we go out instead and I pretend to have forgotten my gloves and dash back inside to turn the dial back down again and save them from boiling alive in the pipe.

I can feel *them* too. Their sound is physical pain and utter joy. I am covered in bruises and full of smiles at the same time. It's hard to explain. We look after each other, they and I.

But at night, when it's cold and dark, after they have sung me to sleep with their lullabies, sometimes the mood changes. Soft tones become harsh and my bed moves with the weight of their anger. They argue – firstly with themselves and sometimes with me. I don't argue back. What would be the point? They are right. They are *always* right. And I wake the next day and I am tired and sore – there are fresh bruises and I can still feel the teeth. Once there were clumps of my hair on the pillow and I had to collect them up and get rid of them before Helen arrived.

But mostly I feel happy. I have been chosen. I am special.

~~~

I deny everything.

Not often. It's not often that anyone ever asks me or enquires after my health or well-being. People *assume*, don't they? I never assume anything. But when Helen asks if I am all right, when she sees a bruise on my arm, I tell her it's nothing, that I fell over in the bathroom and I hear them *hum* approvingly and I know I am safe today. And Helen. Because I have to keep Helen safe too – they don't like her but they tolerate her presence because she looks after me and they care about me. I try never to argue with Helen for fear they might hurt her – she might trip on the stairs back down to her car, or choke on the chocolate biscuit she eats with her cup of Earl Grey that is always served at just the right temperature in a china teapot every morning at exactly eleven o'clock.

But last week, I had to go out for real. Not just to Tesco – I'm used to that – but further afield. I had toothache, you see, and that was down to them too. I'm sure one was inside my head the night before, inside my mouth and fiddling with my teeth. And I woke up with an achy muzzy feeling and my cheek was swollen and Helen took one look at me and got her mobile telephone out and made a call and started talking about me. They didn't like that *at all*. I could feel them gathering around us and I had to try really hard to ignore the way my skin itched with them. And all the while I'm thinking please go away, please don't hurt Helen because who else will come to look after me if she can't? Helen talked for three minutes and sixteen seconds, then gave me a big smile and said she was taking me somewhere extra special today and we might have lunch somewhere different instead of Tesco. It wasn't even a Tesco day and we were *still* going out. And what if this other place didn't have beans and hot chocolate?

So we went down to her red car and they were behind me, screaming at me to stop, come back, it's the wrong day, and I had to ignore them and follow Helen. She drove a different way, on a big fast road and I thought we might never find our way home again. But we parked in a carpark with ten million other cars and got lost in a huge building with lots of people in beds and a man looked at my face and my hair and gave me some green sweets and a cup of water. I said I was fine and I'd bitten my tongue last night and I was all right, really all right. And Helen took me home and told me she would give me some of the green sweets every day for a while and that would make everything better. And I felt sleepy so I went to bed and they stayed away that day. I think they were cross with me.

Helen was right. My face did feel better and the next day she gave me more sweets and they stayed away that day too. And the next day. And the one after. And I was lonely then, so I stopped eating the sweets and just pretended to and Helen was still pleased with me, so I carried on pretending and she carried on being pleased with me and everyone was happy. Except they weren't happy at all at being silenced for so long.

For five nights they kept me awake, pinching and biting and scratching. I had to wear a long-sleeved jumper when Helen came round and she said she'd have to take me back to that place again and get some more sweets because she'd run out now. And that night, they said Helen had to leave me and I cried.

~~~

I see everything.

It's hard for me, because I try not to look and they may be invisible anyway. Sometimes they are all hard shiny white, with big eyes and those sharp – so sharp – fingernails, and other times they are warm and soft and they hug me and love me and I am happy. But mostly I try not to see, because they just are.

And I saw what came next. They told me what I had to do, so I did as they said and told Helen I didn't want her to come around again and I didn't need her. I could walk to Tesco by myself and I'd watched her make sandwiches enough times and it didn't look hard and I could clean too. Helen laughed and said don't be silly and we'd go to Tesco after she'd drunk her tea and eaten her chocolate biscuit. Beans and hot chocolate day. I said I make the tea every morning, don't I, and she said there was a bit more to life than cups of tea, which seemed a bit rude since I'd made her an extra special cup of tea that morning and added all the uneaten sweets which I'd saved up specially for a treat. I didn't think she'd eat them if I just offered – she's too nice for that and she knows how much I like sweets – so I'd squashed them all underneath a plate and added them to the teapot. I even said I didn't want any tea myself so she could have all of it. They approved of that. *This is good*, they said and patted me on the head and I wondered whether maybe they'd decided they did like Helen after all and I would be allowed to keep her. It had been so hard to choose between them.

Helen and I went to Tesco then in her red car and we did some shopping and had beans and hot chocolate in the café like we always did on Thursdays. But on the way home she seemed a bit funny and her voice didn't sound right. Just as we got close to my flat, she took both hands off the steering wheel – I don't think you are supposed to do that, are you? – and the red car hit the kerb and bounced into a road-sign. I thought she was dead and I was sad because I thought she liked me and it wasn't my fault that she had to leave me. So I got out of the car and walked home by myself, but the front door wouldn't open as I didn't have a key. And then I cried and the door opened and they let me in and patted and stroked me and made me smile again and I knew it would be all right.

~~~

I regret nothing.

Regrets are pointless. They mean you wish it hadn't happened and where's the point in that? Wishing things were different is a waste of time because they're not – things are the way things are and there's an end to it.

There are people everywhere in my flat. Lots of people – some in uniforms and some dressed all in white like ghosts. They came before eleven o'clock so I didn't have tea brewing and anyway I don't have enough teacups. A lady who looked a bit like Helen said I would have to tell them what happened and I said that was easy because I could remember. I remember everything. And they didn't like that. At all.

WE DO LIKE TO BE BESIDE

Peter Sutton

And the doors open and we are out and we are running. The dog,
Tyr, streaks far ahead. I couldn't keep up with him if I tried. Little
God, mother calls him. My sister, older, longer legs, is next, her
yellow blouse like the Tour de France jersey; then me. I look back
to see my parents getting the things from the car – a brand-new
beige Austin Allegro – windbreaks, blue plastic picnic cold box,
foldable chairs. And then my feet on are on sand and I put my
head down and pump my arms and fly as fast as I can to try and
catch up with my sister. And there's the sea, the open, blue,
glittering sea. The dunes bump against it, and running in sand is
hard and climbing the dune is hard and I'm panting.

The dog is barking and my sister has stopped and I'm
catching up and that's when I see, when I crest the top of the
dune. Our dune. There's someone else there; that family – father,
massive, glistening in the sun; the mother small, Irish hair; the
children, excessive amounts of them. How I hate that family.

The father lies, his bulk in stasis, his hump of a belly proud of
the sand. The wife looks up to where my sister holds the dog,
straining at its collar, barking. The children don't cease in their
tumult but I sense they've seen us. They know us. We live so very
near them after all.

"She's a witch," my sister says. Has said a thousand times

before. Almost proud of the fact.

And still the mammoth father does not move. They have our spot in the sand and I look back at my own parents trudging across the beach towards us. I glance at my sister. At the line of her mouth.

"This is our place," she spits out.

"It's public," I say.

"Go and tell the olds they have to set up somewhere else," she says, narrowing her eyes. I've seen that look far too many times. I take one last look at the family below, the children shrieking, their mother staring at us in open curiosity, the father unmoving. I shudder, they have brought their clutter with them. The sand littered with the same sort of crap they fill their front yard with. Bamboo poles with woven wool dreamcatchers, brightly coloured cloth bags full of God-knows-what, and stacks of curling paper. Do they not want a break from what Dad calls "the detritus of their failed lives"?

"Go on," she growls, her voice blending with the dogs. Tyr's upset too. I spin on my heel and run to where my parents are slowly, too slowly, walking to where we always set up when we come to the beach.

As I get closer I hear them arguing.

"She's your daughter," Mum is saying.

"I'd like to think that by now you'd consider her yours as well," Dad answers back.

Then she spots me and says, "Toby."

"What is it, Toby?" Dad asks.

"There's someone in our spot. It's that family from the corner," I tell them. They know immediately which family of course.

"Then we'll just have to choose another spot," Mum says.

Dad sighs.

"Can you go and look for another sheltered area please, Toby?" she asks me.

I nod and look back to where my sister still waits at the top of the dune; the yellow of her blouse standing out against the pure blue of the sky. The dog now sits quietly beside her.

"Amy is angry," I tell my parents. They share a look. I put my fingers in my mouth and whistle and see the dog jump up and turn to face me. I whistle again and he races towards me. My sister glances back at us once then walks down into the bowl of the foot of the dune. That's brave of her.

I race off knowing Tyr will catch up. I know that the flat part of the beach will be packed so I have to run up and down the dunes. It occurs to me that another family may get anywhere I find by the time I get my own family back there and wonder what to do about that. I can't think of one thing.

I immediately find another nook with shade for Dad and close enough to the sea for me and out of the wind for Mum and with an area to sunbathe for Amy. It's perfect. It's the next dune to where we usually plonk ourselves anyway. I climb to the top to signal to my sister and parents but they're not there.

Above, I notice that the seagulls are flying in a circle. Their raucous cries suddenly loud, as if the lee of the dune I had been in had blocked their noise. Even better. We all hate seagulls. Last year, on this beach, we'd bought chips from the chip van parked by the concrete toilet block and were mobbed as soon as we brought them on the beach. Mum said that next time we need to eat them near to the van where they had bird scarers. But next to the van smelt like toilets and I wanted to eat mine this year on the beach again but with no seagulls.

I take off my t-shirt and hop-jump down the dune to where I've chosen for us and then place it down on the ground and find a few stones to weigh it down. Just to show that someone has chosen this spot.

"Watcha doin'?"

I spin from where I was assessing my handiwork to come face to face with one of the ragged tribe of children from that family. Well, his face is around my chest-height really but chest to face doesn't sound right. Close up my nose wrinkles to the sour milk and biscuit smell of unwashed body. The child smiles a gap-toothed smile. Younger than me, stick legs and baggy shorts, looking like Micky Mouse. Looking like me at that age but dirtier and with hair that needs cutting.

"Making sure no one takes our spot," I reply. I think a second and take out a lollipop I was saving and give it to him. He smiles shyly and squirrels it away in his filthy shorts.

He puts a finger up his nose and has a good root about. Ignoring the grimace on my face he pulls it out with a slimy green globule at the end which he immediately puts in his mouth. He cocks his head and taking his finger out points behind me. "He sick?"

I frown, and look to where he's pointing. The dog had come back without me hearing, tail between his legs and, as I watch, he heaves, once, twice and then a thick stream of purplish vomit comes out. What the hell has he been eating? A stench of rotten fish rolls over me, my stomach contracts, and I taste acid.

"Are you okay, Tyr?" I ask and walk towards him. He whines and pants. I need to get him some water. Where are my parents? Amy?

"Can you stay here and make sure he doesn't run off?" I ask the boy and when he nods I run up the dune again. Like before, the seagulls wheel through the bright blue sky, screaming to each other. I still can't see my sister, or my parents.

I jump-skip down the dune. "Does your family have any water?" I ask the child. Again he nods. "Come on, boy!" I call to the dog but he just whines. I have to pick him up. Gosh, he's heavy; a good sheep-chaser Dad had called him when we first got him.

"Come on," I say to the boy and lead him around the front of the dune, past the cleft between their dune and the one I'd staked out. The dog's rancid breath wafting up, his heart racing fast, squirming a little in my arms. I look up the small valley between dunes and still don't spot my parents.

The kid remains silent, keeps turning to see if I'm following, his eyes wide. We round the corner, the squealing of the gulls our intro music, and his family aren't there. No, mostly aren't there. No mother, no horde of children, but there, in the centre of the clearing, the patriarch, unmoved and unmoving, a hillock of pink.

The kid scoots over to a plastic bag and takes out a sand-encrusted bottle and holds it out to me. I lay the dog down, my legs and arms screaming from the weight, and grab the bottle. I don't bother asking for a bowl, whatever this family has is covered in grime anyway. I pour a small amount of water into my hand and hold it out for the dog to lick, which he does enthusiastically.

Last year he'd drank seawater and gotten sick too. This year he must have eaten something bad. After a few handfuls of water he starts to look a bit perkier. And I scan around. In among the dirt and jumble there's an intricate display of sandcastles and trenches surrounding the man where he lies. I watch the sand flies hover and a glossy black beetle wend its way across the sand.

"Thanks for the water," I say loudly. The kid grins. The bulk in the middle of the maze doesn't move. "Is your dad okay?" I ask and the kid nods vigorously.

"He's dreaming," the kid says.

I stroke the dog's head and he wags his tail a bit. "Ready to get up?" I ask him and he sits up.

"Well ... I'd best go find my family," I say. I stand and wipe my hand on my shorts. "Can I take this?" I ask giving the water bottle a shake to slosh the water inside a bit. The kid nods again. Not much of a talker.

"Thanks." I turn. "Thanks mister!" I say.

I take a step in the direction of the man and stop, he's asleep, must be to be so still. Best not disturb him.

I scan the top of the dune and only spot a circle of gulls. Time to go.

Back to where my shirt is staked out on the sand. The dog looks done in. "Stay!" I order him and he flops down on the t-shirt and rolls to his side. I give Tyr another cupped hand of warm water and then close the bottle and put it next to him. "Guard!" I order. He lifts his head but then lets it fall back on the sand.

I go to find my family. It feels like a long time since I've seen them – but I don't have a watch, the strap broke and it's at home on my bedside table. I stride to the top of the dune – three steps forward, one slide back – and stand at the top blowing. Carrying the dog took a lot out of me. There's no one in sight. I march down the side of the dune and up the side of the one we usually camp out, disturbing the seagulls that all leap to the air screeching like witches, calling to each other like drunken sailors.

Below: the dome of the man's belly, solid, stately, still. The kid is off at the side of the dune, poking at something with a twig. I try to see the man's features but his bald head is partly covered, his face obscured with a scrap of brightly coloured cloth.

I retrace my path back to the car, which is burning hot in the midday sun, so hot it scalds my hand when I try the door handle. There's no one inside anyway.

I stand on the wall separating road from beach and turn in a circle. I can't see Dad's red t-shirt or Mum's blue beach dress or my sister's yellow blouse anywhere. I run down the road to the concrete toilet block, ash-black and shaped a bit like a shoebox with a too-large lid. My family aren't here either, nor by the ice cream van. I wander onto the beach and decide that they must have got fed up waiting for me and found somewhere else, maybe even on the flat bit.

I'm a bit worried about Tyr. Maybe I should go back and get him before going for another look? But that would take too much time. So I walk up and down the beach, the flat bit, searching. I walk past families and couples, kids and adults, other families with dogs, and people listening to the radio, a bunch of friends on lilos, and a couple of guys throwing a Frisbee. But not my family.

I'm starting to get real worried now. Where could they be? I know they haven't left because the car is still there. I go to where the sea sucks obsessively at the shore. I like the sea, usually I'm the only one who goes paddling, or swimming, on a day as hot as today. I think the rest of them are mad not to have a cold dip.

I shade my eyes and try to spot who's in the water. Dad never goes swimming; Mum says he's afraid of the water but he says he's not afraid of water, he's afraid of drowning, which is different. My sister says he saw someone say that in a film once. I think it's sensible to be afraid of drowning but that it shouldn't stop you swimming.

Dad doesn't like the family down the road, avoids them as much as possible. It was him who first said their mum was a witch, something my sister repeats often. My mum says that he should know, but I don't know why.

I can't decide what to do. I should go back to the dune and find the dog and then go sit by the car. They'll find me at the car. Eventually. As I walk back, the buzz of music and people talking, playing, laughing, surrounds me but something a teenager says to his friend catches me up.

"What did you say?" I ask.

The young man, first moustache trembling atop flaky lips, gazes up at me. "Huh?"

"Just now. You said someone's been arrested?"

"Uh-huh,"

"When? Was it here?"

The dude smooths his 'tache and nods. "Just over there." He's pointing to the dunes. To where I've left the dog. To where the family from down the close were. To where I'd last seen my parents, and sister.

"What happened?"

"I don't know, man, they dragged them away, there was a bit of a crowd. Something about it not being natural?" The two youths exchange a glance.

"What's it to you?" The other one asks.

"Oh nothing," I say. "Nothing." I nod a thanks and walk away. Arrested? I'd best get Tyr and then... And then? Do something – surely Mum and Dad would have said something about me. Nah, it can't have been them arrested. Unnatural? What did Mum mean earlier that Amy was Dad's daughter? What did Dad mean by she should have accepted her by now?

My mind races as I run down the beach, back to the dunes.

The dog's gone when I return. The t-shirt I took off too. There is a gull eating the dog's vomit. That makes me gag. I need help. I go to the where the man from the corner house is, maybe the family has come back.

Around the corner the girth of the man remains unyielding. I edge closer. There is no child here now. The maze is deeper, the mounds I'd taken to be sandcastles now apparent as just heaps of unburied sand. I edge closer – the bulk does not move. The trenches, narrow and deep, wind around the flat foot of the dune. I edge closer and venture a "hello" and still no movement. A squirt of seagull poo lands on my foot and soon I'm kicking sand as I try to wipe it off my trainer. I kick a mound of sand over and into the dug-out labyrinth.

There is a sound behind me like air leaking from a tyre. I turn and the wife is there, her children tucked in behind her like kittens. She beckons urgently. I give my shoe one last scrape across the sand and walk gingerly to her. She places a finger, blackened by who knows what, to her wrinkled lips. I frown but keep quiet and when I reach her she places a hand on my shoulder and grips me hard. It hurts a little and I start to struggle.

"Your sister is waiting for you," she hisses.

"Where is she?" I ask and stop struggling.

"Come with me and find out." Her grip does not lessen as she marches me away from the dune. The kids skip in and out and around us. I'm scared, but also really want to see my sister. I hope the woman isn't lying to me.

"What have you done with my sister?"

The woman turns piggy eyes upon me. "Done? Nothing, she wants you to come too. Prevailed upon my better nature, she did."

"What do you mean?" I ask.

"You don't belong. She does. But she convinced me that we can make you belong too. Once the Dreaming is complete."

The boy I gave the lollipop to skips ahead and looks back at me smiling. His siblings keep their distance.

"Dreaming? The man, your husband, he—"

"We like living near you, you know," she says.

"What?"

"We do like to be beside you."

"Thanks…?" I wonder why she feels like telling me this. I try to shrug out of her grasp but her hand is like an iron claw. We are heading back to the carpark.

"There's only one problem," she continues. "Your mum's innocent, we don't see that much of you but—"

"But what?"

"Your father." She glances at me and I see disgust in her eyes.

"What about him?" We are getting nearer the cars. She's not turning to go towards our car though. I spot their campervan, dirty-white, battered, leaking oil no doubt, like it does on our road.

"He's… Well, he's always staring. At us."

"Is he?" I'm flustered, the lady from down the road has been walking me at a quick pace, and we are now nearing the camper. I can hear the dog whining and scratching.

"It's not polite. It's not nice. You're his blood too, that's how she convinced me. Your sister." We come to the van and she pulls a set of keys from the pocket of her tatty dress. The keyring is unidentifiable, a purple blob that might once have been furry. She fits a key to the lock and pulls the door slightly open. Without letting go of me. With her foot she shoves the dog further inside and then opens the door enough to push me in. Tyr, ready to go for her, jumps ecstatically at me instead.

"Wait—" I say but she's slammed the door behind me and locked it. I try the handle but it won't open, and the van's interior – stinking of old chip fat, soiled, sweaty linen and an underlying rusty, oily odour – has no method of getting into the van's cab.

"Hey!" I shout and bang on the door, giving it a good few kicks. "Hey!"

But nothing doing. She's gone and locked me in here, with the dog, but not with my mum or dad. Or sister. How dare she say Dad wasn't nice. She didn't say anything about my sister at all.

There isn't much room inside – a soot-blackened kitchen, some pots and pans, a couple of bunkbeds and several cupboards locked with padlocks. There is a door to the small chemical toilet, and the windows are high up and thin. I sit on the edge of the bed and wonder what to do next, absent-mindedly stroking the dog.

After a while of kicking the door and shouting I realise that no one is going to come and rescue me. I grab a saucepan as a makeshift weapon – I can find no knives or other cutlery – I sit on the bed to wait. My gaze wanders and alights on an old cardboard suitcase with an advert for laundry on it. Held closed with leather straps. I grab it. Maybe there'll be something useful inside? I struggle to open it. Inside are hundreds of photographs. Photographs of our street, of our house, of our family, of us on the beach, of our car, our dog, of my sister. Many of my sister. In each one with my parents in, Dad's face is erased. Scratched out. That's horrible. I spend a long time looking at the photographs.

After a while I lie down, just to rest my eyes. I've no idea how long I've been asleep but I leap up having heard the van's cabin door open then someone climbs aboard. My hand searches the bed until it lands on the saucepan handle. "Ready, boy?" I ask Tyr. He's sat up too, ears pricked.

The door opens a crack and a child eels inside – I leap to the door and try to push it open as the engine starts. The door springs open and I leap out, past a startled dirty child. The whole horde is there but the parents are in the cab. The child I'd talked to earlier gestures from the door and the horde disappears inside. At his command they leave me alone. He raises the lollipop I gave him to his mouth.

I don't wait around. I run, the dog with me. No one raises the alarm. I glance back and all the children have climbed inside. The child who gave me the water bottle waves from the open door which swings shut as the van lumbers away. As the van turns the corner I glimpse yellow in the passenger seat. Amy! I need to tell my parents they've taken Amy.

It's almost night-time. The light slowly fading into the

summer evening. I stop and watch the van pull away. Have I escaped? Now what?

I run over to our car. It's still there. It's still empty. I again go to the chip van. I wish I had some money because I'm starving. At least I can get a drink at the water fountain outside the toilet block. No sign of my parents here either. I ask the chip-van man if he's seen them, describe them to him, but no. He's also not seen the police arrest anyone. Said that was a rumour passed around by stoners.

The beach is emptying of families. Young couples will turn up soon and walk up and down because it's "romantic". I need to find my family. I hurry back to the dunes and there's no one at the place I'd staked out for us. I climb the hill and look down to where we usually stay and the man has gone and all that's left is the weird maze-pattern in the sand. I sit down and put my head in my hands. I'm going to have to ask a grown-up for help, to call the police.

The dog barks and gallops down the hill. Where the man had lain all day was a smooth circle of clear sand. The dog races across the bottom of the dune to this circle, barks again and runs towards the sea. I watch for a second then start down the side of the dune and I realise something. The weird pattern? It's the street plan of the estate I live on. The central bit being where our house would be – and theirs is blank. Where the man had lain dreaming all day.

I hurry down the dune and see the dog racing towards a figure dressed in blue. The sweat I'd worked up running now cools unpleasantly on my skin. It's Mum! I race to her and grab her in a hug. I've started crying but I'm not embarrassed like I'd usually be.

"Toby. Where have you been, I've been worried sick!" She strokes my head.

"The family from the corner have Amy!" I blurt out. Mum frowns. "Where's Dad?" I ask through the tears.

"What's got into you? Who's Amy? And your dad … your dad is in our hearts, where he'll always be. He did used to love it here though, didn't he? Beside the sea." She gazes at the sea.

"Amy is … is … what do you mean? Dad is dead?" I'm frowning, it's hard to think, my mind feels foggy, what's happening?

She ruffles my hair. "Wake up sleepy head."

I shake my head. I had something important to tell her. What was it? I can feel my mind being rewritten, settling into a new groove, history and memory reconfiguring, I try to keep hold of it. Amy is my sister. Dad isn't dead. Amy is… Dad…

The dog barks and runs at the waves and I look up and the sun is sinking into the sea and I wish that Dad hadn't died, a heart attack at forty, and that we'd not buried him last year. I shake my head, falling asleep in the sun has meant I've awoke confused, that's all. "Amy was just a girl in my dream. She wore yellow." I give Mum a quick hug, dry my eyes and run to play with the dog.

FOOTPRINTS IN THE SNOW

Eygló Karlsdóttir

It's snowing, and like always the snow comes with a bit of magic.

The large flakes descending so slowly it's as if the world is moving at a different pace than before. The snow isn't solely responsible for that feeling though, and if it weren't for the fact that I am still able to do everything at the same speed as before I'd be convinced that something had come along to push pause on the world.

Perhaps that's it. Perhaps I'm the only one still here thinking things can go back to normal. If we just make the effort.

There are no birds, just tiny footprints in the snow indicating movement. It's not a long walk to the grocery store but it can be disconcerting when the ground is white. The pavement gets slippery and my feet freeze in the cold as I wade through the big heavy snowflakes to get some food.

They are here already, the ghosts of our past. Some are standing on the pavement, some are inside people's gardens, others are huddled on people's doorsteps. They are pale, broken-eyed, staring up into the air at nothing in particular, most of them letting the snow pile up on their cold faces.

I shouldn't be surprised to see Dead-Eyed Jerry lurking outside the shop, but I am. He is standing there, shoe in hand, his head turned up towards the clouds as if he's slowly trying to catch snowflakes with his mouth. He doesn't move, just stands there, mouth open.

Julia greets me as I enter the shop. She looks worn, the shotgun resting on the table next to her.

"Having troubles?" I ask her as I pick up the shopping basket.

"Nah, but he freaks me out," she says and points to Dead-Eyed Jerry outside. I just nod my head and proceed down the aisle where a smell of newly baked bread greets me. I choose a rye loaf with caraway seeds and then I load my basket with anything I can find – butter, cheese, and a piece of dried meat amongst other things.

When I arrive at the counter Julia is reading her book. It's called *Notes on the Apocalypse* by Peter Johnson.

"Cheery book you're reading. Enjoying it?"

"This is my fourth time reading it," she says. "I like to remind myself that things could be much worse."

I laugh at that and start unloading the basket. She puts the book down underneath the counter and uses the old-fashioned cash register to sum up my total.

"Slow day, huh?" I ask, looking around.

"It's snowing," Julia says in a low voice, stating the obvious.

"Your mom isn't here to keep you company?"

"She's upstairs – didn't sleep well last night," Julia says and sighs. "He's such a drag." She nods again towards Jerry outside.

"I'm sorry, I know it's hard," I tell her, "but he is your dad."

She looks at me and shakes her head.

"No way," she says firmly. "He's an empty shell, a ghost. My dad is dead. You know Mom is planning on having him removed next time they come to cull." She says this as if she's talking about the weather.

"Really? Isn't that a bit harsh?" I ask surprised.

"No way," she says again, this time with passion. "It will make our lives easier and it's not like it's really Dad."

I nod my head reluctantly, put the groceries in the tote-bag I brought with me, pay Julia in cash and exit the shop with the cheeriest smile I own plastered on my face.

Dead-Eyed Jerry is still staring up at the sky, seemingly without having moved a muscle.

"Hi Jerry," I mumble in a low voice as I walk past him, heading back home. There isn't a single person on the streets beside me and them, remnants of people standing still on patios, or by windows, staring into empty space or at things I cannot see. They don't move, they don't communicate. They just stand there, reminding us of what was.

~~~

The house is covered in snow, the pathway only vaguely showing the footprints I made when exiting the house. The snow has already made a good attempt at wiping out my trail. It would wipe me out entirely I'm sure, if I'd let it.

"I'm home," I yell to the house when I enter. It's as strangely silent inside as it is outside, as if the snow doesn't only settle on the streets but inside our minds as well.

"Was the trip alright?" Bryan appears in the kitchen door, quietly, like a ghost treading air, startling me. I whisper a silent curse and hand him the bag.

"It was fine," I tell him. "They're there, Dead-Eyed Jerry too, standing by the store with a nervous Julia alone inside."

"She was alone?" He asks, surprise emanating from him, rising into the air like smoke.

"She was, her mom was upstairs sleeping."

"Christ!" he exclaims in a muffled voice. "I wouldn't let my teenage daughter stand alone at the register on a day like this."

"She seemed in good spirits." I try to sooth him. "She was reading."

He looks at me as if I've gone a bit insane, and perhaps I have, but I only smile at him and head into the kitchen. The smell of newly brewed coffee greets me and I look at him and then at the coffee maker. Then I shrug my shoulders and pour myself a cup.

"We have to move," he says as he is unpacking the groceries. "I can't stand this."

I don't answer him. We've had this conversation before. In fact we've had it so often it's become a routine. Thankfully one that doesn't result in much. And it's always the same.

"There was no sight of her tonight," I eventually say. "Maybe it's over."

"But you saw Dead-Eyed Jerry. What is the chance that this is ever going to be over?" he says, and I can hear his anxiety rising. His anger aggravated by the fear I know all too well.

"We'll be fine," I tell him. "We're not in any danger."

He just shakes his head, draws in the smell of the bread he's holding in his hands before he puts it in the bread box. He leaves the room and I hear his muffled footsteps on the stairs, the door to his study opens and then closes with a thud.

I cut myself a piece of bread, butter it and add a big slice of cheese. It's been a while since I had cheese in the house and the taste is divine. It's not wrapped in fancy paper that tells you all about it, like we used to have. It comes in a simple clear-plastic bag and I can only guess that it comes from Peter or Tina, two local farmers who are still keeping the town with supplies. The stores get deliveries occasionally, but not often during winter.

I watch the snow falling outside the window, the big flakes reminding me of my grandmother. She used to call it dog-paws. Her way of translating her mother's tongue into ours was charming, albeit a tad confusing for five-year old. She always told us how we lived in different times, how things had changed and for the better. I often find myself wondering what she would make of today's world and the animated corpses that come alive every time it starts to snow.

"There is magic in the world when it snows," she used to say when it was pouring down in the early winter, and she would longingly look at the mountain tops in the distance, dreaming herself away.

It takes me a while to get into the spirit of doing some work. I turn the knob on the old radio Bryan got for Christmas many years ago. It was supposed to look retro, but now it looks right at home with the times. There is a local broadcast I tend to tune into while I knit. I get wool from the local farmers, mostly from Tina, who have sheep. Tina is nice and she knows how important the extra income is to me.

The broadcast isn't on at the moment though, so I tune into one of the bigger stations that still broadcasts. It doesn't have live commentators but there is music and so I listen to old tunes while knitting a sweater that I will hopefully be able to sell at the local market, or to one of the stores in town.

After lunch it stops snowing, but the layer is thick and my trail from the morning has completely vanished. I keep an eye on the gate but there is no life on the street today, even the mailman has, apparently, decided it's not the right time to deliver.

I start making dinner before it gets dark. It's nothing fancy – a soup, some leftovers, and a slice of bread. I volunteer to abstain from my evening portion since I stole a slice during lunchtime but Bryan just shakes his head, smiles, and tells me that the bread will get stale anyway, we might as well eat it. So we binge and take two slices each during dinner. Bryan seems in better spirits than before. Hopefully that means the conversation we touched on has left his head for the moment.

When it starts getting dark he locks the house, puts the security bolt on both the front door and the back. I let him do the work, spending my evening by the living room window where I can see the front gate.

It hasn't been moved. There is no trail in the snow still.

We crawl into bed early. Bryan reads a book but falls asleep with it on his face. He snores, so I am not as easily cradled by unconsciousness. I put his book on the nightstand and spend a while staring at the ceiling.

"There is magic in the snow, Elsa." I can almost hear my grandmother's voice. "It brings fresh ideas, it colours everything white, makes things new and clean and gracious," she would add, cuddling up to me during bedtime. Then she would read me a story or sing me a song.

I am thinking of her when I hear a noise from outside the house. It's the gate creaking softly, a very delicate sound, but in the silence of the snowy night I can hear it loud and clear. I feel it so prominently that I fear it's going to wake Bryan.

I stay still, listening intently for any other sound. The house is old and so it gives the occasional gasp, a creak here and a groan there, but when it has snowed I get sensitive about the noises and keenly aware of the differences between the elderly moans the house makes and anything else that might be creeping in the night.

When I hear a second sound I start to move. Bryan is easily stirred when he sleeps so it takes me a long time to emerge from under the blankets and get up from the bed. I put my slippers on, pull the robe from the door hanger, and then I brace myself. The hardest part is to open the door without it making the sound that will usually wake him up.

I take my time, but quietly, ever so slowly, I manage to pull the door open enough so I can slide out sideways. I leave it open, hoping there will be no other noises to alert him. I tip-toe down the stairs and into the living room from where I can see the gate and the path that leads to the front door.

The gate is open, as I suspected it would be, but I can't see anyone in the yard or by the door. There is however a small space on the porch that I can't see from where I am standing, no matter how hard I lean towards the window, and so I go to the hallway and brace myself.

There is no way of seeing who is at the door from inside, no peephole, no windows here. The only way to see if there is anyone is to open the door. I take a deep breath, listen into the house to hear if Bryan has woken up, but I don't hear a thing.

I turn on the porch light and then I open the door.

She is standing there. Of course she is. What else did I expect? Who else would be here at this hour when it just snowed?

I'm so relieved, and at the same time completely terrified. She looks different from the last time I saw her. She is still wearing the dress. A white long-sleeved thing made of cotton. It had looked so pretty on the mannequin in the store – now I wish I had chosen something else entirely. It's dirty, torn, and looks so thin to wear in this cold weather, but to be fair I wasn't expecting to see her dressed in it more than once.

"Hello baby," I say, and I can hear my voice shivering. I try to keep it low as not to wake Bryan, but at the same time I don't want to give the impression that am not pleased to see her.

She doesn't answer me of course. Just stands there by the side of the door, facing away from the house, staring at the clouds, or perhaps it's the mountains she's looking at.

"Did you have a good summer?" I say, knowing very well that she will tell me nothing. I notice that she has lost a shoe and her pantyhose is torn. The other shoe is thankfully in its place, but her knee is out on that leg too. I pull a jacket from the rack and put it on, push my feet into Bryan's boots, and then I step outside onto the snow-filled porch to take a better look at her.

"Don't you want to come inside and get warm?" I ask her.

Her hair is dirty, her fingers are brown with mud, her fingernails torn and I can see that one has fallen off. There is no blood, but that's not to be expected.

I brace myself and look at her head. It's always hard to look into her face, into those cold-dead eyes. It's still her. She still has her blue eyes, though they are glazed with a white hue. Her lips are blue and the colour of her skin disconcerting as always, but there is one distinct difference from the last time I saw her.

There is a wound on her head. It wasn't there last winter. It is large, covering the top of her head and to her left eye. The skin is flapping loose, the bone bare in places.

Alarmed I almost fall flat on my ass down the stairs into the snow, but manage to grab a hold of the rail. I stumble inside and close the door behind me.

My breathing is heavy and uneven, my pulse is racing, but I'm still trying to be careful not to wake Bryan. I just sit on the small chair in the hallway until I've calmed down.

It's bad. This is really bad. We can't have her standing there during the snowy patches of winter, not like this. But what exactly is the alternative?

I open the door again and take her cold little hand. "Diana darling, won't you come inside and get warm?"

She doesn't say anything, doesn't answer me and doesn't

react until I tug at her hand. Then she slowly moves in the direction I pull her. I drag her into the laundry room and sit her down on a chair. Then I tell her to stay put, turn her towards the window, and I go back to bed. Bryan is still asleep. He won't be happy about this but I can't see that we have any other choice. I can't imagine leaving her standing on the front porch.

Adrenaline is still rushing through my veins, however, and I can't sleep. Instead I'm tossing and turning, worrying what Bryan will say. Worrying that she'll start to move around in the house if the snow starts to thaw. Worrying she will start to rage, what we've all been terrified of since the whole thing started over two years ago.

I don't know if it's my tossing and turning that wakes Bryan, or my sheer agony that she's in the house, but he's looking at me. His eyes slow and sleepy in the hollow darkness.

"What is it?" He whispers through the silence.

"Nothing that can't wait till the morning, love." I can feel my voice trembling. My body is shaking so violently that it's almost impossible not to show it.

He raises himself and leans onto his elbow. "She's here, isn't she?" he asks and gets out of bed quickly. "What did you do?"

"Nothing, Bryan," I tell him. "I put her in the laundry room. She's sitting there. I couldn't leave her outside."

He looks at me, tilting his head, maybe out of compassion but at the same time I can see the contempt, the devastation, and the anger shining out of his eyes.

"Please Bryan, can we just sleep?" I plead with him.

"And what if she suddenly snaps? What if she suddenly—" His voice breaks and he buries his head in his hands, runs his fingers through his dark hair, shakes his head. "I can't do this anymore, Elsa. I just can't do this anymore."

"What do you want me to do?" I'm on the verge of tears, but it's useless. He's at the door, rushing down the stairs, on his way through the kitchen towards the laundry room before I know it. I follow him, running down the steps so quickly I almost fall. He meets me in the kitchen, key in hand.

"I just locked the laundry room," he says. "I knew you wouldn't do that, and I can't sleep with her potentially going rampage in the house! This is the least we can do."

My sigh of relief is so monumental that I collapse to my knees and start crying. "Thank you," I whisper but I don't know what I'm thanking him for.

"Let's go to bed," he says and we hold each other like two people condemned to death, on their way to the gallows. I never want to let go.

"Remember we should be happy that she comes here," he sighs. "It's a good sign."

I don't say anything. I know what he means because we've had this conversation before. She was just fourteen years old, and that she comes here means she loved us, it means that the remnants are still there, bringing her to us. I've held onto that thought with everything I am and everything I felt since the whole ordeal began.

Bryan tries to coax me into bed but I go to the window and gaze out. The snow is everywhere, the entire backyard is white, the branches are heavy with the weight.

"Magical," I whisper and find I am still shivering.

"What did you say?" Bryan whispers. He's under the covers, his arm over his eyes. He might fall asleep that way – he is equipped with the superpower of being able sleep under any circumstance – but the hand over his face means he's deep in thought. I know from the way his quilt is covering his feet that he is also ill at ease, that he might even be at the end of his tether.

The notion terrifies me.

I stare at the sky again, a quilt wrapped around my shoulders. I stand there wondering why this is happening. Why have my best wishes come to pass in the worst of ways? I stare angrily at the stars that are peaking through gaps in the clouds that are slowly traversing the sky. The night seems to worm itself forward gradually, the seconds become minutes, the minutes hours, and when the first hint of dawn strikes my window I feel endlessly tired.

I don't wake Bryan. Instead I head down into the kitchen, make coffee and prepare sandwiches. I haven't looked to see if she's still sitting in the laundry room. I know that she is. I would have heard the ruckus if she'd tried to get out of the room and Bryan still has the key, hidden somewhere.

When he comes down I can see it in his eyes – the fear I've had since all this started is about to come true.

"Is she still in there?" he asks.

I nod my head. "I suppose so," I say and hand him a cup of coffee.

"Elisabeth," he says and that's never a good sign. I feel the tears well up in my eyes, my heart gives way before he even says the words. "I can't take it anymore," he says. "I have to leave. Please Elisabeth, please come with me."

I look at him. I feel every bone in my body scream, every fibre of my being wants to shout yes, but then I think of the little being in the laundry room. Her split head and her dazed, unknowing gaze.

I look into his eyes and between us we exchange all the information we need. He knows I can't leave and I know he can't stay. We're at an impasse.

"You know I love you, Elisabeth," he says. "I'd do anything for you, except to continue to do this. Please come with me. We'll be happier elsewhere. We can come here during the summers." It's his last plea and I recognise it. It's his last attempt at negotiation, his last attempt to hold us together.

I just shake my head. The tears running down my cheeks. I try my best to swallow the sobs, but I can't stifle them, can't put a cork in it.

"We could find another town somewhere, not too far from here. We don't have to go so very far, you know that," he says.

I can't muster up the words. We've had the discussion a thousand times before. She'll be all alone here then. She'll be standing on the porch of the house she used to live in all alone during the entire winter, or she'll go out searching like a few of them do – and what then?

But I don't say the words. He sighs and pulls the key out of a drawer. He pushes it into the keyhole and opens the door. She's sitting on the chair, just like when I left her last night. The wound on her head is grotesque, the look in her eyes terrifying, and the notion that she might attack us at any moment makes me shiver. Because though most of them are peaceful, still, frozen in time, some of them do snap. It's been known to happen. There have been reports. Some of them do bite. There are always a few bad eggs, but most are just like her, quiet, pale as the snow, and dirty.

For some reason they only appear when it snows. Only a few years back that would have meant you were safe near the equator, but not anymore. The weather, like death, has become completely unpredictable.

"I can't take it anymore," Bryan whispers. "I'm sorry, I just can't." He says this sternly and leaves the kitchen. I hear him walk up the stairs to our bedroom. I know he is pulling out a bag and I can imagine him throwing a few things in it, shirts, pants and other necessities.

I enter the laundry room and look out the window, trying to see what it is she is staring at. The sky, the clouds, or the trees next door. It's impossible to tell. She doesn't move, not unless I tug at her. Then she will follow me until I stop tugging, and then she will stay motionless until the snow melts away, or until something snaps inside that dead head of hers – and then she'll start to attack the people closest to her. I've heard they are relentless once they start.

Bryan comes back downstairs, puts his knapsack on the floor beside the fridge and stands behind me. He puts his arms around me, buries his head in my hair and whispers the words I always like hearing. "I love you, Elisabeth," he says. "Please, please, please—" But he says no more and I'm thankful for that. Because if he had made a final plea I might have gone with him. I might have left my home and my dead daughter and I might have followed him to the end of the world – and I would spend the rest of my days hating myself, and him, for doing so.

"If something changes, I'll come to find you," he whispers. "I might be back in the spring." And he repeats: "If something changes, you know I'll come to find you."

I just nod my head but I know he won't.

"I'm sorry," he whispers and I turn around to see tears streaming down his face. "This is horror that I didn't sign up for. It was bad enough to lose her—" He hugs me tightly as if he's not ever going to let me go again and then he kisses me warmly on the mouth. He holds his lips on mine for an eternity, or until something in the laundry room moves, and we both jump, turning our attention towards Diana – she is still sitting on the chair but now she is staring at us.

"Elsa, move back into the kitchen slowly," Bryan says.

But I can't move. She is looking directly at me. She has never done that before.

"Baby, can you hear me?" I ask, hoping that the sound of my voice will wake her up from the grasp of death.

"Elsa, go into the kitchen now!" Bryan says. There is terror in his voice. This is why he's leaving. Because while she is here he is constantly terrified that she's going to attack us, bite us – maybe even kill us. But I know she won't attack me. I'm her mother. I gave birth to her. I've known her since before she was born. I carried her in my womb – and I laid her to rest. I chose the clothes she is wearing now – and every winter since she died I've agonised over that choice, because I know she would have hated it.

Bryan pulls at me and for a moment I feel like giving in, just let him lead me away, just like Diane let me lead her into the house.

Instead I stand strong. "It's fine Bryan," I say flatly.

He looks at me and then at Diane. He shakes his head, tears streaming down his face once more. I want to plead with him not to leave me in this nightmare, not to make me go through this alone, but I can't muster up the words.

Instead I kiss him one last time and then he is out the door, making footprints in the snow.

I'm left in the house with my daughter who died in a car

accident a little over three years ago. She was fourteen years old. I thought my prayers had been answered when I first saw her coming back. I thought all my wishes had come true.

I was wrong.

BLACK NORE

Tim Jeffreys

Hunter hadn't been out along the bay in years.

"You used to love it over there," his mother would say when on previous visits he'd refuse a walk along the seafront. "Floating your little boat on the lake. Feeding the ducks. Watching the ships sailing up the estuary."

"I don't have a little boat to float anymore, Mother," he'd tell her, aware that his irritation was masking something else, something like fear or foreboding. "I'm thirty-six."

"You could get a real boat, a proper boat, sail it across to Cardiff or up the Avon to Gloucester."

He would shake his head and scoff at this.

"What the hell would I want to go to Gloucester for?"

Often she would look at him for a long moment when he said things like this, in this tone, and he'd wonder if she was seeing the same thing he saw when he looked at pictures of himself these days. A man he didn't recognise. His hair turned grey above the ears and thinning on top. Face serious and scrunched-up as if against a bright light. A fixed expression of irritation or some buried anger. *Think too much*, he would say to himself when he saw the pictures. *Stop thinking too much. Just smile.* But his smile didn't come as readily as it once had. Was his mother wondering the same thing he did? Was she wondering what happened to the blue-eyed boy who looked out at the world with wonder and expectation? Where was he that boy? Gone. Lost. And it seemed to Hunter that he'd gained nothing in the passing years; that nothing worth anything had replaced all that boyhood wonder and expectation. Just weariness and irritation. Shouldn't there be wisdom? Some kind of wisdom?

Once you'd passed the lake grounds the sky dominated your vision. Today it was full of tall clouds. Again he wondered what had driven him out that way. Perhaps he'd been looking to escape. Escape his mother or escape from himself. She'd started talking about Reece again. Always the same. What would Reece look like now? What sort of man would he have been? Would he have married? Given her the grandchildren Hunter had so far been unable to provide?

There isn't even a woman in his life. Hunter had overheard her telling his father once, a few years ago. Or perhaps she'd meant for him to hear. *I'll never be a grandmother at this rate.*

Reece would have done it, though, she was sure of that. Reece would've given her those grandkids she so craved.

He paused on Beach Road, staring out across the bay. Seeing the clay-coloured expanse before him, he felt suddenly cold. *Get a real boat, a proper boat, sail it across to Cardiff or up the Avon to Gloucester.* Ugh. The thought of being out on that water made him shiver. There was only a ripple of reflected light – a shimmer, somehow sinister – to mark where the mudflats ended and the sea began. Other than that it was all the same slick sickly beige, more like slurry than seawater.

In an attempt to avoid thinking about Reece – memories as deceptive and treacherous as all that mud and water ahead of him – he fixed his gaze on the Welsh coast, hazy with distance on the other side of the estuary. All he could make out were wind turbines, factory chimneys and, beyond, rolling green hills. Shifting his gaze, he watched a woman walking a dog in the narrow area of long grass high up on the beach, ahead of the mudflats. She talked on a mobile phone, apparently oblivious to her surroundings. He worried for her a moment. For the dog too. Was it safe to walk there? He wondered if he should say something, warn her. But likely she was a local and would know the area better than him, he who hadn't visited this spot in more than twenty years.

Without thinking, he turned to the left and began walking across an area of grass which ended in woodland. He knew where this direction would take him, if he entered the trees and followed the footpath, if he kept walking. Did he really want to go there? Did he really want to see it again – the lighthouse? Black Nore. Was it even there, still? Perhaps it had been dismantled and tossed into the sea. But no. Hadn't he read recently, in some local paper he'd found lying around his mother's house, that it had been sold to a conservation trust? That it was getting a new paint job?

A woman around his own age passed him, another dog walker. She said hello, then gave him an odd look. He realised he'd been scrutinising her face too closely, and at once shifted his eyes away. He often wondered what would happen if he bumped into Leah Appleton again. Would he recognise her? And she him?

She still lives in town, I think, his mother had told him when he'd asked about Leah, as casually as he could. *Though not on the farm anymore. They sold that. Lives over on the other side of the marina now, I think. Your dad used to see her.*

Did he? Where?

Just around.

Is she married? He'd quickly realised his mistake in asking this.

His mother had looked straight at him, a smirk curling at the corners of her mouth. *Oh that's right. You had quite the crush on her when you were a boy, didn't you? You used to write her love letters.*

No I didn't.

You did. You used to leave them at the lighthouse for her to find when she went down to wind the mechanism. I don't know how you knew she'd find them, and not one of her brothers. Unless those letters were meant for one of the brothers. They weren't, were they?

You're confused. That wasn't me. And this sort of talk is why I don't travel down and visit you as often anymore.

The liveliness had left his mother's face then, and he'd regretted the last thing he'd said even though it was true.

Well, she'd said, dropping her head. *You could always go and look her up. I'm sure somebody must know where she is.*

I'm not going to go look up Leah Appleton, Mother. It's been twenty years.

And you wonder why you're still single. She isn't going to come knocking, you know.

Mother…

You could have the house. Shove me in a home and live here in this house together, you and the Appleton girl.

Stop it now.

~~~

He followed the footpath even though he knew where it led. Before realising it, he arrived at the cove with the little shale beach where Reece and his friends used to come to drink beer and smoke cigarettes. A shallow cave under a gnarled outcrop of rock had been their hideout. Looking that way, Hunter half-expected to see his brother and his gang there, jeering and laughing, or shouting threats at him the way they often did. Mocking him as he went to leave another letter for Leah on the lighthouse steps. Reece had snatched one of the letters from his hand one day, and read it aloud to his cronies.

I always felt alone until I met you. I was like a ship out there in the dark. And you're the light guiding me home. But you know I want more. So please blink your light and give me a sign…

Just thinking about this brought a rush of blood to Hunter's face, not just because of the awful teenage poetry but because he could remember Reece standing as if on a stage, on a cluster of rocks, and reading it aloud to his guffawing friends.

~~~

Though Hunter had seen Leah Appleton at school where she was in the year above, the one between his and Reece's, and knew her as the girl from Black Nore farm, his infatuation with her didn't begin until the summer he was fourteen, when he started walking the family dog Sasha along the footpath, where he would sometimes run in to Leah as she made her way to or from the lighthouse. When he'd thought about her he remembered her sun-lightened hair and tanned face and arms. It was she who had first spoke, calling out to him one morning as he gazed out over the estuary.

Ahoy, there! Hey. Aren't you Reece Kersey's little brother?

He'd told her he was.

She'd smiled. *Help me*, she said, reaching out a hand as she climbed the slope towards him. It was a thrill to take her hand in his, to feel her warm skin.

Wanna see inside the lighthouse? she'd said. *I'm on my way there now to wind the thingimajigger.*

He had no idea why she was being friendly with him. By the time he was fourteen, his friends at school had ostracised him. Everyone had. He'd become, for some reason, untouchable. The older kids knew if they pushed him around Reece wouldn't defend him. Reece might even encourage it. So he kept to himself. Most days, he'd felt adrift. He'd even had a few mad thoughts about going up to Battery Point and throwing himself into the sea. Now here was this lovely girl, tossing him a lifeline.

Sure.

Come on then.

They'd walked together back down the slope until they reached the lighthouse. Then he stood and watched as Leah took a set of keys from the pocket of her shorts and started to climb the ladder.

Come on up, she'd said as she fiddled with a padlock securing the hatch on the lighthouse's underside.

You have to do this every day?

Yeah, because it's on our land. Sometimes Billy or Patrick does it. But usually it's me.

Like a good deed, he'd said, glancing out to sea. A small cargo boat had been making its way up river.

She'd looked down at him and smiled.

I suppose you could say that. Come on, get up here.

He'd followed her up the ladder and through the hatch. In the cramped interior they had to stand very close together and he could smell the soap and sweat on her skin, feel her breathing in and out when she pressed against his side. It sent a jolt of pleasure down his abdomen. A pulse of exhilaration.

The winding mechanism was a tall hollow grey metal box containing what looked like large cogs. Leah explained that these were the gears. A long handle jutted into the cramped space. As she worked the handle he couldn't help but notice the motion of her hips. Heat rose to his face.

You have a go, Hunter.

Me?

Just turn it until it stops. She'd put her hands on her hips and said in mock seriousness: *Hey, there are ships out there depending on you, young fellow-me-lad.*

Which way?

Towards you. That's it.

After that day, he began to time his walks with Sasha in order to meet Leah at the lighthouse. He'd wanted to make it appear as if they met by coincidence but sometimes when he didn't see her he would sit on the platform under the lighthouse and wait. Even then she sometimes didn't appear. Or it would be one of her brothers, Billy or Patrick, taking their turn at winding the mechanism. The brothers would look at him with suspicion or irritation, or sometimes just plain indifference, but Leah, when he did see her, always seemed pleased to see him.

Just can't stay away, huh? she would say. And the look on her face said something else, something he couldn't quite read but which made his pulse quicken.

I love you, he had wanted to tell her. *I love your eyes. I love your smile. I love your laughter.* But he couldn't say it and so, with September and the threat of a new school term looming, he wrote it in a letter and attached it to one of the rungs on the lighthouse ladder using a bit of blue rope he found on the beach. He didn't sign his name just in case one of her brothers found it. If it was Leah who discovered it he was certain she'd know who it was from.

~~~

Are some people born bad?

Hunter often wondered about this. It seemed to him that Reece, two years his senior, had hated him since the day he was born. There was even a family story their father liked to tell about three-year-old Reece, caught holding a pillow over his infant brother's face. For some reason everyone thought this was hilarious. Reading the letter meant for Leah Appleton was not the worst thing Reece had ever done to him, certainly there had been innumerable unasked for beatings that had left Hunter bruised and bloody nosed; there was the time Reece had tried to drown Hunter in the toilet; and once, when Hunter was ten years old and he twelve, Reece had taken out a knife and threatened to cut Hunter's ear off, and Hunter had cried to their mother because Reece looked so serious he thought he'd actually do it.

Throughout, Reece had somehow managed to remain the apple of their mother's eye; and Hunter was somehow able to shrug off Reece's cruelties, perhaps thinking he deserved them. He'd always been the weaker one, as his brother had loved to remind him, preferring books and words and drawing where his older brother loved sport, wresting in particular, in which he'd entered various tournaments and won numerous trophies which his mother still kept behind glass on a cabinet shelf in the living room. Or perhaps Reece had imagined that all brotherly relationships were like the one he and Reece had. In boyhood photos he was always smiling; his face that mixture of wonder and expectation, as if he couldn't wait to find out what life had in store.

How? How had he borne it all? The daily tortures and humiliations. How had he been able to keep smiling? It was only now, now that he was older, that he saw it for what it was. Abuse. Yet, amazingly he thought now, at the time he'd been able to suffer it all. Suffer, that is, until that day at the lighthouse. At Black Nore. That day that finally broke his spirit. Reece's final cruelty.

He left the beach, pebbles crunching under his feet, and found the dirt track through the woods again. When the trees broke, the sight of the lighthouse took him by surprise and he caught his breath. There was something incongruous about it, but it wasn't just this that stopped him in his tracks. A sudden rush of memory hit him like a blow to the chest, knocking the air out of him. He was fourteen again, following Reece after he'd taken off with his letter, saying he would present it to Leah Appleton himself. And there was the lighthouse, and there was Leah stood at the foot of it, paused in the act of climbing the ladder, blinking at Reece as he ran towards her.

Shaking his head to clear the surge of images, Hunter looked again. The lighthouse stood alone. He remembered the vague fear it had instilled in him as a boy. It looked sentient somehow. He'd often imagined it as an alien spaceship, standing insect-like on its six legs. Squinting, he thought there was the silhouette of a person pressed against the glass of the one window, but when he got closer he saw that the ladder up to the entrance hatch had been fitted with a metal panel to prevent climbing. Still, as he passed underneath, he thought he heard, for a moment only, the sound of footsteps on the rungs of the narrow platform that ran around the circumference of the lighthouse about two thirds of the way up. And he could feel it, feel someone staring down at him. He looked up, alarmed. But, although the sun was in his eyes, he could clearly see there was no one on the platform. He had imagined it, that's all.

He remembered that day Reece had taken his letter and run to meet Leah Appleton, and how he'd found them when he finally reached the lighthouse. Reece had her pressed against one of the lighthouse legs. He remembered how Leah had screamed at Reece: *No! Get off me! Get off!*

But Reece wouldn't get off. Reece never got off.

~~~

He often wondered if it had been his intention to kill Reece, or if he was lashing out, meaning only to hurt him. He had borne all the cruelties his brother could dish out but he would not tolerate him hurting Leah. He would not.

In that spot where he'd chosen to ambush his brother there was a break in the trees lining one side of the path, with a clear drop down to the sea. He could remember the weight of the black stone in his hand. He could remember the hot tears on his face as he crouched beside a bench next to a dip along the path where Reece wouldn't have seen him as he returned from the lighthouse to join his friends on the shale beach. Perhaps Reece had been planning to tell his friends what he'd done at Black Nore, to brag about it. But he never got the chance.

As soon as Reece passed the spot where he hid, Hunter rose to hit feet and struck his brother as hard as he could over the head with the rock he'd been cradling in two hands. He could remember how Reece crumpled without a sound before staggering sideways. Hunter had felt his heart lurch as Reece tumbled towards the short drop. He might have reached out for his brother. But then Reece slipped and fell. The brown water took him. Within seconds of Hunter striking him Reece was gone. Though Hunter watched the water his brother never reappeared. Hunter had never known if the blow had killed Reece, or if he had drowned in that muddy seawater soup. Sometimes he told himself that this had never happened at all. That he'd imagined it or dreamed it. How could he have done that? How could he have killed his own brother, then never said a word to anybody? He took part in the searches. He sat and watched his parent's anguish. But he never said a single word about what he'd done.

Though he had fretted and waited over days, weeks, months, for some announcement – body found, washed up somewhere – none came. All anyone apart from himself knew, was that Reece had merely vanished.

~~~

"It's a strange thing memory," his mother said. She looked at the television, not at him, as if she wasn't actually talking to him. He felt that it would've made no difference if he were present or not. She would still go on talking. To him. To Reece. To her husband two years in the ground. "Sometimes memory gets all mixed up with fantasies. We remember things the way we choose to, or the way we prefer to, not the way they actually were."

"When I was a baby he tried to smother me."

Now she turned her head to look at him and laughed. "He was only a baby himself at the time. You can't blame him for that. He didn't know any better."

"What about the time he threatened to cut off my ear?"

"You don't think he would have actually done that?"

"He said he would. He had a knife."

"He was just trying to frighten you. You should be grateful."

"*Grateful?*"

"Having a big brother toughens a boy up." She must have noticed his outrage; it must have shown in his face. But before he could respond she pursed her lips and changed the subject. "Guess who I bumped into in the Post Office today?"

He stared hard at her. "You honestly think all those nasty things Reece did were good for me?"

"Oh let it go," she said, her face for a moment showing genuine anger. "You're exaggerating it all. Boys will be boys. He's dead and you're alive, but you're still whining on and on about how he used to bully you."

He turned his head from her. He wanted to get up, collect his belongings together and leave. If he hit the road now he would be back in Exeter by nightfall. He'd have three full days to relax and get his bearings before school started again. Then he thought of all those children, eager and restless after their holidays. Children he would have to make interested, make silent, buoy up somehow. Just the thought of it made him tired.

His mother spoke, her voice calm again, casual. "Do you want to know who I met in the Post Office or not?"

"No."

"The Appleton girl."

He swivelled his head around. "Leah?"

"Only she's not a girl now, is she?"

"How... How's she doing?"

"Ask her yourself. I told her to stop by tomorrow."

"Stop by? What… What did you do that for?"

"I thought you'd want to see her. She's not married anymore. Separated. And you're—"

"What?"

"You're available. Aren't you?"

"Mother, you can't just… People don't just…"

"What's the matter?" she said, half rising from her chair. "She's put on a bit of weight, but she's still pretty."

~~~

He tossed and turned most of the night. Somewhere in the tangle of sleeping and waking he dreamt about his brother. He was standing on Beach Road looking out over the estuary, just as he had a few days before, when a movement down by the waterline caught his eye. It was a figure emerging from the sea, clawing its way out, and crawling up onto the mudflats, hauling itself along on its hands. He glanced around. No one else appeared to have noticed anything untoward. An old couple sat on a nearby bench eating sandwiches. A woman walked her dog along the grass bank below.

Look. Look. There. Look. Someone…

Hunter wanted to point, to cry out, but for some reason he was becalmed. The figure lurched and struggled over the mudflats, moving up the beach towards him, and despite the figure being slick with mud he was suddenly sure that this was Reece. Reece, returned from the sea. Reece, coming back to reclaim his place as their mother's favourite. Coming back to start the cruelties he'd once inflicted on Hunter all over again. Reece crawled on all fours over the mudflats, sank and disappeared for a moment, one arm flailing, reaching, then heaved himself up again, spitting mud and seawater, crawling forward again, dragging himself across the mud, his eyes fixed on Hunter. Even from a distance Hunter could see the fury in those eyes.

Just you wait…

Just you wait till I get hold of you, little brother of mine.

Bro…

You'll see…
You'll see what I'll…

~~~

Come morning, Hunter had decided to pack his bag and leave for Exeter after breakfast. His mother would grumble but so what? Let her sit and talk to Reece's school photograph. Despite his resolution, and his suitcase in the hall, he delayed his departure until mid-morning, and in the end the doorbell rang before he'd had a chance to say his goodbyes.

Was it dread that rooted him to the spot?

"Answer it," his mother said, irritably.

When at first he opened the door he was able to breathe out and let go of the flutter of panic that seized him. The woman standing on the doorstep was not Leah Appleton. This woman had short bobbed brown hair, and the kind of doughy complexion that could render a person almost featureless. But as he looked into her face he realised that it *was* Leah. He recognised the humour and the inquisitiveness in her eyes and the set of her mouth. He'd always imagined her being haunted by what Reece had done to her that day at the lighthouse. How does a girl get over something like that? But here she was with the same mischievous expression she'd had as a girl.

"Come in, come in," he said, ushering her inside.

"Hunter, right? I remember you from school. You were always kind of quiet."

His heart dropped. Was that all he was to her? Didn't she remember the rest, their time at the lighthouse that summer? His letters?

"Yes … I suppose I was."

His mother appeared and spared him any more awkwardness, sweeping Leah through to the living room, sitting her down on the sofa and asking what she'd like to drink. Coming back up the hallway, heading for the kitchen to make tea, she scowled at Hunter who still stood by the front door with his hands in his pockets, stuck there unable to move like a ship run aground.

"Go and talk to her."

Hunter took a deep breath and went to the living room.

"So," he said to Leah. She sat in an awkward position on the edge of sofa, with her hands on her knees. "How are you keeping?"

"Good. Yeah. I work for an estate agent now. You?"

"Ah… Teaching."

She nodded. "Like it?"

"Not much. Don't know what I was thinking, really. I hated school when I was a boy. I hate it now too, to be honest."

She smiled. "It must be your good deed."

So she does remember, he thought. She remembered their meetings that summer at the lighthouse. He wasn't just a face she knew from school. And if she remembered that, perhaps she remembered his letters.

She looked beyond him. "What a lot of trophies."

He turned to the glass cabinet.

"Reece's. You… You remember Reece? My brother?"

"Oh yes," she said, smiling. Why was she smiling? Why would she smile after what he'd done to her? "I've been to see his grave a couple of times."

"Grave?"

"His grave. It's in St Peter's, right? I've been to see it. To pay my respects."

"There's no grave. Not for Reece."

Leah squinted her eyes, tilting her head to one side as she did as if to say: *You sure?*

"There's a memoriam but there's no grave, no headstone. Reece's body was never found."

"Really? I'm sure I… No body? What happened to him?"

"No one knows for certain. They thought maybe some kind of accident. He fell in the estuary and drowned, somehow. He used to go down there and drink with his friends quite a lot. You can ask my mother."

"No, I…" Leah turned away from him, looking inward. When she faced him again her expression had changed to one of concern and, he thought, distrust.

"That's weird."

"What? What's weird?"

"I heard it was a car crash. I heard he was a passenger in a stolen car that crashed going eighty down Nore Road. It was Simon Usher driving. Remember him? Proper tearaway." She glanced down at her feet. "But I must've got confused. Been misinformed, or—"

"No, we're fairly sure Reece went in the estuary and drowned." Hunter nodded his head as if to put the seal on his words.

Leah raised her eyes to him. "So sad."

"Sad? You're sure you remember him. He was…"

"Oh yes, I remember him." She smiled again, her face lighting up. "How could I not? He kissed me once at the lighthouse, you know."

"Kissed… Kissed you?"

"Yes. He used to write me these letters, you see. So sweet. I still have a couple of them somewhere. One day he just handed one to me, and then he kissed me." She laughed. "A long time ago."

"No. No, it was … are … are you sure he only kissed you. I thought…"

Her face darkened. She drew her head back. "Of course I'm sure. What're you saying?"

"No… Nothing. Just that Reece. He could be … well … he could be a bit of a bastard."

She made the same gesture of disbelief by drawing her head back again. "Really?"

"Yes, he…"

"I always found him very sweet."

It's a strange thing memory.

"Sweet?"

"Yes, a lovely sweet guy."

"I remember that day. At the lighthouse. Your lip. It… It was bleeding."

"What?"

"I was there. Don't you remember? Reece, he…"

"You were there when he kissed me?"

"You ran. Don't you remember? You ran, and your lip was bleeding. And your skirt, it was torn… He must've…"

His mother reappeared carrying a tea tray. She must have sensed some odd atmosphere in the room as she switched a questioning look from Leah to Hunter.

"What's he said to you? Has he upset you?"

"No," Leah said. "We were just talking about Reece. Those are his trophies, right?"

"Yes." The old woman looked at Hunter and narrowed her eyes. He could say nothing, his mouth opened and closed, but no sound came out. He felt as if time had stopped. He was afloat in the middle of the sea with no shore in sight. Nothing. Just blackness all around him. His mother turned back to Leah, laying the tea tray down on the coffee table alongside the sofa.

Leah said, "Seems we remember things differently. Hunter was saying…"

"Oh, don't listen to him," Hunter's mother said. "He always was jealous of his brother."

HENRIETTA STREET

Gail-Nina Anderson

"I do not think of myself as a fussy man ... nobody could accuse me of being a hothouse flower..."

We looked at David with frank admiration. He is a large man, built on a scale suggestive of Edwardian municipal banquets, and assuming a style vaguely reminiscent of that period. His torso is expansive, his abdomen even more so. He *might* just conceivably be viewed as a hothouse flower, but it would have to be one of those gigantic exotic blooms whose petals looked worryingly like animal tissue.

On the other hand, he most definitely *is* a fussy man. He could – frequently does – quell a room full of aggravating students or stare down a burglar (and he's done that too, but that's another story and even he would admit that the polychrome glory of his dressing gown may have played its part in undermining the man's spirit). But a detail out of place or a small unexplained noise grates on the delicate equilibrium of his nervous system to an extent – well, to an extent that everyone else has to know about it, to understand his plight, to enter into the minutiae of the minute problem.

And we had known *that* when the field trip was suggested. Three academics taking an out-of-season holiday cottage in Whitby, each with their own excuse to link the excursion with the holy grail of *research*. Gerard was looking at the way early Christian history was repackaged and sold via the heritage industry, which provided an excuse to visit the Abbey; I, of course, was examining the means whereby Victorian photographer Frank Meadow Sutcliff had shaped our preconceptions of the town; and David was considering – only *considering*, mind – the possibility that a rather rousing new biography of Captain Cook might be a suitable project for the early retirement which he was beginning to see in the distance (and actually had no intention of taking). So we persuaded ourselves to while away the start of January with this modest break from the university staff-room where we usually met, and yes, we knew from the start that Gerard and I would accomplish the planning, booking and driving, while David would permit himself to be invited, cajoled and automatically be given all to himself the one sizeable double-bedded room in the cottage as though by right. I have no idea why we allow ourselves to play to his whims, but we do – that's the game. If nothing else, time spent with David allows us to observe how surprisingly sane, temperate and grown-up *we* are by comparison – and invariably provides enough top-class anecdotage to see us through till the next time.

"I do not think of myself as a fussy man..."

We held our breath. So far, everything had gone well. The weather was bracing to a fairly extreme degree but the town looked enchanting through the crisp coldness. The cottage was tucked down a tiny side street along from the bottom of the cliff where St Mary's churchyard was slowly crumbling into the sea.

Our holiday let was a compact little dwelling dating from a period when town planning and Health and Safety Regulations were alike things of an unimaginable future. Its plan was idiosyncratic, so that it felt folded in upon itself, the space inside offering more nooks and crannies than seemed altogether feasible, the whole thing modernised just to the extent that major inconvenience was avoided without character being sacrificed. The stairs to the first floor were so narrow and steep that it felt safer to come down them backwards, like a ship's ladder, but that was part of the fun, as we had told ourselves several times already. Gerard and I were sharing the family room, and David had just emerged from the en suite double bedroom he had so effortlessly appropriated.

"It's just that" – he continued – "there's a noise."

Did we stifle our snorts of laughter? One of the advantages of David is that you don't really have to. He knows and appreciates the fact that to have his idiosyncrasies, his past triumphs, recollected with amusement puts him centre stage. But he didn't join in.

"No, it's a mite worrying – not that I'm actually complaining…"

"What sort of a noise? Old house noise – squeaky floorboards, that sort of thing? We *have* been moving about down here, *sorting things out in the kitchen*…" (While there's actually no point in dropping hints about the just division of labour we still do so, more out of habit than anything else.)

"Or old house in cold-weather noises? Beams contracting and expanding, that sort of thing?"

He shook his head mournfully. "Nooo – I don't *quite* think that's it."

As he hadn't conclusively dismissed this convenient possibility, we went on with it.

"The cottage *is* over four hundred years old, you know, and it's only just been renovated. We're the first people in since they installed the new central heating and did the rewiring" (I knew this because the letting agency had advertised it with some pride. They had obviously had their eye on this prime piece of saleable quaintness for some time, waiting like vultures for the demise of last remaining member of the local family whose home it had been. Indeed, the renovation had been much featured in the local media, I was told, because of the tactful way it had been undertaken, with the local historical society allowed in to document its progress, and none of the original structure spoiled by the work.)

"The agency did say that the property wouldn't suit *all* holiday tenants, but for three reasonably fit and responsible men with well-developed historical perspectives—"

"*And* we've already learned not to fall downstairs more than once a day!"

David was coming round. "You're probably right – central heating turned on, on a cold day and all that – but it did sound rather more ... organic than that. You don't suppose it could be rats?"

"Rats *inside the walls*? Possible once upon a time, but not after all the work that's been done – and why upstairs and not down? David, old man, this isn't going to be another *grenade attack*, is it?"

As ever, the grenade story had the effect of instantly reconciling David to his own glorious history of mistaken obsessions. The man is more like Mr Toad than I can say. When we were staying at a heritage holiday home on a forested estate just before Christmas one year (the usual excuses of research interests having been trotted out to justify this) we had enjoyed the rather moving spectacle of David becoming enthused over the notion of gathering woodland decorations suitable for the festive season, impeccably natural and (incidentally) completely free. After returning with arms full of Nature's cast-offs, we had all anticipated a night of deep restful sleep – until the early hours of the morning when David had leapt onto the landing to avoid *the grenades* that had gone off in his room.

"It must be – or illegal fireworks at the least! Something has been stockpiled in that airing cupboard and now it's started to explode – God knows how much of it there is!"

I can't remember which of us had braved the airing cupboard to discover that the pinecones collected earlier for decorative purposes, all tightly folded in, had been set by David to dry out next to the boiler and were now obligingly opening up with loud pops, crackling as the wood and seeds responded to the heat, with explosive results. Ever since then, the pinecones had become our favourite David motif. As could have been predicted, the story at once put David's Whitby noise into perspective.

We *did* go up and listen in the room, but mysterious sounds are notoriously diffident when it comes to singing out on request and we heard nothing.

I draw a veil over the massive plates of fish and chips that constituted the evening's entertainment, but after the meal and the walk and the ensuing conversation, I know we should have earned a good night's rest. But Gerard slept fitfully – I know because I was awake for much of the night and could hear him. Next morning, preparing breakfast in the kitchen, we compared notes.

"Bloody *dreams* – the sort you can't remember – and you?"

"Just anxious," I admitted, "about nothing at all – after all, we're on holiday."

When David emerged, the circles under his eyes told their own story.

"Wish it *had* been pinecones in the airing cupboard," he admitted. "There's nothing to see but I did just seem to *hear* something – you know, on the edge of hearing. Irregular, scrabbling. First I thought it was one side, then the other, then over by the chimney."

"Was it close to you?" (I wouldn't admit it, but it did just strike me that the rat theory was a possibility – and the thought of little clawed feet tippy-tapping their way across the floor towards the bed was not a good one, whoever it was happening to – though the ensuing legend of *David the Mighty Rat Strangler* would be one to cherish)

"Oh no," he said, flatly. "It was definitely *confined*. That's the problem. It's not a bad noise, you understand – just a noise in the wrong place. Maybe wings, I thought, then something more regular, like a heartbeat. But I don't want to *fuss*. I realise that some things you have to live with."

This sentiment was so unlike the David we knew and loved that we might really have started to worry, but luckily our late start meant that breakfast had to be seen to, and suitable distraction was at hand. The kipper smokehouse down the street had by this time started up so supplies could be purchased and cooked at once, in a culinary experience so authentic that it should probably have earned an award of merit from English Heritage. The ensuing fug of smoky aroma (and actual smoke – our kitchen skills were not of the most accomplished) restored our faith in the cottage.

"I bet it always smelled like this – that they all did."

"With tar and pipe smoke and coal fires thrown in. My God, it must have pickled their lungs!"

Why did that make us laugh? The mild hysteria of a sleepless night, perhaps.

"It's enough to dry out a pinecone…"

We were off again, and the humour carried us out and around the town. It's not difficult to amuse yourselves with a combination of tourist tackiness, historical sites and pubs galore.

"We must save something for tomorrow."

"Well, the Captain Cook Museum, of course," said David, "I need to be fresh for that – and Whitby Museum – that's supposed to be a real cabinet of curiosities, virtually unspoiled."

David has decided opinions on modern museums, with which Gerard has long since learned how to disagree in amused silence. The words of disapproval are *gimmicky* and *educational*, spoken with equal contempt. At this moment we were in the Visitors Centre (snort of disgust from David at the very thought) of Whitby Abbey, where computer screens provided taking heads to expound, with lightly worn learning, on the town's history. We had heard Abbess Hild and assorted ecclesiastics, and were now standing in front of an actor playing the role of Bram Stoker, explaining how a holiday in Whitby had given him one of the key settings for his novel *Dracula*.

David wandered over and we waited for the explosion of exasperation. He likes to say that being a Victorian at heart he sees *Dracula* for what it is – a cheap shocker designed for an under-educated audience avid for sensation. But he listened in silence until the Stoker monologue was over.

"Where did he stay, on this holiday that was supposed to have inspired *Dracula*? You'll know—" turning abruptly to me "—you've read all the Tourist Information material – where was *Dracula* born?"

"*Transylvania!*" we both chorused, and even David joined in the good humour, but it was Gerard who had taken in the way the town built up its own mythology, and could actually answer his question

"Other side of the harbour," he said with conviction. "Across in those rather elegant terraces."

"Oh." David was obviously disappointed. "Nowhere near our cottage, then?"

"No – it would have still been a fisherman's cottage then, down in the smelly part of town. Though Count Dracula presumably flitted all over the place. He was certainly around in the churchyard…"

"Not interested, dear boy. The vampire count is an imported motif, nothing to do with the place itself, just the creation of a literary hack with an eye to the main chance. Simply wondered what he saw of *old* Whitby, that was all…"

The Abbey ruins – and the way they were effectively sold to us – plus St Mary's church and churchyard took up the rest of the daylight, and food and drink happily occupied the evening and… Was it just me, or was there a general reluctance among us to go to bed that night? We drank whiskey till late and it was well past midnight when eventually we retired, or tried to.

Gerard was just going up the steep stairs when David, who had been the first up to bed a few minutes earlier, suddenly lumbered down again, moving with surprising speed and almost crashing into him.

"Sorry, so sorry, dear boy – just occurred that I really shall need a *tumbler*. Very dry up in that room – and whiskey doesn't help. Really ought to do it now – throat is very tickly."

He coughed a pathetic little cough, as though to convince us, squeezed past and padded into the kitchen to fetch a glass. I shrugged. Gerard had been caught on the hop, though, and responded with quite uncharacteristic ill-humour.

"Don't you just want something to throw at Count Dracula when he flies in at your window?"

"Very funny old man – just a water glass, I assure you." (David was already sipping at the one now in his hand. It occurred to me later that I doubt I had ever before seen him drink water voluntarily).

A spirit of mischief had got into Gerard and he persisted.

"No, that *was* it, wasn't it? Dracula's out to get you, you old disbeliever. Not so much a scrabbling as a *fluttering* – wings was what you heard!"

I tried to defuse it. "Shouldn't think so – big black capes don't make the same sort of noise."

"No", said Gerard, persistent now, his rarely revealed claws well into David's nightmare. "Scritchy scratchy – what was it that you said? Scratch, scratch, scratch – can't vampires turn into rats, into bats? Was it really in the walls? Are you sure it wasn't *coming down the chimney*!"

David had frozen into stock stillness for a moment before he managed to laugh, but with an obvious effort.

"Tell you what, how about another whiskey – one for Stoker and the Count?"

~~~

We never did see Whitby Museum, not on that trip. It was a year and more later when I finally caught up with it, long after we'd settled as penitently as possible with the holiday letting agency (though I imagine we're still on a blacklist – when I eventually came back, I stayed in a hotel). The trouble was, we never had any explanation to give them. David was a respectable academic in fairly easy circumstances – he may have been a fussy man, but he wasn't really a neurotic one, and certainly not *destructive*. And the final upshot wasn't even all that dramatic. True, he *did* take very early retirement, and *didn't* write a book on Captain Cook, but nothing worse. Except that he gave up drinking, but that could happen to anyone.

~~~

Once we'd gone up to bed, the second – and final – night of our stay was, so far as Gerard and I were concerned, notably uneventful. The extra whiskey worked and we slept like the dead, rising to a spectacularly late start. David, of course, was not in sight as we moved around the unfamiliar kitchen sorting out coffee and toast.

"He's already been down, though" said Gerard. "Look…"

The wall cabinet in which an array of suitably sturdy crockery had been left for the use of the tenants was open, its doors pushed wide. There had been a row of glass tumblers – now there was only one. As Gerard took it down, scrutinizing it as though some explanation for its solitary state might be forthcoming, David lumbered into the room behind us. He looked appalling, slack-skinned and greyish, still wearing his pyjamas, and strangely dusty about his hair and beard.

"Need that old man," he said, taking the glass out of Gerard's hand. "Thirsty work, awfully dry."

He filled the glass and began instantly to drink as he moved back to the stairs. We were momentarily speechless.

"Err … better get a move on. David – take a shower, it will wake you up."

He didn't look back.

"Bad night I suppose – looks as though he's been rolling about the floor."

We turned back to the tasks in hand and began to nag at each other as old friends do to give the unnameable tension a focus.

"When did we say we'd get the keys back?"

"How long will it take David to do the museum – both museums?"

"Well, do you want to lunch on the way back or get some more kippers and call *that* lunch?"

What we really wanted to say was, maybe we were mistaken. Maybe something really had gone wrong in the en-suite, recently modernised, completely rewired, double-master bedroom that David had appropriated.

Between our jagged comments and the water boiling and the

crockery clattering it took a while before the other sound cut in. That is, of course we did hear noises from upstairs, but David never was a quiet person so we took no notice. But this was a *little* noise that came and went and would keep on coming back, a little noise that scrabbled or scratched, scratched, scraped – wings perhaps, or feet, little feet or fingers scrabbling....

Suddenly it was too obvious to be resisted. Did we call out to David before we ran up the stairs? I can't remember, but it wouldn't have made any difference. He turned when he heard us enter the room, but without urgency. He was still at his task, but we could see he knew it was hopeless. All around the skirting board stood glass tumblers containing water.

"Dry you see, dear boys, thirsty work. Need to put some moisture in the air ... all dried out, like the kippers."

And David had methodically, gently, as quietly and carefully as he could, as though not to disturb what might be behind it, cut into the plasterboard of the smooth modern wall and pulled it away, leaving a ragged trail of dust and debris along the carpet and revealing the older structure it masked, of brick and timber. And now he was crouching by the chimney and using his bare hands to scrape away at the old brickwork, trying to loosen chunks, to get into the structure of the cottage, to somehow get behind what we saw.

He didn't protest when I took his hands and pulled him away. Indeed, he was almost instantly his old self

"Not usually fussed, you know – take things as they are, put up with anything for a quiet life." (We didn't even smile.) "But thought I could hear it. Not so very silly, you know – pigeon might have got in down the chimney, don't know how the space has been messed about with, heard it scratching behind there, thought if I could just let it out...."

He saw now how he looked and the devastation he had left around the room. We led him into the family bathroom to clean up and while he did so we packed his things so that we could all go straight to the car. I won't tell you how grateful I was that Gerard dealt with the letting agency. They were, he said, less surprised than you might imagine

~~~

It's an old practice, according to the label in the Museum. And when I saw it, it did sound vaguely familiar – websites, documentaries, information you pick up somewhere. The cat walled up will keep the devil at bay – presumably because it's such a good hunter by night, chasing off vermin even after death, or perhaps because it's the Devil's own animal and its corpse will scare him off. The one they found in the cottage, when they were doing the renovations, had pride of place in a display labelled *Recent Finds*. I wasn't looking for it – I was still following up ideas about Victorian photographs, hence the return visit to Whitby, this time alone. The cat was pathetic beyond belief, a dry little corpse, angular in its stiffened state, curled in on itself. The museum did not offer a postcard of it. A shame, I thought – they could have sold it in aid of the RSPCA.

David might have said that had he seen it but I was glad he hadn't. It's like a genie and a bottle – shouldn't be in there but once you take it out, the world – or at least one little corner of it – has been changed. But David was rather more of a hothouse flower these days – a little more delicately tuned – and this would certainly have given him something to fuss about.

EVERY BAD THING

Sharon Gosling

1
Four hundred years and ne'er a change.

It had taken Willa two lifetimes to realise that her problem was not that she did not understand people, but rather that she understood them too well. She read them like poems, and each had a cadence that told her far more than was comfortable to instantly know about another human being. Their personalities swelled towards her, the good bright and blinding, the bad dark and cloying, both unavoidable, both suffocating. She had developed defences – *don't look, don't look* – but only later in life. As a girl, as a young woman, it had been one more unnavigable consequence of a life stained by a strangeness for which no one, least of all her, had been prepared.

They say bad things come in threes, but in Willa's experience that was a woeful underestimation of the world's basic state. Tonight, for example, she would be starting work with a shiver because the weather had suddenly turned colder than a witch's tit, which by her count made at least five things that could be legitimately considered bad in her day. She came into the kitchen through the side door and hung up her coat before walking into the goldfish bowl of the restaurant beyond. Not yet five o'clock but outside it was almost dark, rain hissing against black tarmac and grey concrete, the lights of neighbouring businesses glinting valiantly through the misery of an early Cumbrian winter.

Meg was already there, putting in the till and humming to herself. Willa couldn't remember being that young and was no longer sure she ever had been. Friday night wasn't her usual shift. In the year since she had taken the job at La Trattoria she'd generally worked lunchtimes, which were quieter, safer. But Ben was on holiday and Lucy was off sick. They were stuck for staff. Meg had begged for her help and Willa hadn't felt able to refuse, knowing how difficult it would be even if she said yes. Tonight the restaurant's front of house staff would consist of Meg, Willa and Odette.

As if thinking of her face had conjured her to appear, Odette arrived in a flurry of apologies, her accent lancing through the air as she left the kitchen staff behind with a raucous laugh.

"I'm sorry, so sorry," she gushed, as she hurried in and hugged both Willa and Meg hello. "I did not mean to be late. It is busy out there already, eh? The bus…"

"It's fine," said Meg. "I think we'll be busy tonight, though."

"Aye," said Willa. "Or maybe the rain will keep everyone at home."

This idea made them all snicker. As if northerners were known for their deference to adverse weather at any time, but especially at a week's nether end.

Elizabeth I had decreed that the border city of Carlisle must close its gates to travellers after dark and so instead a street of taverns had sprung up on the last mile of the old road from London, an area owned by a Flanders man called Botchard. Four hundred years later, Carlisle on a Friday and Saturday night was so notorious for its revels that for decades Botchergate had been closed to traffic from early evening so that drinkers could spill between the doors of the numerous watering holes without being mown down. La Trattoria was just around the corner: the chippies would fill first, then Nandos, but there would come a point when the Italian would be just as appealing.

Willa crossed to the mirror that elongated one end of the room. She wrestled with her hair until it was a manageable enough to fix in place with a band. She had vowed to hack it short the minute the red waves began to fade, but despite a strand or two of silver the colour had yet to dull and she was vain enough to love it despite all its impracticalities. It was a rabbit's white cottontail, unmistakable and glaring: *Missed me the first time? Here I am again.*

The restaurant opened its doors right on time at six, but the table of twelve were already outside. They poured in, fractious and wet, blaming Willa and Odette for their state. Willa retreated to the bar and kept herself busy with their drink order. She looked up briefly as the second early booking came in, also wet with rain. Behind them came another couple, then another. The rain fell, on and on.

2
Stars like flowers, opening in the dusk

By seven they were full save for the booking expected to arrive last. Meg had to turn several groups away.

"They all come at once, they'll all leave at once," Odette muttered as she slipped behind the bar to retrieve another bottle of white. "Why are they all so *grumpy* tonight, eh?"

It was true. Willa could feel it, a gathering weight in the air. "You okay?" she asked, quietly.

Odette nodded, mustering a smile. "It ends," she said. "I just keep telling myself that – no matter what, the shift, it always ends. Eventually."

The restaurant door opened, bringing in rain and nine broad noisy lads who looked as if they'd already been up and down Botchergate at least once. Meg rushed over, anxious to get them into their seats. Willa watched as one of the men rested his fingers on the young woman's shoulder, leaning too close to speak something into her ear. Willa felt a stab of anger spike in her chest – *don't look, don't look* – which only grew as she saw Meg make a tiny movement, dipping her shoulder beneath his touch, but he did not remove his hand. Perhaps he was already too drunk to register his bad behaviour, or perhaps he was just in the habit of ignoring women's discomfort. Something in that touch made Willa think of Elin, and her stomach clenched hard at the unexpected equation. *Don't look,* Willa told herself, turning away. *Don't look.*

"I go to help," Odette muttered, setting the wine bottle down on the counter and hurriedly scooting out across the floor.

Willa realised that both Meg and Odette would be occupied for a while and took the wine herself, working her way around the empty glasses. It was obviously a birthday party for the matriarch seated at the head of the table. When she reached the birthday girl the old woman touched two delicate fingers to Willa's wrist. Her skin was like paper, pale and thin. The touch made Willa look at her face and the old woman smiled.

"Thank you, dear," she said. "It looks as if you're having a busy night."

Willa smiled in return. "Happy birthday. Is it today?"

"It is! Ninety. Where does the time go?"

"Well, you don't look a day over eighty," Willa said, and the old woman laughed with delight, a great gale of sound incongruous to her frame. The familiarity of it took Willa by surprise. She should have walked away then, should have moved on and let the moment pass – *don't look, don't look* – but instead she lingered, trying to smooth out the creases in that old face, to turn back time. The woman looked back, her gaze straying to Willa's hair.

"Have we met before?" she asked, the smile faltering into a faint frown. "You seem very familiar."

A sliver of light illuminated the depths of Willa's memory. She took a breath, already knowing it was too late. She should not have looked. Pull at a loose thread and the next will come undone. Bad things do not only come in threes.

Stars like flowers, opening in the dusk. Two women, hidden in the tall white wheat beneath an apple tree. Their fingers are tangled together amid the stems, and they are sharing sorrows.

How? How is it that you never look any different?

"I've worked here for almost a year now," Willa said, her voice brittle. "Perhaps on a previous visit?"

The woman shook her head, still looking up at her. "This is the first time I've been here."

"We'll have the dessert menus, please." It was the woman's daughter, her voice splitting their communion like a whip-crack.

Willa blinked, smiled, stepped back, the woman's fingers dropping from her wrist. "Of course."

She escaped to the bar just as the kitchen bell rang for service. Willa caught Odette by the arm as she went to answer it, pushing a handful of dessert menus at her instead.

"I'll run the food," she blurted. "You take these to table three."

Odette frowned, opened her mouth to ask —

"*Please*," Willa begged.

Odette nodded. Willa went into the kitchen, for a moment envying the frenetic activity within – the steam, the clatter, the heat. She took a breath, trying to ground herself, wishing for air and earth and water when there was none to be had, not a stone's throw from Botchergate on a Friday night in the year two thousand and twenty.

"Willa! Table eight, please."

Tony was staring at her as if he'd said her name more than once, pointing to the plates on the pass. She nodded, picked up all four, and backed out of the kitchen.

The old woman was in the corridor, making her slow way towards the bathrooms. Their eyes locked.

"Willa," Meg called from the bar, "could you do me a latte for table seven please? I'm just adding it on now, but I need it quickly... Thanks!"

"Willa?" the old woman asked. "I knew a Willa once. Such an unusual name. She had red hair too. And green eyes. She..." Her voice faltered as her gaze dropped to the half-hidden flash of silver at Willa's throat.

"My grandmother," Willa said, quickly. "I'm named for my grandmother."

She turned and walked out onto the floor to deliver the plates she carried. Then she went back to the bar and let herself be consumed by the list of drinks, her head ducked behind the silver hulk of the coffee machine, letting it fill her horizon.

When she looked up next, her checks had cleared and the woman's daughter was at the till. The rest of the table were leaving. The old woman was already outside, in the rain.

Her daughter did not leave a tip.

3

For every action, an equal and opposite reaction

She had been the death of all her mothers. The woman who birthed her had been felled by the knell of her first cry and Willa had been cursed from that point on. Even as an infant she had put the fear into those around her. Her first baby screams revealed teeth already in place. When she unscrewed her face enough to open her eyes, they were green and focused straight out of the womb instead of a blind wash of blue. Her strength was unnatural, her bite unholy, her eyes unsettling, and her entrance into the world unlucky. The husband of the barren woman to whom she was given called her Devil Child before he had owned her for a day and tried to douse her more than once. He swore Willa's lungs worked as well in the beck as they did in the air and consequently water could not end her life.

The village left her high on the fell to be taken by wolves or wildcats or eagles, but instead she had been found beneath a wild raspberry by a woman called Elin Bray. The baby had been wet and cold but as vibrantly alive as when that first scream had killed her own kin. When she had been old enough to understand words, the first story Elin had told her was Willa's own. *I found you with a rattle of bones tied by a bird's beak, a snippet of meat in your fist, a rabbit pelt under your little buttocks. You were a fell child and the fell will never be a place you need to fear.*

Elin tried to teach her that the anger was something to be contained, controlled. There were consequences if Willa didn't and she had learned this, too. Never at Elin's hand, gentle Elin. It was simply the price Willa paid for being what she was. For every action, an equal and opposite reaction, borne by her own flesh. It was just the way of the universe. God – Elin believed in God with the kind of simple firmness that was as unshakable as her belief in the seasons – had given the child this burden to bear, this test to end all tests, and He would reward Willa for passing His challenge. But the fury in Willa remained rampant, for like her teeth her memory had come early. She remembered what the village had done to the orphan baby she had been and she did not forgive, no matter how much she loved Elin, no matter where it could lead. *If they come for me I will kill them, every one,* she vowed to her small, uncomprehending five-year-old self. *They will not touch me.*

But it was not Willa for whom they came. Elin Bray had kept her strange child a secret from the world, high up there on the fell in a hut she'd built with her own hands. Dear, sweet Elin, who of all people had not deserved to depart the world the way she did, who was still calling for Willa to trust in God even as the village men dragged her away through the sucking mud, because a woman without the need for a man could only be due an ugly death.

"Keep to Him, little one," Elin had cried, out making her captors think she was addressing her familiar. "Our reward will be in the next life, where we shall see each other again. Live, little one. Live!"

It should be me, Willa had tried to scream, as they had tied the old woman to a barrel, as they had coated her naked buttocks in thick black tar, as the men had laughed and dripped it on the coarse grey hair between her tied-apart legs. *Don't you recognise me? It was me, all of it, every bad thing. You deserved it and it was me.*

But Elin took the blame for every moment of fury her adopted daughter had ever had and in the aftermath of that night Willa's body gained more scars, bad ones that would never fade. She had lost the little of God she'd had, her anger incandescent. It raged hot enough to reach the heaven Elin had hoped for so fervently, or at the very least the village where Willa's cursed life had begun. It also took every soul in it not fast enough to outrun the flames.

Once the inferno had died, though, the guilt set in. Willa had done this, after all. Elin's blood was on her hands. If Willa had passed the test to which she'd been born, Elin would still be alive. The failure was in Willa's very bones, her blood. She did not know how to atone – there *was* no way to atone – and so she withdrew into the fell mists, into the hidden clefts and valleys of the wild borderlands between England and Scotland. She'd learned to hide. If she hadn't, she'd have been killed, one way or another – drowned, hanged or burned. Assuming, of course, that any method of death would have been effective against her Devil's flesh.

Years later, with time moving on, she'd had to abandon the fells. Roads came, then trains. The world grew smaller. Willa could not hide as she had once done, could not live by forage and herb knowledge when even the emptiest land was parcelled, partitioned, surveyed and owned. Plain sight and constant motion became her only option. She tried to avoid people but loneliness sometimes trumped reason: *stars like flowers, opening in the dusk.* Willa travelled far and wide but she always missed the fells. She always wanted to go home.

Centuries of self-control held her in good stead. Sometimes the rage bubbled but it never again quite overflowed. Somewhere on a distant mountain in a distant land she had learned to narrow her evil into one form. The denarius at her throat was both personal symbol and reminder of what she must never again do. It was fortunate, really, that coins were rapidly becoming a thing of the past.

Willa had worked hard not to be herself. Yet nothing good ever came of thinking about her early years or about Elin Bray, about how a man's hands were so often involved in the end of a woman's life.

4

The kind of soul that casts a long shadow

The noise from the drunken lads became a problem, swelling to drown out the happy conversation of the other tables. Meg asked them to keep it down, and they were apologetic and promised to do so but within a few minutes the level had risen again. Outside, the rain hammered blows against the city, on and on, on and on.

Willa retreated to the bar and kept her eyes on the task at hand, turning out coffee after perfect coffee. The rhythm she established began to settle her. She enjoyed watching the milk as it plumed beneath the heat. The lattes were her favourite. Willa took pride in the ephemeral patterns she drew across their surface. A leaf, a flower, a whirlwind swirl, a string of broken hearts floating through a cloud of foam.

It's all right, she told herself. *It was just one encounter, that's all. She probably won't even remember it tomorrow. And if she does come back, wanting to know more about my grandmother, I just say she died years ago. It's not the end of the world.*

She had weathered worse, Willa reflected, as the tension in her gut eased. Perhaps she wouldn't have to move on after all. For all the worries this job carried with it, she liked working with the people here. This place suited her, and Willa was tired of moving.

She felt the sudden change in atmosphere like a drop in the temperature, as if ice had rolled in to coat the walls. She faltered, looking over the coffee machine towards the front door of the restaurant. A figure was looming through it, shoulders glinting with rain. Big, bulky, a stranger, yet recognisable. He was the kind of soul that casts a long shadow. *One of those,* she thought, and shivered, cold gathering like a storm front in her gut.

There was a woman with him – small and birdlike, she fluttered in his wake clutching a tiny black bag. Eminently breakable, she was shivering with cold in a denim mini-skirt and cropped top. Her open-toed heels were wet, they and her bare legs splashed with dirt from the road and rain.

Don't look. Don't look.

The man ignored the "Please wait to be seated" sign and strode straight to a table. The woman tottered after him, probably a little worse for wear. Not a lot, just a little. When she reached the table she stumbled against his outstretched leg and he lifted one hand to grasp her arm. A second later she was in her seat, as if he'd deposited her exactly where he wanted her. Willa's heart constricted. She could feel the impression of those fingers even if there were no marks visible. The truth of that face was hidden behind a mask of make-up, impeccable despite the rain she had been dragged through to get here. *She's tired*, Willa thought, trying not to look but seeing anyway, *tired in more ways than one*.

Her boyfriend turned to survey the restaurant as if wanting to demand why he hadn't received service yet. Willa averted her eyes, busying herself with the next coffee order.

"New people on table four," she said to Odette as she passed.

"Right," said the younger woman, grabbing a couple of menus.

"Odette," Willa said quietly. "Be careful."

Odette met her eye and then glanced over her shoulder towards the newcomers. Looking back to Willa again she gave a tiny nod. Willa tried and failed not to listen as Odette arrived at the table. The waitress handed out the menus, pointed out the specials board, and went to move away.

"Don't go anywhere," he said.

"I'll just be a couple of minutes, sir," Odette said. "I need to take an order from another table."

"I'm ready now." The man looked up, challenging her to see how difficult he could be.

Odette smiled and took out her order pad. "Of course."

Her studied deference seemed to win him over. He smiled and Willa's skin crawled at the glinting charm in it. She'd seen that before too. How nice a man like that could seem, how nice he could *be*, when he felt like it. When it served him.

He reeled off an order involving rare steak that Willa could have written without him even opening his mouth. Odette nodded, smile in place, then turned to his companion. The woman was still looking at the menu.

"Just make a decision," Willa heard him say. "It's not that difficult."

She looked up at Odette, smile twitching like a touched nerve. When she spoke her voice was barely even there. "Please, can you tell me if the sea bass—"

"Have lasagne," her partner said, speaking over her. "It's what you always end up with anyway."

The woman hesitated then looked back down at the menu.

"Lasagne," he said. "With salad. No dressing. That's what you want, isn't it? Come on, Stella, get on with it."

"Yes," said the tiny woman called Stella. "I'll have the lasagne. Salad, but no dressing. Thank you."

The man twisted around in his seat and looked directly over at Willa. "I'll have a double Jack on the rocks. She'll have a glass of red."

Willa pretended not to hear. His order could go up on the tab grabber, in line like every other check.

Odette smiled again. "Thank you, sir."

"Don't keep me waiting, eh?" he said, with a wolfish grin. "I'm hungry." His eyes lingered on Odette's legs as she walked away.

5

Strung out across year after bloody year

The evening continued to uncurl like the fingers of a clenched hand pried slowly open. More diners left but the ones Willa would have been glad to see the backs of remained. Meg had established that the raucous lads were on a stag weekend and were lining their stomachs, for their night was only just beginning. They continued to be loud but for the most part they were genial. Their happy bluster was countered by the heavy storm cloud squatting at the other end of the room. Every now and then, after a gust of fresh laughter from their table, he would turn and look over his shoulder at them. He seemed partly angry at their loudness, partly envious that he wasn't in their all-male circle. Willa suspected this was a pattern for his life.

When Odette cleared the couple's plates she asked if either he or Stella would like dessert.

"I'm not sure what I'd really like is on the menu," Willa heard him say, and it wasn't just the words that turned her stomach or his smile at Odette as he said them, but his tone.

Odette gave a laugh of her own. "We always try to please, sir," she said but Willa could read her discomfort in the tip of her shoulders, in the turn of her feet away from the table.

"I bet you do," he said, with another of those animal smiles while his girlfriend looked on with her own expression frozen in place.

"The roulade is very good," Odette said, ignoring him.

"Bring me one of those, then."

"And for you?" Odette asked, turning her attention to Stella.

"Just bring an extra fork, she can have a taste of mine if she really wants one."

Odette's pen hovered over the pad, hesitating. Then she nodded and smiled again before turning towards the kitchen. Willa followed her out and through the door.

"He's a pig," the younger woman shuddered as she tore the order from her pad and put it up on the pastry station. "My skin, he makes it crawl."

"I know," Willa said, "mine too."

"Poor woman. I bet he hits." She swore in Russian, a sharp, angular word that needed no translation.

"Men like that are too sly to use their fists," Willa said. "To begin with, anyway. Do you want me to take over?"

Odette shook her head. "They will be gone soon. And he would notice, eh?" She smiled and squeezed Willa's shoulder, heading back out onto the floor.

Willa went back out to the bar to find Odette behind it

pouring another double Jack.

"Can you do a large cappuccino for her?" she asked, quietly. "No chocolate."

Willa nodded. "Did she order it?"

Odette raised an eyebrow. *What do you think?* "I don't think she's drunk," she added in an even lower whisper. "I think is on drugs, maybe."

Willa glanced over at the table again. Stella was staring into space.

"Fuck knows I would be," Willa muttered.

Odette laughed, an involuntary sound louder than she intended. It drew his attention with a look sharp enough to catch the waitress putting her hand quickly over her mouth. Willa saw his expression blacken and all her senses rang an alarm at once.

"Leave the whiskey," she said, not wanting Odette to go back, not just then. "I'll take it with the coffee."

The kitchen bell rang and Odette went to answer it as Willa carried the two drinks to the table.

"What's her problem?" the guy asked, nodding after Odette.

Willa projected a puzzled expression, glancing up the corridor. "Sir?"

He shook his head, taking the glass and slugging a shot straight into the ugly slash of his mouth. Odette reappeared with his dessert, stopping by the cutlery hopper to pick up two forks and two napkins before setting it in front of him with a bright smile. Willa moved away but her hackles were up. A faint buzzing had started up in her ears, as if somewhere deep in her brain a radio had lost its tuning. It was a sensation she hadn't felt for a long, long time.

Breathe, she told herself. *Calm down. Just—*

She heard, rather than saw, the unmistakable sound of something striking clothed flesh, followed by a faint gasp from Odette. Willa turned sharply to see the waitress twisted to face the table with a rising flush on her cheeks. The guy was focused on his plate as he forked cake into his mouth. Stella's face was the tell-tale. She looked on, her vacant eyes suddenly wide and worried.

"What happened?" Willa asked.

"He slapped me," Odette said, not bothering to keep her voice low.

"What?" said the guy, his mouth full of cake. "No, I didn't."

"You did," Odette insisted. "And is not okay."

He dropped his fork onto his plate with a loud clatter, on his feet in a second. "You calling me a liar?"

Odette raised her chin. "Yes." She looked at Stella, sitting huddled in her seat, the steam from her cup of coffee tracing patterns in front of her face. "You saw. Didn't you?"

His girlfriend looked between the three of them, her eyes large with terror.

"He didn't mean anything by it," Stella blurted, begging for something no one could give her. "He's just had a bit too much to drink, that's all."

"You stupid bitch," he said, three words coated in such venom that they could have poisoned the world.

The woman he was supposed to love shrank back in her seat, and Willa saw, as if it had been fixed in a neon sign over her head, the quality of this woman's life. Of the escalating damage strung out across year after bloody year, of the pleas and then the screams, of the quiet sobs and the hidden bruises, a myriad tiny humiliations followed by a myriad larger, terrible hurts, a burning that would consume her slowly but with no less agony than had she been tarred and tied to a barrel with her bare legs forced apart.

"What's happening?" asked Meg, appearing beside Willa.

"This man just assaulted Odette," Willa told her.

"Assault?" he barked with a laugh of disbelief. "It was just a tap on the arse."

"That is not acceptable behaviour, sir. We'll have to ask you to leave," Meg said quietly but firmly. "We'll take the cost of your dessert off your bill as a gesture of good will."

"Good will?" he spluttered. "She's a liar."

"I'll get your bill now, sir."

His lip curled. "Insult me and expect me to pay for the privilege? Fat chance."

"In that case we'll have to bring the police in," Meg told him, "and report theft as well as an assault. There's a police van at the end of the road."

He stared between the women before him as if he couldn't believe their nerve. Meg crossed to the till and printed the bill.

"Here you are, sir," she said as she held it out to him. "Cash or card?"

"She's been leading me on since I got in here," he snarled, nodding at Odette. "Look at her, the slut."

"Oi, mate," said a new voice. One of the stags had come closer. Willa recognised him as the one she'd noticed earlier, the one resting his fingers on Meg's shoulder. "That's enough, eh?"

The man spun, a snarl on his face. "What's your problem?"

The younger man held up both hands, placating. "No problem. But maybe let this one go. For now, eh?" He gave a smile, a conspiratorial gesture of male solidarity. *Women, what can you do? Men, we can't win.*

For a second Willa thought Odette's attacker was going to throw a punch at the interloper. Then he dropped his shoulders. Willa watched his hands as his fingers fumbled in his wallet. *Cash,* she willed. *Use cash, you big, pig-ugly bastard. For once in your life do something worthwhile. Use cash.*

He pulled out two twenties and threw them in the vague direction of the counter. Willa ducked to pick them up before Meg could react and was at the till a second later. It pinged once as Willa punched the button, a silver coin in her hand less than a second later. The buzzing in her ears had reached a crescendo. The man turned back to look at Odette standing silently behind Meg.

"You'd better be watching for me, bitch," he said, his voice low, the grin on his face even more terrible than the words coming out of his mouth. "You'd better be waiting."

He headed for the door, not even waiting for Stella to stand.

"Just a minute," Willa called after him. "Here's your change."

He turned on his heel and stared at her then came back to the counter. Willa put the coin into his palm, hot from her own hand. Stroked it right down his lifeline and then turned it on its edge. She let it go and the buzzing in her ears ceased, just like that.

He turned his shoulder and walked away. Stella skittered after him. He tugged the door shut behind him, almost hitting her in the face. A second later they were gone.

Silence reigned for a second or two, a tableau of relief. The lad who had intervened turned to look at Odette.

"You really shouldn't go upsetting a man like that," he said.

"Odette, take a break," said Meg. "Go and get some air."

"Maybe she never learned to say 'thank you' in English, eh?" the guy said to Odette's back, as she headed for the kitchen.

"Do you want the bill for your table, too, sir?" Willa asked him. "Take a seat and I'll bring it right over. Cash or card?"

6

Maybe they all had it coming

"Right," said Meg once the last table had cleared. "That's it, I'm locking the door. Why don't you check on Odette?"

The rain had slowed but not stopped. Willa found Odette just outside the kitchen door, leaning against the dank wall of the passageway where they kept the bins, wrapped in Tony's oversized red mac. Her face was half in shadow, the rest of it painted a sickly orange by the single streetlamp overhead. She glanced up as Willa opened the door, then raised a nervous hand to remove the cigarette between her lips.

"Sorry," she said. "I be back in a moment."

"It's fine. Meg and I can finish up. You should go home."

Odette let out a breath as shaky as her hands. The smoke of her exhale twisted up into the smudge of night sky above them, sliced to ribbons by the incessant rain. "Tony is going to drive me home," she said and Willa hated it, the coil of fear around this woman put there by so insignificant a man.

Somewhere beyond the passageway a shout echoed followed

by a hysterical laugh that was soon joined by another, and then a chorus of terrible singing. Just another Friday night in Carlisle.

Beside her, Odette sighed. "Maybe I should just give up, eh? Go back home to Petersburg now, before it all gets even worse."

Willa shifted, lifting her face into the rain. "You mean there aren't men like him in Russia?"

Odette laughed again, her lips around the cigarette. "Good point."

"There will always be men like him," Willa said, eyes closed, rain on her face. "There always have been. Perhaps, after all, that's why there are women like me."

Odette was silent for a while and Willa opened her eyes to find herself being watched with open curiosity. Odette looked as if she was about to say something when a scream echoed to them from the street. It was a man's voice, bright at the edges and dark in the middle, a cacophony of terror exploding like fireworks as one scream crashed into another, then another.

There it is, Willa thought. *That's him. Squeal, pig. Squeal.*

"My God," said Odette. "What's that?"

There were more sounds now. A woman's voice pleading for help. The sound of running feet.

"A fight, probably," Willa said, wanting a cigarette although she had never smoked. *Well, not deliberately,* she thought, with a little bubble of silent laughter. She was a little dizzy, a little euphoric. *This is me,* she thought. *This is what I am for.*

She felt the cut, then. It slid open between two ribs, narrow but deep. There was pain, but it was familiar. She wondered what scar this one would leave behind, amid all those older healed hurts. There was blood too – Willa could feel it welling out of the wound. She bent forward hoping it would stop before it soaked her white work shirt. The scar she was resigned to, the pain was commonplace, but blood was such a nuisance.

Still the screaming lit the sky.

Jesus Christ, Willa thought. *Just die, you piece of shit. Just die.*

"Should we call an ambulance?" Odette asked, but Willa caught her arm before she could reach for her phone.

"I wouldn't bother," she said. "It's too late."

Odette looked at her, her face suddenly unsure. Willa smiled. So many centuries, but humanity never changed. Any excuse to burn another human being. In her day it had been more literal – but still. They all had it coming. Maybe there needed to be consequences. Maybe she existed for a reason. After all, bad things never did just come in threes.

"Why don't you take tomorrow night off?" she said to Odette. "I feel like doing front of house for a while."

I LEFT MY FAIR HOMELAND

Sarah Ash

Elindultam szép hazámból

The man paused to adjust his homburg to fit more snugly, tightened the scarf neatly knotted around his neck and continued his walk. Even though spring blossoms dusted the cherry branches with pink and white, a chill wind blew across the park from the Hudson. Every day he came here in his lunch break to walk beside the lake, in the vain hope of convincing himself that he was not really in this alien, foreign city, but was back home, strolling through the central park in Budapest. Hidden from sight by the trees was the great city with its skyscrapers, roaring traffic and surging crowds. He passed other walkers, mostly women: mothers pushing baby carriages; elegant women of a certain age parading yappy little dogs on leads; only the occasional rowdy shouts of sailors on shore leave gave any hint of the terrible war raging abroad.

In spite of the crisp freshness of the air, he was tiring already, finding it harder to put one foot in front of the other. He could feel the stones in the path through the thin worn leather soles; he must find a cobbler soon as there wasn't enough money to buy a new pair. But in spite of his sore feet he forced himself to keep going until he reached the lake. The waters were grey today, mirroring the troubled clouds overhead, speckled with windblown petals where the wind had ravaged the early blossom. He eased himself onto a bench and stared out across the water, grateful for the restful, dull light. His eyes ached; he had been burying himself in his work at the university library, laboriously notating the Serbian-Croatian folk music archive recorded in Yugoslavia, before war broke, out by two American scholars. Even as he sat there, the traditional melodies of his homeland and neighbouring countries, now devastated by invading armies, still twirled about his brain. He was grateful to the university to have been given the job but the pay was hardly enough to cover the rent of their four-room apartment, let alone food and clothing. In their haste to leave Budapest he and Ditta had brought so little with them, just the bare essentials.

He closed his eyes, tilting his chin upward to feel the wind on his face. Here he could no longer hear the distant roar of the traffic, could forget the bright yellow taxis and their garrulous drivers, gum chewing, always asking who was going to win the game that night, as if he cared.

What use is a composer who doesn't compose?

His music had dried up from the moment they arrived in New York. At first he had assumed it was a temporary interruption, brought on by the stress of displacement and war. His identity, his very reason to live just … melted away.

He had hoped that the contact with the raw folk music, recorded out in the Eastern European countryside in happier days, might have triggered the urge to compose something new. But the weeks had passed and the block was still there.

While his eyes were closed he heard a distant snatch of song. A woman, her voice low and throaty, like the purr of a dove. He knew the song instantly. How could he forget it – or the singer? It was one of the first he had transcribed, the start of a life's obsession.

A warm summer's day in Békés County, under the crumbling walls of Gyula castle. The young man carefully puts down the Edison phonograph he's lugged from the station and wipes the sweat from his face. Cicadas are churring in the linden trees close by; bees buzz around the fragrant blossoms.

And then he hears a woman singing, her voice low and sweet, like the throbbing call of a turtle dove. The words of the song are imbued with homesickness and the melody has a wistful lilt neither major nor minor, but cast in an ancient folk mode, steeped in a sadness, centuries old.

Just what he has been travelling the countryside to capture: the old songs that will soon be lost forever if no one records them, swept away by the fashion for Austrian waltzes, polkas and military marches.

"I left my fair homeland..."

He opened his eyes, blinking as he gazed around to see if he could spot the singer. The path winding around the lake was empty. A thin mist had begun to drift over the grey waters.

I must have nodded off. He was still lost in his memories of that distant hot day when he was young and filled with idealism. *Zoltan and me, trekking from village to village, persuading the villagers to sing the old songs into the horn of our phonograph, recording them for posterity on those fragile wax cylinders...*

How could he have known when he first heard that song that the words would be so prophetic and he would be forced to flee Hungary?

~~~

As he opened the door into the department library he heard music. And not the refined baroque polyphony of Bach or the lyrical rococo counterpoint of Mozart, as he might have expected, but the rough, honest singing of a Yugoslavian peasant, captured on an aluminium disc in a village tavern. Students looked up from their work, frowning at the disturbance. The duty librarian, stern-faced Miss Carson, had already left the central desk, and was tap-tapping briskly on sharp heels toward the source of the music.

As he reached the doorway of his little room he saw her standing staring at the phonograph, scratching her head. The hissing sound emanating from the horn told him it had come to the end of the recording and the needle-tip was grinding against the metal. He walked past the glowering librarian, lifted the arm, and turned off the revolving mechanism.

"Doctor, I'd appreciate it if you made sure—" she began in a furious undertone.

"Someone has been tampering with my equipment." He picked up the disconnected headphones and showed them to her.

Honeyed scent perfuming the air…

Had a cleaner been in, wiping the desk and shelves with some sweet-scented wax polish? It was possible they had tinkered with the phonograph and then fled in panic as music blared out.

"Didn't you lock the door when you went to lunch?" Behind the horn-rimmed lenses her eyes narrowed. Obviously it was his fault; the absent-minded academic had neglected to observe the usual security protocols, resulting in the peace of the library being rudely disturbed.

He thought about assuring her that he had indeed locked the door and that the keys were still in his pocket. But he had been preoccupied when he left; the hire firm had threatened that morning to take away the second piano if he didn't pay the rental and he and Ditta needed both pianos to practise together for concerts, if and when the promised bookings began to materialise, for it was surely only a matter of time…

Sweet scent of linden blossom, wafting on the summer breeze…

He realised that the librarian was still staring at him.

"Well, please make sure this doesn't happen again," she said frostily and stalked away. He closed the door behind her and began to hunt around for clues.

His papers lay where he'd left them, the half-notated song, his fountain pen, neatly capped, pencils, an eraser, the usual paraphernalia needed to facilitate the transcriptions.

He picked up the sheet of music paper, looking at the notes he'd written down earlier that day – and stared again.

"I left my fair homeland…"

His mind must have been wandering for him to have sketched out that song from 1906. Perhaps there was a similarity which had caught his attention between the two melodies, the one recorded by Professor Milman Parry and the song he had recorded himself below Gyula castle? A musicologist could not help but be fascinated by the way folk melodies sometimes crossed centuries and borders, taking on a new identity along the way.

The library staff had hung a couple of framed black-and-white photographs on the wall: one of Professor Parry with a smiling, moustachioed peasant singer, proudly holding a fiddle, taken only six or seven years ago – and the other, in his honour, he assumed, taken over thirty years ago. 1906. He was forced every time he looked up from his work to see his younger self, hair still dark, with the famed Edison phonograph, surrounded by villagers in their local costume. And staring solemnly at the camera, two girls, arms linked, patiently waiting their turn to sing for him.

Lidi.

He stopped to stare back.

"No, you're not Lidi, neither of you. Lidi Dósa was the first to sing for me, the year before Zoltan and I got our hands on the phonograph," he told them.

~~~

Late that night, back in the apartment, the nostalgic flowery perfume haunted him still. Had the librarian dabbed on some lime flower-based perfume? Or was it just in the wax used by the library cleaners? It was far too early in the year for the heavy, honeyed scent of yellow-and-white linden blossom, sweet yet with that subtle, bitter undertone. And yet the memories it had conjured up from his past...

The weak electric light in the apartment was making his eyes ache. He took off his glasses and pressed fingertips to closed eyelids to relieve the discomfort. When he opened his eyes again, blinking, the sheet of manuscript paper on the desk in front of him was still blank, the staves empty of notes, his pencil lying where he had left it.

Another day gone and no new work achieved. He closed his eyes again, leaning back in the chair, trying to ignore the distant roar outside, of the city that never slept.

He had brought the sound of a modern city to life, the endless roar of traffic, the discordant parping of car horns, the relentless to-and-fro of crowds of faceless strangers, all portrayed in an orchestral score for a ballet that critics had labelled so shocking, immoral and avant-garde that performances had been banned, forcing him to rescue some – but not all – of the music as a concert suite. But that was nearly twenty years ago. He had written much more music since then, synthesizing the rhythms and clashing harmonies of the folksongs he had collected into his own unique style, until—

Until war had broken out, forcing him into exile. And now he could not compose. He had nothing to say. It all seemed pointless. He could no longer hear the melodies that used to wreathe around his mind, intriguing and tormenting him in equal measure.

A gentle tap at the door roused him; Ditta appeared, wrapped in a blue blanket; she looked as worn and tired as he felt himself.

"It's late, Béla."

"Go to bed," he said, not unkindly. "I'll follow soon."

"Shall I make you a tisane to help you sleep? Chamomile? Or lime blossom?"

"Lime blossom," he said automatically. When she reappeared with a steaming cup some minutes later she smiled as she set it down on the desk.

"I wish we had some madeleines for you to accompany the tea," she said, a little wistfully. He nodded in appreciation. Proust was one of his favourite authors and as he sniffed the fragrant steam arising from the cup he found himself making a wish.

If only the scent of lime flowers could release the music in my mind along with the memories.

"They offered me a sponge cake called a 'Twinkie bar' at the grocery store but it has some kind of vanilla cream in it." She pulled a face. "I didn't think you'd like it."

He suppressed a shudder at the thought; he detested any food or drink with ersatz flavours and America factory-made food seemed to rely on such staples. Still, in wartime, at least they had food where others back at home were suffering terrible deprivation. As he sipped his tea he closed his eyes again, trying to recapture that hot summer's day beneath the castle walls ... and the lilting voice of a young girl singing.

<center>~~~</center>

"I left my fair homeland..."

His heart missed a beat. A woman was in his office, her back to the door, and the phonograph turntable was spinning. For a moment he thought the music issuing from the horn was not one of Professor Milman Parry's Serbo-Croatian folksongs, but instead the one he had recorded himself on a warm summer's day beneath the old walls of Gyula castle. So similar...

He opened the door to the office and the song filled the darkened library. The woman turned to him as the needle reached the end of the disc and the song faded into hissing. In the yellow-ochre electric light he saw the librarian, Miss Carson, her eyes dull and unfocussed behind the thick lenses of her horn-rimmed spectacles. She moved unnaturally slowly, as if she were a puppet controlled by an unseen hand.

"Why did you choose that song?" he asked, his voice strained and hoarse as he carefully lifted the needle from the disc. "That one in particular?"

"I— I don't know. It was one *he* liked to listen to."

"He? Professor Milman Parry?"

"I'm so sorry." She seemed flustered. "I should have asked your permission. It's— When I heard you playing it this morning, it brought back ... memories."

"You were appointed to look after the archive," he said politely, "so you have as much of a right as I to explore the recordings."

"Why were *you* listening to that song, Doctor?"

"Me?" The directness of her question took him aback.

"Is there something different about it? Something unusual?"

He considered his answer carefully. "I thought I detected a

similarity in the construction of the melody with an old song I recorded in Békés County long years ago. Sometimes songs travel from country to country."

"It's just—" she fiddled with her spectacles, as if searching for the right words "—after the professor's tragic death there were … rumours."

"Rumours?"

"Silly, unsubstantiated stuff. Unworthy of scholars, if you ask me, spreading such superstitious nonsense."

"Such as?"

"That there'd been a curse laid upon him by some gipsy woman in Yugoslavia. Because he'd dared to 'steal' the old songs by recording them."

"Or preserving them for posterity?" He felt himself smiling wryly. If Professor Parry had been cursed for stealing the old songs, then surely he was equally culpable.

"Although Albert Lord said that one of the peasants warned him that one of the songs brought 'bad luck'."

"Mr Lord? Parry's assistant?" He had met the young man, recently appointed a Junior Fellow, but nothing had been mentioned about songs that brought misfortune. There was the rumoured curse of the Ninth Symphony, of course, as so many composers – Beethoven, Schubert, Bruckner, Mahler – had not lived to complete a tenth. *But I'm no symphonist and never have been. And at this rate, my list of compositions is already complete.*

~~~

As he turned the corner of the street he saw three removal men struggling to carry an upright piano down the steep steps of their apartment block.

He stopped, staring, as did several passers-by, including a couple of children who started pointing and jeering at the sweating men. It could have been a comical scene, bringing to mind countless slapstick sequences from the movies, the hilarious antics of Laurel and Hardy or Buster Keaton – and the children were doubtless hoping to witness something similar. But there were no cameras turning, no bright lights – only one woman watching from the front door, silhouetted against the electric light in the hallway, her hands covering her mouth as if suppressing the urge to call out, "Please, be careful."

He recognised Ditta and realised with a sinking feeling it was their upright piano that was being taken away. They had not managed to raise enough funds to pay for another month's rental and this was the consequence. Now they would have to take turns to practise on the single remaining instrument – and any hopes of securing engagements to play music for two pianos were dwindling fast.

He turned away from the scene. He could not bear to see the distraught expression on his wife's face as the removers manhandled the piano into their waiting van. Instead, tired as he was, he set out to walk once more around the block, hoping that the removal men would have gone by the time he returned.

~~~

"A letter for you, Doctor." The music librarian on duty today was Miss Carson again. She handed him the envelope without a comment, not even meeting his eyes. So he was still in disgrace. He took it, seeing with a quickening of the pulse that it had been forwarded from another major orchestra via his publishers, and hurried into his office to read it.

"Thank you for offering us the opportunity to perform your…" The standard acknowledgments, polite but distant. But then followed those words he had read too often in the past months. "It is with great regret that we are unable to proceed; the current world situation means that to perform any work from a composer whose home country is currently in league with the Nazi regime would be wholly unacceptable to our sponsors and…"

Another rejection.

He set out on his daily stroll through the park. He passed the usual nannies with their perambulators, the elegant socialites promenading their tiny dogs… The letter weighed like lead in his pocket. How was he to break the news to Ditta? She would be so disappointed. One after another, the orchestras had turned down his works, refusing to play them – even though he and Ditta had fled Hungary to escape arrest, and their son Peter had enrolled in the US Navy. No performances meant no income. One rental piano had been taken away; how soon before the other would be removed as well?

And then he caught a breath of flowery perfume. He glanced up, confused. It was far too early in the year for that heavy, honeyed scent of yellow-and-white linden blossom, sweet yet with a subtle bitter undertone.

It must have been the perfume wafting from one of the New York women who had passed him by on the path around the lake, elegant on their high heels, with their little clutch bags and scarlet lips, chic, self-assured and utterly oblivious of his presence.

~~~

"Good day."

He glanced up, startled. He was certain there had been no one about; even the noisy ducks on the lake had fallen silent. Yet there she was, a young woman, smiling at him.

And then, blinking into the harsh grey light, he recognised her. "It's *you*." Lidi Dósa.

"I told you we would meet again." There it was once more, the shy smile that had bewitched him so many years ago. "Béla."

She knew his name. But how could she be the same girl? Nearly forty years had passed yet she looked – to his tired eyes – as pretty as she had back then, with her soft brown eyes and arching dark brows.

It had to be a prank, set up by some of the music students. He'd barked at them more than once to keep the noise down in the library as he struggled to make sense of the scratchy recordings. They must have plotted this; even now they were probably hiding in the bushes close by, smothering laughter.

"Lidi?"

She reached out and caught his right hand in hers, turning it over to stroke his palm with a swift feather-light touch.

"Tell your fortune?" A mischievous gleam lit her dark eyes.

"You're not a gipsy." He tried to extricate his hand. He didn't like to be touched by strangers. Although this girl's grip, surprisingly strong for one so slender, was not displeasing. He glanced toward the bushes behind her, expecting the students to make their presence known, pointing at the bemused old man and the girl – and laughing.

But no one appeared.

Then he blinked, seeing, as a thin cloud passed across the sun, the shadow of a hollow-eyed skull beneath the pretty face. Startled, he tried to jerk his hand away but she held tight, leaning in close until he was afraid she was going to kiss him.

She laughed and as the cloud drifted away, the grinning-skeletal vision faded. Was he still awake? Or was he dreaming?

"Who— No, *what* are you?" he asked. "You're not— You can't be ... Lidi."

"I think you already know," she said softly. "Sometimes the yearning for one's country is so strong it becomes a sickness. A mortal sickness. The seeds are already sown within you, Béla. You know it, don't you? The longer you're absent from the life-giving air of our homeland the more you're wasting away. You're so tired, so very tired..."

It was true. But what choice had there been? If he and Ditta had stayed behind they would have been imprisoned, even dead by now.

"Did you come to warn me?"

She drew a little closer and, answering his question with another, said, "If you could make one wish, what would it be? To be well again? Or to reawaken your gift? To write music again?"

That proved it; he must be dreaming. He smiled. "You have to ask?"

"I can grant that wish. Just as my singing you the old songs my grandma taught me did back then. I kindled that flame in you, Béla. I can re-kindle it. But it comes at a price."

"And that price?" he asked although he had already guessed what it would be.

She leaned in and pressed her mouth to his. He tried to pull away, tasting at first a foul, foetid aroma on her saliva, bringing back the savour of the smothering kisses he had tried to wriggle out of as a child from elderly great-aunties, the taint of their rotting gums half-concealed by the violet comfits they liked to suck. But then the sickly sweetness sharpened, flooding his mind with a kaleidoscopic burst of sounds and memories. The rhythmic stamping of peasant dancers, swirling in their Sunday best, building to a torrent of forgotten songs, a musical map of his homeland unfolding before his eyes, rich and vibrantly colourful.

She drew back from him slowly, lingeringly, her dark eyes still fixed on his, and said, "There. It's done. You wished it so and I granted your wish."

He stared at her, still hearing the wild skirling of lost melodies, as if a troupe of wandering Magyar musicians were passing by, playing fiddles, pipes and drums, travelling from village to village.

A gust of wind ruffled the surface of the lake, stirring up little eddies of dust from the lakeside path, setting his eyes watering. He fumbled in his coat pocket for his handkerchief to wipe them and when he could see clearly again he was alone. The ducks were quacking loudly from the choppy water, two pug dogs were yapping at each other further along the path, and he could hear the distant, ever-present roar of the traffic once more. The scent of linden blossom was gone, replaced by the odour of the lake, mud mingled with waterweed.

She was gone. But he became aware of the ghost of a melody at the back of his mind, one that felt at once familiar yet also strangely fresh and new. He took out his little notebook and a stub of pencil and began to scribble it down before it eluded him. And the more he scribbled the more the music welled up from the depths of his homesickness, a passionate elegy for his homeland that he was now permanently exiled from.

Later that evening he sat down at his desk in the apartment, took out the blank stave paper and began to write, feverishly trying to capture the essence of what he had experienced by the lake. The musical language was a distillation of all his years wandering, collecting, notating, assimilating, and now he was making it into something uniquely his own.

He was so absorbed that he did not even hear Ditta tiptoe in until her shadow fell over his work.

"Are you feeling all right, Béla?" She placed her hand on his forehead, the touch of cool fingers sending a shiver through him. "You look flushed."

"Just a little tired after a long day," he said, taking off his spectacles to pinch the bridge of his nose. His body ached; he must have caught a chill in the cold wind by the lake.

She gazed over his shoulder at the spatter of notes filling the staves and then at him. "But this is new...?"

He nodded, not daring to jinx the first bars he'd written in months by confirming it to be so, not out loud. It was merely the seed of an idea, one that would need careful nurturing – but it also felt like the keystone, the heart of something on a much grander scale. Perhaps even that elusive symphony.

"That was Jozsef Szigeti on the telephone just now." He had not heard the phone ring but he caught the tremor of excitement in her voice. "He thinks that maestro Koussevitzky might be interested in commissioning a new work from you."

He smiled up at her. "Jozsef is a good friend. He wants to help, but—"

"He's performing the Brahms concerto with Koussevitzky and the Boston Symphony Orchestra. Such an opportunity! And he's going to suggest your name to the maestro. So, don't give up hope just yet." And then she said, "You hardly touched your food at supper. Would you like a warming drink? Tea?"

"Lime-flower," he said, distantly. "Linden blossom."

As he sipped the fragrant yellow-green tea, inhaling the scent of summers long gone, he looked over the notes he had written, hearing the plangent reedy plaint of the oboe, the sobbing strings...

Elegia.

She had said there would be a price. But what a gift she had given him in return. To carry the spirit of the forgotten music into a new land, to new listeners...

~~~

Bartok's Concerto for Orchestra was commissioned by Serge Koussevitzky and first performed by the Boston Symphony Orchestra in December 1944. It has five movements, of which the third is called "Elegia".

Béla Bartók, Hungarian composer, died yesterday morning at the West Side Hospital after a long illness at the age of 64. One of the most important composers of modern music, he was also an outstanding specialist in musical folklore and a teacher of wide repute.
<div align="right">

New York Times, September 27, 1945
</div>

DIGGING IN THE DIRT

Mike Chinn

The place had changed. He'd expected that after eighty years. Didn't seem to be for the better, though. Last time he'd been here you could see the Manhattan skyline to the west; now, although that skyline was quite a few storeys taller, the view was blocked by a busy road bridge. Plus there was a thin mist obscuring the few buildings he could see, despite the bright, hot sunlight. Pollution, he'd been told.

"And this is where it all started."

He glanced back at the blue-eyed woman standing on the sidewalk, dressed in a jumpsuit the colour of her eyes, a matching purse hanging from her left shoulder by a gold chain. She'd changed, too. She'd kept her hair blonde though, even if it now fell halfway down her back. And she'd never have gotten away with that slinky blue number back in the day.

They'd flown straight up from Florida, stopping just to buy him clothes that didn't make him look like an extra from an old movie. T-shirt and cargo pants. He felt underdressed next to her.

"For you, maybe." Damian Paladin returned his attention to the deserted gas station spread out before him. It was stripped of all brand logos, the gas pumps vandalised, canopy sagging, bracketed on three sides by vacant lots. Everything looked forlorn, forgotten. On the far side of the street was a stretch of what once might have been warehouses, or some kind of factory. The rows of windows were blackened and blind, some of the panes broken. The peeling white walls were daubed with colourful symbols and letters. A private code. There were even sigils – old and powerful patterns – which managed to not look out of place among the graffiti. That intrigued him. He wondered how whoever had splashed them up there had known which ones to use. Or had they just been operating on gut level? Tagging the neighbourhood with ciphers dredged up from a collective unconscious?

"Didn't there used to be a sign?"

"Just there." She pointed at a spot right in the middle of the cracked road.

"You sure?"

She flashed him a smug grin. "Who's the one with the eidetic memory, O returning hero?"

Eidetic memory? Sounded like somebody had swallowed a dictionary sometime in the last eighty years. Paladin returned his attention to the run-down gas station. Some of the sigils had been painted on the building's bleached sides. They didn't look as fresh as the ones across the street: they were discoloured, flaking. Burned.

A car horn tooted. He turned in time to see a large silver two-door coupe turning onto the cracked weedy forecourt. He recognised the double-R insignia and hood ornament, if nothing else. The last Rolls Royce he remembered seeing was a fussy rich maiden aunt; this looked like a predator.

The coupe pulled to a halt; both doors swung open and two men stepped out. The driver was dressed in an expensive looking pale-grey suit, the other an open-neck black shirt and flared pants, with unruly hair and eyes in the same colour. Just like Paladin's.

"We get you out of bed, Raven?"

Andy Raven glanced down at his clothes. He made an elaborate head to foot gesture. A moment later he was dressed in faded black hoodie and jeans. "So how was the lakeside vacation, junior?"

"Deathless beings from beyond time. Crazy acolytes. The usual. You'd've loved it. Good to be back, though."

Grey suit took the woman's right hand and kissed it. "How are you, Miss Oswin? It's been too long."

"Leo." She let the so-called Count Saint-Germain paw her a little longer before taking back her hand. "And I've gotten used to Adrestia."

"Ah yes, your ascent to near godhood." Saint-Germain took a step back. "Immortality suits you, my dear – although I trust we won't need to call on your vengeful alter-ego today. Eternals bring me out in a rash." He glanced meaningfully at Raven.

Leigh – she'd always be Leigh to Paladin, not Adrestia, not Ludmilla Tatiana – looked uncomfortable. Paladin regretted he hadn't been around during the years when her dual nature was asserting itself. She'd done okay, though, growing into her new identity. Even jumping feet first into the kind of cases they'd investigated together, or so she told him. The new name was just another from a line of aliases, adopted after World War Two was over, when "Leigh Oswin" started to get inconvenient. There'd always come a time when people wondered why she wasn't getting any older while they grew grey and wrinkled.

"Time's a-wastin', people." Paladin led them towards the empty building. He didn't go more than a couple of yards before he felt it, a warm prickle along the scalp, a twinge of unease in the gut. The sense that someone, or something, was just behind him, matching his footsteps. The traffic noise all but died, too.

Inside, the station was stripped bare. What had once most probably been a small convenience store was just floor, walls, and glass front. The shelves, counters and registers long removed. It smelled musty, and old. The only marks on the floor were their own footprints in an inch of dust.

The sense of unease was more intense. Paladin felt like he could cut himself a slice of it. He turned to face them all. "Everybody want to get in position?"

All four spread out in a small circle, facing inward. Consciously or not, they had arranged themselves with their backs to the cardinal points of the compass: the Count in the north position, Raven south, Leigh to the west, and Paladin east. The silence intensified.

"Raven, you're up." Leigh's voice was at once both familiar and unfamiliar. There was an authority which hadn't existed eighty years ago. Paladin guessed that after riding tandem with an aspect of divine vengeance, something was bound to rub off.

Raven rubbed his hands together, clicking his neck from side to side. "Hold onto your hats, ladies and gentlemen."

Saint-Germain sighed theatrically.

Spreading his hands wide, Raven took a deep breath. Then he brought his hands close together, palms almost touching. He exhaled softly. Between the facing palms Paladin could just make out a glowing sphere of light. Gradually, as the group's breathing fell into synch, the glow brightened. Raven drew his hands apart, inch by inch. The sphere grew by degrees, becoming the size of a golf ball, a basketball, a car tyre. Eventually a dazzling orb floated between Raven's hands, his arms stretched as wide as they'd go.

He spoke a word.

The orb expanded to fill the whole room, losing none of its radiance. Paladin felt his clothes and hair ripple as it engulfed him. For a moment he was blind – then the brilliance snapped off. Around them the floor and walls sparkled, the window had taken on a mirror sheen. There was a smell like ozone.

Raven dropped his arms, flexing his fingers. "That's it. We're sealed in. Whatever happens here, stays here."

Saint-Germain raised an eyebrow. "Is that meant to be a movie reference? My turn, I believe?"

He unbuttoned his suit coat. Underneath was a gold vest decorated with a variety of alchemical and masonic symbols. He tugged at its front and the whole vest came free. Kneeling, Saint-Germain spread it across the floor, unrolling it like an oddly shaped carpet. Once in place it took the form of a pentagram, the symbols forming two inner circles, the vest's edges the angles.

Saint-Germain stood, re-buttoning his coat. "Do you have any idea how much that cost...?"

"Real joy comes not from ease or riches or from the praise of men," Raven quoted, "but from doing something worthwhile."

The Count sniffed. "Have I ever told you how much I hate you?"

"Not since we stepped out of the car." Raven turned his dark eyes on Leigh. "My Lady Adrestia?"

Leigh gave him a brief nod and reached inside her purse, taking out a hand-sized object that was part hammer, part throwing star. Its intricate patterning seemed to fold in upon itself. She raised it to eye level. As she did so her face altered, becoming more angular, paler, harsher. She blinked and her eyes turned to ice – with vertical pupils. Jagged electric discharges walked across the raised weapon. Paladin heard the crackling. The sweet smell of ozone thickened.

She flung the purse aside, bending low with a fluid motion. The strange weapon descended; lightning trailed in its wake. It struck Saint-Germain's pentagram vest dead centre and a huge rent split the floor. Light poured out of it: actinic white, shot through with spears of cold blue.

There was the sound of colliding worlds, a rumble as deafening as the light was blinding. Paladin didn't think he lost consciousness, but the sensory deprivation was just as complete. For an eternal moment he neither heard nor saw.

His vision returned slowly, blurred purple dots swirling, gradually resolving into three figures. Leigh's mouth was moving.

"—Damy, your turn at bat."

They appeared to be standing on nothing. Where there should have been concrete, dirt or foundations, was a dim void. Paladin wasn't looking at what lay under the gas station any longer. Stretched out at his feet, in all directions, was just a step to the right from the reality containing the empty convenience store. Sideways on.

"C'mon, junior," said Raven. "We don't have all day."

Paladin eased a kink in his shoulders. "I hate this bit."

Way back, before he'd crossed paths with an on-the-run girl calling herself Leigh Oswin, there had been a disused airfield right on this spot. He'd effectively been squatting there, along with a couple of beaten up kites left over from the so-called Great War. Nearby, Leigh had hidden a pile of – not exactly stolen – Russian jewellery that needed laundering. It had set them both up. He'd never let on he knew all along where she'd buried it, but then he had a secret of his own. His own stash hidden under the airfield. Things he'd acquired over the centuries: some useful, some best left buried and forgotten. He'd never meant to leave them, always intending to put them somewhere more secure. A *one day* that never came. In 1937, events took over and he never got the chance.

The stash was well guarded so he'd never worried someone might dig it up by accident. The deserted gas station, vacant lots and sigils dotted about the place attested to his wards' effectiveness. Still, it was time to move it on, with the help of Raven, the Count, Leigh, and their various talents.

But he had to dig the stash up first. As the one who'd buried and warded it in the first place, only he could do that. Except the wards weren't always fussy, and after a while they grew forgetful. He'd have to tread carefully.

"Ready or not, here I come," he muttered, and took a forward step. His foot dipped a little below the invisible surface. Another step, another few inches lower. Step by step he appeared to head westward, yet never moved so much as a fraction forward. Only down.

He sank lower. Leigh, Raven and Saint-Germain rose above him, their tense faces tracking his descent. There was a last glimpse of Leigh's high-heeled sandals, then blackness.

Paladin pulled a small flashlight out of his pants and snapped it on. It cast a beam which speared the gloom, fading into an invisible distance. The darkness felt thick and solid – he still walked on *something* – but nothing intercepted the flashlight beam.

"*Yehi 'or,*" he murmured, using the words just for old time's sake.

A faint glow grew around him, turning the blackness to grey, then a dark opalescence. He stood at the centre of a universe where there were no points of illumination, just an overall background glow. Nothing flashy like Raven would have conjured, with rainbow stars, blazing comets, and brilliantly lit floating paths. But it worked. He pocketed the flashlight.

Paladin continued walking although he had even less sense of movement. He was suspended in the dim glow, a cartoon figure going through the motions against a stuck background. He felt the wards, alerted by his presence, outraged. One by one he deactivated them. Like falling off a log…

A more intense point of light grew in the distance, gradually resolving into an old battered suitcase. Ridiculously mundane. Within moments it was at his feet, held up by the same nothing he stood on. Paladin gave it a quick inspection: it was kicked around some, scarred, its corners scuffed. The kind of thing you took on vacation and left there.

He grabbed the brown handle and raised it, carefully. The case was heavy, like someone had packed a few gold bars for the trip. Wrapping both arms around it he turned and, he hoped, retraced his invisible steps.

Easy. Maybe he didn't need the others after all.

The background glow wavered for a second, almost winking out. The dull glow flickered again, this time changing to a deep red. It was like walking through a vast photographer's studio.

He tried to remember how many wards he'd deactivated. Clearly, he'd missed one.

Paladin speeded up. The light darkened. If blood could glow, this was what it would look like. He hoped he was near the exit; he wouldn't know until his head broke free. He glanced over his shoulder though he knew it was a pointless action. It could be coming from any direction. It could be right in front of —

Ordinary daylight half-blinded him. His head was raised up

through the convenience store's floor. Leigh, Raven and Saint-Germain were still looking at him.

"You get it?" asked Raven.

Paladin nodded, trying to haul himself up out of the void quicker than he'd entered. "I'm not coming back alone."

Raven muttered something under his breath and reached down. Paladin rose almost to waist level. The man in black grabbed the suitcase handle and pulled. Paladin was hauled free of the floor. Raven swung him aside before dropping both him and case untidily.

"Seal it, quick!"

Leigh's axe and Saint-Germain's vest had reappeared. They snatched up both items. The floor quickly lost its transparency. All four backed towards the door.

The floor erupted. Concrete and dirt showered the empty room. Something huge and shapeless and the colour of putrefying meat oozed through the hole. It reared, scraping the ceiling with a blunt heaving mass which might have been a head. There was a yawning hole in there, constantly swallowing itself and reforming.

"Your pet looks pissed," commented Saint-Germain.

Leigh raised her odd weapon. It reflected the cold fire in her eyes. "Did you forget to feed it, Damy?"

Raven reached behind him, hand closing around something Paladin couldn't see. As Raven pulled his hand back, a long delicate rapier slid out of the air. Its blade was jet black.

The Count looked impressed. "Neat trick."

Raven grinned. "I like to keep it handy."

The thing slid further out of the hole. Its squirming body ebbed and flowed in a way that made Paladin's eyes ache. Raven and Leigh stepped forward, their weapons raised. Both spilled light from spectrums alien to Earth.

Paladin dropped the suitcase to the floor and clicked open both locks.

The guardian surged towards them. Leigh and Raven sliced at its squirming form, hacking off chunks which flopped to the floor, only to flow back to the main body and reunite with it.

"You're just making it mad," the Count remarked.

"Feel free to join in any time." Raven ducked as a thick limb groped for him.

Paladin rooted through the suitcase. It was far too large inside, the contents enough to fill a dumpster. He found what he was looking for – two silvery twists of metal that could have been jars, or handles – and tossed one to Saint-Germain.

"Hold it up, Leo!"

The Count did so. Paladin stepped to the far side of the window. Now the thing was almost equidistant between him and Saint-Germain.

"Leigh! Raven! Get down!"

They ducked without question. Paladin raised his twisted piece of metal and yelled a simple phrase. *"Jatuh mati!"*

The surging mass paused. Its amorphous head appeared to turn Paladin's way.

"You heard, ugly. Do what you're told. *Jatuh mati!*"

The thing split. The halves flowed up towards the hand-held shapes, moving with all the grace of cooling lava. Paladin felt the impact as it made contact with the object in his hand. It pulled, reluctant to surrender. Paladin's feet scraped against the floor.

"Hold on, Leo."

"That had never occurred to me."

The thing gave an abrupt surge, its halves flowing, shrinking, disappearing inside the twists of metal. Once it was gone Paladin gestured to Saint-Germain. The Count threw his object across.

Catching it, Paladin snapped both pieces together. They fitted smoothly, with no sign of a join. The resemblance to a bottle was even stronger. Sighing with relief, Paladin dropped it back into the suitcase and snapped the lid shut.

"There," he said to Raven. "All yours."

Raven lowered his black rapier. "And why should I take it?"

Saint-Germain stepped forward. "I'll have it if—"

"No, that's okay, Leo." Raven hefted the case like it weighed next to nothing. "I'm sure junior knows what he's doing."

Leigh grinned. "Guess there's a first time for everything."

"Well, if that's it?" Raven included them all in a glance, nodding farewell. A moment later he slid out of view. Before he vanished he seemed to age, his jeans and hoodie flowing into long robes.

"That was rather rushed and enigmatic," said Saint-Germain. His vest hung carelessly from one hand. "Even for him."

Paladin opened the door and stepped outside. The sound of traffic was instantly loud and intrusive. "Thanks, Leo. Couldn't have done it without you."

"I know you couldn't." He shook Paladin's hand and kissed Leigh's. "*Adieu*, to you both." He slid into the Rolls Royce and drove slowly away.

"And then there were two." Leigh glanced at the deserted gas station. It looked sunken, about to collapse. "You have any plans – apart from catching up on eighty years' history?"

He shrugged. "I guess Damian Paladin died years ago. No point bringing him back. Besides, I hear this Adrestia dame has pretty much put him out of business."

"Woman, please." They started to walk towards a black Chevrolet SUV parked fifty yards away. "Although she could always use a partner."

"I left my hero suit in Florida."

"It would have been out of fashion, anyhow." She looked him up and down. "How do you feel about spandex? And a cape?"

He had no idea what she was talking about. And he was frightened to ask.

THE PRIMORDIAL LIGHT

John Howard

Strandby was a quiet place, and cheap. Those considerations fulfilled my main criteria. It was also easy to find. As I drove along the narrow lanes the alternatives seemed to gradually and inexorably reduce, with no effort needed from me. As long as I kept on heading towards the sea – the direction in which the sky was tallest and deepest – and avoided taking any of the diminishing number of turnings that presented themselves, I felt reassured that I could not get lost. And so when the road ran out there was nowhere else I could be but my intended destination.

The road broadened out into a combined turning circle and car park. There were a few other cars there, and I parked mine with plenty of room to spare, manoeuvring so that I could drive straight out again with no fuss or bother. The sound of the engine was replaced by that of the breeze coming off the sea, and I sat still while my mind adjusted.

My shoes scrunched on gravel and decayed tarmac as I walked round to take my holdall from the back of the car. Leaving the car park there was still only one direction to go, unless I wanted to walk back the way I'd come. Beyond the parked cars, wire fencing that had seen better days prevented me from walking to the left or right across rough windswept grass; I was channelled onwards, towards the cluster of low buildings that was Strandby.

As the term had approached its end, I had been longing for the time when I could take a short break. Now the academic year was finally over it had become a necessity. A few days, a week, would be enough. I just wanted to get somewhere away from all students, and where I could not possibly meet certain pompous colleagues or self-important administrative staff. I wanted to walk where no one could possibly know me or care, or wander on a stretch of beach where I could see anyone else coming from a long way off. I wanted not to have to do anything – even to get out of bed – unless I wanted to.

The internet is a wonderful thing – even as I dreamed of being beyond its reach. I searched for short-term holiday lettings and cancellations, and short-listed a number of possibilities. Then I'd mentioned what I was planning to one of my few friends. He is a native of Lincolnshire, and although he hasn't lived there for decades, never misses an opportunity to sing its praises. He thought for a moment before launching into a reminiscence of a childhood holiday on the Lincolnshire coast, at a place hardly anyone had heard of – then, at least. A couple of decades ago, apparently, Strandby was quiet and little-known. For a teenager on holiday with his family it was torture. My friend was tactful enough not to say that for someone like me, who wanted to get away from it all and at minimum cost, it should be ideal. Assuming Strandby hadn't changed beyond recognition, of course.

"It's a remote place – and yet isn't," he said. "Not in miles from anywhere, anyway. It's paradoxical. People forget how much of the county there is east of Lincoln. And along that coast there are areas people still don't really bother to seek out. You'll have no trouble finding Strandby, and you'll be just about the only one who does. Everyone else seems to prefer somewhere like Skegness or Mablethorpe – real Babylons."

Although I have lived well inland all my life, I have always been drawn to the coast. The few holidays my parents had been able to afford for us during my childhood and adolescence were spent in seaside resorts. I particularly remembered staying in Brighton over successive years: the steep shingle beach, the miniature railway, the pier. From our hotel in a side street near the then incomplete marina I would walk into the centre of Brighton along Marine Parade, staying on the seaward side, before walking back along the beach. Sometimes I'd do the reverse. I particularly liked to walk into Brighton in the evening, when the sun was setting over the Palace Pier and the single tall block of flats that dominated the seafront beyond it.

On the beach I would look for driftwood and pieces of sea glass – those remnants of broken bottles and jars buffeted and smoothed by the tide until worn and rounded. I would hold them up to the swollen orange sun. Most of the pieces of glass had been clear, and then been scoured to a consistently dull grey-white, the colour of winter clouds; but I sometimes found fragments that had kept something of their original colour. I prized these scarred and frosted jewels in green, brown, blue, and red. I must have collected a boxful of them over the years before I lost interest and my parents made me throw them away.

Education and work ensured that I remained inland. I found myself living in a place of rolling hills and steep dry valleys, as close as I could afford to the remaining woods and fields. But even as I lived in a high place, I never quite lost my affection for the sea – or, rather, the flat border strip of stones or sand between it and the land.

~~~

Light battered me. Its intensity was almost physical. It didn't only pour from of the glaring eye of the sun, now a little past the meridian, but it also seemed to flood out of the entire sky, from all directions at once. And this was while I was still wearing my dark glasses! Although the light swallowed me it was not at all hot. There was a steady breeze off the sea, not itself cool but keeping the blue air from muffling all in a transparent shroud of heat. I strode on, feeling more and more alive with every step. I could not yet see the sea but it was close by and made its presence felt. Gravel crunched underfoot.

As I walked past the first building, a large wooden hut, a sunburned man emerged into the sunshine and nodded at me. The hut was a general store, presumably mainly for the convenience of visitors. I wondered if it stayed open throughout the winter as well. Next to the shop was the pub, the Sovereign. I had imagined strolling there for a quiet meal and drink after a long walk on the beach – when I could be bothered to leave the bungalow I had rented.

Most of Strandby was an outcropping of holiday bungalows, reasonably sturdily built by the look of them. They partially surrounded the original hamlet, which consisted of the pub and a few stolid cottages. Most of the bungalows stood between the older buildings and the beach. According to the directions I'd been sent, my property for the week was located off the footpath leading to the steps down to the beach. The key would be under the mat.

The interior of the bungalow was clean and white – as intensely white as the freshly-painted exterior, which had shone, almost painfully, in the sun as I approached it. There were some small prints on the walls, cheaply framed and faded by exposure to light. The furniture was pale; the curtains and rugs were as faded as the pictures. My first impression was of whiteness, tempered by patches of washed-out colour, where pattern and design had not been able to maintain themselves against the onslaught of light.

It was in the kitchen that I had a shock of colour – and memory. Standing on the windowsill, in the full glare of the early afternoon sun, was a glass dish. I reached out to move it; I recalled being told that it could be dangerous to let the rays of the sun focus through glass, as it could start a fire. In the bowl were what I first thought were a few boiled sweets: green, red, white, they glowed in the sunlight, lighting up the dish and providing the only proper colour I'd so far seen in the bungalow. I didn't ask myself why the sweets hadn't melted in the heat. When I picked up the dish the sweets revealed themselves to be rounded, smoothed pieces of glass. I immediately recognised them as being pieces of sea glass. That was the shock to my memory. I still moved the dish out of the direct sunlight, and as I unpacked the few things I'd brought with me I remembered the holidays on the coast I'd had as a boy, my wanderings on beaches, and the box of sea glass fragments I had once had.

~~~

I quickly slid into a routine. I bought some basic supplies at the shop so I could make breakfast and sandwiches for the day. In the evening I went to the Sovereign for a hot meal and drinks. During the day I wandered up and down the beach. Sometimes I sat down and rested away from the sand, in the shade of bushes or by one of the embankments built against flooding. I emptied my mind, letting my body cope admirably on its own. The sunshine was relentless; in the shop and pub I overheard snatches of conversation about how good a summer it was turning out to be. I agreed, when I was spoken to. I nodded and smiled, and said how much I enjoyed the light and heat. The constant breeze kept the temperature tolerable; I wore dark glasses and a cap so I could walk outside without discomfort.

I rarely saw anyone on the beach. For some reason other visitors preferred to be lured inland, leaving the beach and the sea to me. Each morning I was woken by the slamming of car doors and the revving of engines, and later observed the almost empty car park. It was as if visitors to Strandby, as well as its inhabitants, turned their backs on the beach and looked to the land to which their houses clung rather than the sea which could sweep them all away. I was fully aware that although the beach seemed unchanging it was shifting continually. The scene changed by the moment even as it looked as solid and enduring as the country built up behind it.

Seen from the beach, the sea and the sky tended to merge. It was difficult to tell where one ended and the other began. Looking inland or ahead provided a distraction as there the boundaries between sky and water and sand were clearly defined. But even so, the penetrating quality of the sunlight – which always seemed to pour down from all around, as if I were under a solid dome – took all colours and textures into itself. Perhaps everything was simply made from light existing in different states.

I criss-crossed the beach in vast diagonals, from the constantly scoured sand at the sea's edge to the tired and dried-out sand, littered with rubbish, at the edge of the sea defences. And I always kept alert for pieces of driftwood and sea glass.

The third morning was hot again. The beach unrolled around me. I wandered the sand. Eventually my mind must have settled into a reverie, because I was shocked into recalling my surroundings. Close by, someone had shouted something. Without realising it I had walked to within a few yards of a man kneeling on the sand. As I approached he stood and muttered something. Then he dropped the object he had been holding, presumably something he had noticed and been examining.

"Good morning," I said.

"Morning. Ah, that was no good."

"Pardon?"

He looked at me as if I should have known what he meant. He was about my height, and much the same age, as far as I could tell. He was lithe and windburned, wearing loose khaki shorts and battered sandals. His shirt had once been a deep red or mauve, but had worn and faded to a rosy flesh colour. Several of the buttons were missing; others were undone. It was splattered with white patches in several places; I was relieved to be able to convince myself that they were no more than paint stains. He wore an old and similarly stained baseball cap, which he swept off his head in a single sweeping movement that reminded me of old films about courtiers and kings. A lock of black curly hair fell across his forehead. His eyes were screwed up against the sun and wind – I soon found this to be the almost invariable set for his features.

"Oh, I said that piece of sea glass was no good. Do you want it? I've noticed you out here the last couple of days."

Without waiting for an answer he picked up what he had thrown down less than a minute before. He held it out to me.

I took the piece of glass. It was almost circular, thick and heavy. It had been a dark blue – from the wine-dark sea, I remember thinking – but the scouring action of sea and sand had webbed the deep-blue glass, obscuring its true colour, which could only remain within and beneath. I held it up to the pale sky, and then turned so I could hold it in front of the sun for a moment. The purple-blue of the fragment shone through before I let my arm fall to my side, hand still clutching the piece of sea glass.

"It's a lovely colour," I said lamely. "I suppose it's the base of a bottle. Are you sure you don't want it? Do you collect sea glass?"

"That's right. I'm always looking for the right pieces. That bit is very nice but not what I want. You take it."

I thanked him. We had fallen into step together, having somehow circled round and begun to walk back in the direction of Strandby, and the steps leading from the beach to the houses and pub.

"Are you from around here?" I asked.

He nodded. "I've got a little place, not far. It's sheltered, cosy. I keep my things there."

As we walked it soon emerged that he earned his living by maintaining a number of holiday homes, and undertaking general decorating and plumbing tasks for the inhabitants of Strandby and the nearby villages. He was clearly well-known in the area as a reliable handyman. Even if it didn't pay much, what he earned was enough for his needs. He had all the free time he wanted – time he said he used to wander the beach hunting for the "right" pieces of sea glass.

The beach steps resolved themselves out of the level, monotonous shoreline. We walked towards them for a few minutes, keeping pace with each other before my companion began slowly to increase the distance between us.

"I'm going on," he said.

I had been considering whether or not to invite him for a cup of tea, but it seemed my mind had been made up for me. There was no hint of him wishing more of my company – and why should he? We were still strangers. And in any case, I had walked enough for the time being.

"Good luck," I said. He looked at me sharply. Did he think I was making fun of him? "I mean good luck in finding the sort of sea glass you're after," I explained. "Perhaps I'll see you around. Oh – and thanks again for this piece." I had still been holding the glass he had given me. I held it up to show him.

He smiled and adjusted his cap. Then he strode off, clearly much more practiced at walking on sand than I was. His path took him gradually towards the sea again, where it foamed and fell back against the land. As I squinted at his diminishing back, in the glaring light it seemed his footprints vanished, fading and filling as soon as he had made them. At every moment it was as if he were without a visible starting point as well as destination. I sat on the first step, shading my eyes with my hand as I gazed after him – and past him at the beach and the sea. He stopped and bent down, picking something up, before turning back in my direction. As if he knew I'd still be watching, he briefly raised his hand. Had he found something, or was he simply acknowledging my presence? I got up and waved once, but he had already turned away.

As I climbed the steps back up to Strandby, I realised that we hadn't introduced ourselves.

Another realisation struck me on my return to the house. I put the piece of sea glass on the kitchen table. Then I caught sight of the glass fragments glowing in their dish on the windowsill, and made the connection. The nameless beachcomber and maintenance man must look after the bungalow I was renting – and did not throw away, or give away, every piece of sea glass that he picked up. I wondered if there were fragments of his sea glass in every house in Strandby. It would be as if a territory had been marked out, a part of the colour schemes the homeowners required of him.

~~~

The long evening slowly unwound itself, leaving the day behind as the light moved and changed. The sun swelled as it sank. Low clouds on the flat horizon became burning ramparts of red and orange fire. I decided against taking another walk along the beach, so struck out along a narrow tarmacked track that seemed to run parallel to the coast. To begin with there were bungalows and mobile homes on the landward side, facing the rough grass and frequently dilapidated fencing separating the road from the coastal defences and beach. After a half mile or so the tarmac gave out, and the road became a dirt track, hardened by the summer heat and scored with deep ruts made by the wheels of farm vehicles. On one side the beach and sea were below me, out of sight. But I could hear the sea, and smell it. On the other side were level fields, extending inland – for ever, it seemed. It was like walking close to the edge of a table. I glimpsed a roof and chimneys in the distance, but the setting sun erased all sense of distance as it did colour.

I approached a group of sheds or huts. They huddled together, forlorn against the flat earth and overpowering sky. As I got closer I could see that they were unpainted: the wood had acquired a grey shading and had become as smooth as silk. I assumed they were agricultural buildings, but as I walked past I found there were three more just beyond the others. These looked like beach huts rather than storage sheds – although why they should be so far from the others and Strandby itself was a question I couldn't answer. They had windows with net curtains, and narrow verandahs – although these faced the road rather than the beach. I thought that there must be a private path to the beach, which must be closer than it seemed.

As I drew level with the third of the huts its door opened. Someone stepped out and into the road. A man almost collided with me, as he shaded his eyes against the low sun. He stumbled; I put out my arm to stop him knocking into me, and then to prevent him from falling to the ground. He regained his footing and we regarded each other. It was the man I'd met on the beach.

"I thought I might see you again," he said. He dug into his pocket. "Here."

He held out a piece of sea glass. It was a pale green, the colour of a newly unfurled leaf in May.

"Thought you might like it," he said. "It's no use to me. Not what I wanted."

I slipped the piece of glass into my pocket. "Thank you." Neither of us moved. "Ah, those pieces of glass in the kitchen of my bungalow – did you put them there?"

"I look after most of them," he said. "I thought they'd help to make the houses different. They catch the light. Do you like them? It's just something I do."

"Yes, they really brighten up the place."

"I spend a lot of time looking for sea glass – for the right pieces."

"What do you want them for?"

He glanced back at his house. "Got a few minutes? Come in. Please."

The hut was much larger than it had seemed from the outside. It was immaculate: bright, clean, beautifully kept. There was a door in the opposite wall to the entrance, which I assumed led to a kitchen and toilet of some sort. In the room there was space enough for a bed, table, and an upholstered chair. There were narrow cupboards and shelves high on the wooden walls. My host waved me to the chair, while he sat on the edge of the bed. I hoped I had done the right thing by agreeing to his request.

He leaned forward, holding out his hand. I'm Peter Lacon," he said. "Pleased to meet you." I told him my name, and we shook hands.

"Now," he said. "Sea glass. We think we know what it is. I know what it really is." He paused. "No – what it can be."

He stood up and reached over to one of the cupboards mounted on the wall. He opened the door, revealing a row of transparent plastic boxes – the type food is kept in. From where I sat I could see the boxes were filled with a kaleidoscopic mix of coloured pieces, like boiled sweets.

"Sea glass?" I asked.

Lacon sat down again. "That's right. I collect it, and store it. If

I don't put it down again or give it away. Well, sometimes I leave pieces in dishes – arrange them so they can catch the light and brighten a room." He laughed softly. "I must be a bit of an artist on the side. Not just the local maintenance man."

"Well, you clearly have an eye for colour," I said. I hoped I didn't sound as uneasy as I felt.

"I collect sea glass because I know what can be hidden in it. Out of all those millions of pieces of glass, there are some, well, *other*, pieces. I'm sure of it, I know it."

"Other pieces? Pieces of what?"

He jumped up. "Exactly!"

This was too much like trying to extract some piece of information out of one of my students. Although I dreaded the possibility, I couldn't help saying it: "I think you should start from the beginning."

Lacon grinned. "Yes, it is all about the beginning. Or 'Beginning' – capital 'B'. You see, most people think they know what sea glass is – and they'd be right."

He spoke as if making a pitch, or giving a lecture to try to convince doubters. Perhaps I should have suggested that we went to the Sovereign; but I thought better of it. The regulars had probably heard it all before, and the landlord would surely not have wanted to give Lacon the opportunity to hold forth and to possibly annoy visitors who wanted nothing more than a quiet time.

"Nearly all sea glass is what we think it is," he said. "But I know different about the rest. That's what I'm looking for."

I remained silent, so he continued.

"I was in the Sovereign one night. The TV was on, but it wasn't sport or some singing contest programme, but one of those science documentaries. I don't know why it was on. It was one of those programmes where they have a young and pretty professor type, all smiles and hair – but also really knows their stuff. A proper scientist – a real professor. Anyway, this time the professor was going on about how old and big the universe is, and how long it takes light to reach us here on Earth. The stars and galaxies we see, all their light takes thousands and millions of years to reach us. So we see things as they were, not as they are. You knew that?"

I nodded. The self-taught man is a wonderful thing.

"So on my way home I thought to myself. I asked myself some questions. What happens to all that light? Where does it go to? Because there's light, from the most recent – like from the Sun, to the most ancient of all, from the first stars to ignite and shine. There's light from all the way back, to when the universe came out of its Dark Age. That's what the professor called it – the Dark Age. How fascinating is that? All that light is still out there. Well, I carried on thinking. It was pitch-black, and all the stars were shining. I've learned them. Sirius, Rigel, Orion: the lot. I've learned about them. And I thought that when the light hits the Earth it must sometimes freeze – solidify. Later I decided that 'congeal' was the best way to describe it. Only a tiny part of all that light must do that, otherwise everything would be covered in it. A lot would go into the sea. And then the idea came to me. It would end up looking like sea glass! Wouldn't it?

"I've always loved sea glass and hunted for it, so I decided to carry on, but only keep pieces of the primordial light. Star glass – that's what I call it. That's what I'm looking for in my spare time."

Lacon gazed at me expectantly. Obviously he wanted me to say something supportive or profound, if not both. I'm not usually one to be lost for words, and can speak for any length of time without saying anything meaningful. I've always found that useful when serving on committees and working groups. But I remembered that I was on my own in a strange place, a long way from anywhere else, with a man I didn't know. The possibilities flickered through my mind.

He must have interpreted my silence as me being overwhelmed – in a positive way. I was about to open my mouth to say something completely non-committal, and to break that silence, when he held up a hand and started talking again.

"I haven't found any star glass yet, but I know it's here. And

I thought a lot more, and read some books. There's the original, primordial light – light from stars and things that have changed completely or burned themselves out and died. And there's more recent light – but also from objects that no longer exist. Do you see? There are nebulas made out of supernovas, when a star blows up. Now we see the light from the destroyed star, but the light of the original one is there too. And if the star glass somehow captures the light, it captures its source as well. I think some of the stars that blew up must have had planets with civilisations on them – creatures, maybe like us. Maybe better, greater – maybe worse. So a piece of star glass from their star would contain something of them, stuck in the light – like a fly caught in amber. It could be like a sort of summary of them. A record of their world, history, geography – everything possible. Do you see?"

I nodded, but said nothing. Actually, I don't think I saw at all – not just then, anyway. But Lacon would certainly make a better lecturer than many of my colleagues. I could even see him being inspirational – in the right context. In another he could be intimidating. But I was getting bored. His room was becoming oppressive, and my back was beginning to hurt. And, lecturer that I am, I don't much care for being lectured to.

Lacon started to talk again. Then I realised he had stopped. I must have tuned him out – I hoped I hadn't made it obvious, but I am good at doing that in committees, and no one ever seems to notice. But I did take note of his last words, before he sat back on his bed and fixed me with that expectant look: "If I can find a piece of star glass, I want to try to open it."

I stood up – I couldn't stop myself. "I need to stretch," I said, smiling – sincerely, I hoped. I moved my arms and rubbed the small of my back. It was not an act. And I wanted to leave; but at the same time I didn't want to be rude. So I still made conversation, even as I hoped I was making unmistakeable preparations to go.

"How can you open a piece of glass? What do you think would happen if you could?"

He looked at me as if I were rather stupid. "I should have though it was clear enough," he said. "But then, I have been giving it a great deal of thought. I'll tell you."

I sat down. Lacon reached over to a little table by the head of his bed and switched on a lamp. The room was bathed in a warm yellow glow.

"You have electricity," I said flatly. "You live here all year round?"

Lacon reached under the table and pulled out a bottle. He showed me the label: it was a decent malt whisky. The bottle was nearly empty. He produced two glasses.

"Have a drink before you go."

I nodded, dumbly. I was going to have to see this one through, to the bitter end. I sat back in that awful chair and accepted the whisky.

"I haven't found any star glass for sure, not absolutely, but there might be some pieces in what I've kept. They're some of the pieces I leave out in the houses I look after. I like to put them where the light will fall on them – the new young light from our star. What I think would happen to genuine star glass is this. Do you know that line from the poem? Wordsworth's poem? 'Light that never was on sea or land'. It would be like that – entirely different light, and it would manifest itself." He paused, took in a breath and sipped his whisky. "And *how* it would manifest!"

"What would happen is what I asked."

"If I broke a piece of star glass, or ground it down, or just left it in the light of our fresh sun – well, I think whatever's in it, what makes it up, would be so incredibly ancient. It would have been imprisoned in the glass for such a long time. Maybe since the universe was young. Or maybe some of the scientists are right and it would even be from an earlier universe, a different cycle to ours. Think of that! Trapped for aeons of aeons! It would want to be free. I want to liberate it. No more Dark Ages."

Perhaps it was my painful back, and the effect of the whisky, but I was getting more irritated, and I wanted to say so.

"Yes, but what would happen?" I snapped. "A big joyous

thank you from some creature of light you set free? A cache of ancient knowledge we could use to make a better world? Or what? Do you know how exasperated old people can get when they're cooped-up and want to be somewhere else? Sorry, I've had enough – nothing personal. Good luck with your sea glass, I mean space glass."

I didn't want to be nasty. I set down my empty whisky glass on the table, gently. "Listen, I think this sea air is making me tired. They're some ideas you've got. I don't know if they're science, science fiction – or horror."

Without waiting for Lacon to say anything or even to move, I turned and opened the door. I closed it behind me as gently and quietly as I put down the glass. In my pocket I felt the weight of the piece of sea glass he had given me earlier. That seemed from a different time. Outside it was night – or almost so. There was still a pale band of light remaining in the west and north, along the horizon: the faintest hint of sunset and the fast-vanishing afterglow. The sky was a mass of stars.

As I walked slowly along the track back to Strandby, I had never felt so alone, so insignificant. It was so dark, and yet there was all that light up there. I could understand why it had been thought that the Earth was flat and the sky a solid dome, and why some do. I slunk along the border between dull flat land and the chaos of the sea, and none of that meant one single thing, in the long run. Of course, I'd long known that intellectually; it was just that I had never felt it so emotionally. And following everything that Lacon had said... It was too much.

Any effect of the few mouthfuls of Lacon's whisky wore off; gradually I simmered down. I picked my way carefully under the scattered streetlights and past curtained windows. There was so little light, and it was so feeble; I heard Lacon speaking at me rapidly, describing his visions of primordial light and its emancipation into the world. Some light would be welcome. Soon I genuinely hoped that I would see Lacon again before I left Strandby. I hadn't wanted to be offensive, and if I had I wanted to apologise. After all, I was the visitor – a guest, even though a paying one. Back in the bungalow I emptied out my pockets and went to bed.

The next morning I didn't see Lacon on the beach, but I wasn't going to go to that little wooden house of his. I was hot and sweaty when I got back to the bungalow: sunlight was drenching Strandby, the sea and the land. In the kitchen the pieces of coloured sea glass glowed in their glass bowl. As I let the tap run cold, I noticed that they had been rearranged, as if the bowl had been knocked and its contents jumbled-up. I certainly didn't remember doing that. I was sure I had left the piece of sea glass Lacon had given me on the windowsill next to the bowl, and now it was in the bowl with the other pieces. I picked it out, but it slipped from my fingers. I braced myself for the sound of my piece of sea glass shattering, but there was only a dull clatter as it hit the floor. The glass was still intact. I felt relieved; I gently picked it up and put it back in the bowl, placing it on top of the other fragments.

Lacon must have a key to the bungalows he was responsible for. Had he been in mine while I was out? I didn't bother to check if any of my property had disappeared. I hadn't brought anything valuable with me, let alone left anything worth stealing. As far as I could tell, all Lacon had done was to rearrange the pieces of sea glass in the bowl. For all I knew, that was a routine of his. He had told me that he liked to leave candidate pieces of star glass lying in the sunlight.

I drank down the cold water and sat at the kitchen table. I had planned on going along to the Sovereign for lunch and a drink, but that would mean exposing myself to the sun.

While I had been listening to Lacon lecture me on his theories, there had been times when I had despised him. But at other times he had sounded persuasive; he had almost suspended my disbelief.

In a day or two I would be travelling home again. I would be getting away from Lacon and his torrents of words and ideas and images. But my gaze kept returning to the fragments of glass nestling, inert, in their bowl. Had something happened to them?

Had there been a change? I could leave Strandby and manage to forget Lacon – but there would be no escape. Liberation can be like that.

I got up and pulled down the blind. It made little difference to the light, but it was all I could do.

CONTRIBUTOR NOTES

Gail-Nina Anderson is a cultural historian of a Gothic-bent living in Newcastle, where she delivers courses on art history, literature and film. She is an active member of the Folklore Society, a member of the Dracula Society, and a contributor to Fortean Times, and has written and lectured on the links between the Pre-Raphaelites and Dracula. She writes ghost stories for Phantoms at the Phil, a twice-yearly evening of spooky tales delivered in Newcastle's wonderful (and possibly haunted) Literary and Philosophical Society Library.

Sarah Ash trained as a musician but writing fantasy fiction has allowed her to explore her fascination with the way mythology, folklore and history overlap and interact. Learning to play Bartok's piano music as a teenager led to a life-long love of his music and eventually to this story. Sarah's latest published novel is *The Arkhel Conundrum*, the fourth in *The Tears of Artamon* series. www.sarah-ash.com

Debbie Bennett tells lies and makes things up, writing both fantasy (as Debbie Bennett) and dark crime/thrillers (as DJ Bennett). Debbie has also branched out into scriptwriting with an IMDb credit for a *Doctor Who* spin-off DVD. She's currently involved with the scriptwriting and production of a local community radio soap *Eastwich*. She claims to get her inspiration from the day job – but if she told you about that, she'd have to kill you afterwards… www.debbiebennett.co.uk

Mike Chinn has edited three volumes of *The Alchemy Press Book of Pulp Heroes*. His first Damian Paladin collection, *The Paladin Mandates*, was short-listed for the British Fantasy Award in 1999; and an expanded edition is due out from Pro Se Press. Pro Se published a second Paladin collection, *Walkers in Shadow*, in 2017. He has two short story collections in print: *Give Me These Moments Back* (2015) and *Radix Omnium Malum* (2017). In 2018 he published his first Western, *Revenge Is a Cold Pistol*. http://saladoth.blogspot.co.uk/

Peter Coleborn created the award-winning Alchemy Press in the late 1990s and has since (co)-published a range of anthologies and collections. He has edited various publications for the British Fantasy Society (including *Winter Chills/Chills* and *Dark Horizons*), and co-edited with Pauline E Dungate the Joel Lane tribute anthology *Something Remains* in 2016; and in 2018 he co-edited with Jan Edwards the first volume of *The Alchemy Press Book of Horrors*. www.alchemypress.co.uk

Pauline E Dungate is a short story writer, reviewer and poet. She is co-editor (with Peter Coleborn) of *Something Remains,* a tribute volume to the late Joel Lane. When not reading, writing or pottering about in the garden she visits far-flung places in order to photograph butterflies – most recently to Mexico and Colombia. She lives in Birmingham.

Jan Edwards is an editor of anthologies for The Alchemy Press, the British Fantasy Society, Fox Spirit and others. Her short fiction has appeared in many crime, horror and fantasy anthologies. Some of those tales have been collected in *Leinster Gardens and Other Subtleties* and *Fables and Fabrications*. Her novels include *Sussex Tales* and *Winter Downs* (Bunch Courtney book one, and winner of the Arnold Bennett Book Prize) and its sequel *In Her Defence*. She is also a recipient of the BFS Karl Edward Wagner Award. http://janedwardsblog.wordpress.com

Paul Finch is a former cop and journalist now turned best-selling crime and thriller writer, the author of the very popular police-procedural novels featuring DS Mark "Heck" Heckenburg (seven books to date) and DC Lucy Clayburn (of which there are three). The first three books in the Heck line achieved official best-seller status, the second being the fastest pre-ordered title in HarperCollins history, while the first Lucy Clayburn novel made the *Sunday Times* Top 10 list. His first crime thriller from Orion Books will be published summer 2020. Paul cut his literary teeth penning episodes of the British TV crime drama *The Bill*, and has written extensively in horror, fantasy and science-fiction, including for *Doctor Who*. Paul is a native of Wigan, Lancashire, where he still lives with his wife and business partner, Cathy. http://paulfinch-writer.blogspot.com/

Sharon Gosling started out as a journalist. Her first kids' book, *The Diamond Thief*, won the Redbridge Children's Book Award in 2014, and was followed by two sequels. Her young-adult horror *FIR* was shortlisted for Lancashire Book of the Year 2017, and 2019's *The Golden Butterfly* was nominated for the 2020 Carnegie Medal. She also writes non-fiction books about television and film. Sharon lives with her husband in a small village in Cumbria that is also home to the Croglin Vampire. The legend forms the basis of her first adult horror novel, on which she is currently working.

John Grant, is the winner of two Hugos and a World Fantasy Award (amongst others), and has written over 80 books, including *The World* (1992), *The Far-Enough Window* (2002), *The Dragons of Manhattan* (2008) and *Leaving Fortusa* (2008), and the collections *Take No Prisoners* (2004) and *Tell No Lies* (2014). With artist Bob Eggleton he created the two "illustrated fictions" *Dragonhenge* (2002) and *The Stardragons* (2005). For a number of years he ran the Paper Tiger imprint of fantasy art books, bringing him a Chesley Award. His nonfiction includes *The Encyclopedia of Fantasy* (1997, with John Clute), *The Chesley Awards* (2003, with Elizabeth Humphrey and Pamela D Scoville), a series of books on the misuse and misunderstanding of science, and *A Comprehensive Encyclopedia of Film Noir* (2013). He also wrote the website Noirish. John sadly died February 2020. This book is dedicated to his memory. http://noirencyclopedia.wordpress.com.

John Howard was born in London. His books include *The Silver Voices, Written by Daylight, Buried Shadows*, and *A Flowering Wound*. With Mark Valentine he wrote the joint collections *Secret Europe* and *Inner Europe*. He has published essays on various aspects of the science fiction and horror fields, many of which are collected in *Touchstones: Essays on the Fantastic*. He reviews writings from the small presses in *Camera Obscura*, his column for *Wormwood*.

Tim Jeffreys' short fiction has appeared in *Weirdbook, Not One of Us,* and *Nightscript*, among various other publications, and his latest collection of horror stories and strange tales 'You Will Never Lose Me' is available now. He lives in Bristol, England, with his partner and two children. www.timjeffreys.blogspot.co.uk.

Eygló Karlsdóttir was born in Iceland. She studied literary theory at university before moving to the south of Sweden where she lives with her daughter and dog. She never grew up enough to start drinking coffee, but she does know how to pronounce Eyjafjallajökull. She is the author of *All the Dark Places* and the short story collection *Things the Devil Wouldn't Dream Of and Other Stories*. She is also the creator of the experimental zine *The Chestnut*. http://eyglo.info

Nancy Kilpatrick is an award-winning writer and editor in mainly the horror/dark fantasy field. Her 23 novels include her current six-book series *Thrones of Blood*, recently optioned for film and television. She has published over 220 short stories and seven collections. She is also an editor with 15 anthologies to her credit. You can connect with her on Facebook, Twitter and Instagram. Check out her website where you can subscribe to her once-a-month, pithy newsletter. http://www.nancykilpatrick.com

Garry Kilworth was born in York in 1941, just in time to catch the attack on Pearl Harbour. He started writing speculative fiction at the age of 12, but had to wait through school and eighteen years in the RAF before publication. He loves to travel, especially in the Far East and Pacific, and to photograph wildlife. He has written over 90 novels and collections of short stories, one or two of them best sellers. Married to Annette Bailey for 58 years, he has a bundle of kids, grandkids and great-grandkids scattered over the globe. www.garry-kilworth.co.uk

Samantha Lee is a graduate of the Central School of Speech and Drama and began writing while she was still a professional performer. Her output is as diverse as it is prolific, covering both fact and fiction and including novels in the horror and dark fantasy genres, self-development and exercise books, short stories and articles, children's TV series, movie screenplays, literary criticism and poetry. She hosts creative writing workshops at libraries. Her work has been translated into French, Dutch, Spanish, Swedish, Italian, German, Croatian, Greek and Chinese. http://samanthaleehorror.com/

Thana Niveau is a horror and science fiction writer. Originally from the USA, she now lives in the UK in a Victorian seaside town between Bristol and Wales. She is the author of the short story collections *Octoberland*, *Unquiet Waters* and *From Hell to Eternity,* as well as the novel *House of Frozen Screams*. Her work has been reprinted in *Best New Horror* and *Best British Horror*. She has been shortlisted three times for the British Fantasy award. www.thananiveau.com

Jim Pitts started submitting artwork to fanzines back in the early 1970s. David Sutton was the first to accept his work for Shadow Press, closely followed by Jon Harvey for *Balthus*. He has since worked extensively in the UK, European and American fantasy and horror fields. Jim has long been involved with the British Fantasy Society and twice won the BFS Award for Best Artist.

John Llewellyn Probert's latest book is the British Fantasy Award-nominated *The Last Temptation of Dr Valentine*, the second sequel to the British Fantasy Award winner *The Nine Deaths of Dr Valentine*. He won the Children of the Night Award for his portmanteau book *The Faculty of Terror* and his current projects include two more titles utilising the same structure. He is also at work on two novels and a new book of film reviews while continuing to write about current releases on his website House of Mortal Cinema. After all five books have been finished he intends to sleep for a bit. http://www.johnlprobert.com

Peter Sutton has a not so secret lair in the wilds of Fishponds, Bristol, and dreams up stories, many of which are about magpies. He's had stuff published, online and in book form, including a short story collection called *A Tiding of Magpies* (Shortlisted for the British Fantasy Award 2017) and the novels *Sick City Syndrome* and *Seven Deadly Swords*. Pete has also edited eight anthologies and is a member of the North Bristol Writers. Twitter: @suttope

CPSIA information can be obtained
at www.ICGtesting.com
Printed in the USA
LVHW031954060420
652381LV00002B/167